A Love to Keep Me Warm

GINA ARDITO

The following is a work of fiction. Any resemblance to actual persons, living or dead, is purely coincidental.

A LOVE TO KEEP ME WARM

DEDICATION

For all those who believe in the magic of Christmas…

A LOVE TO KEEP ME WARM

Pronunciation Guide For Polish Terms

Bardzo dobry: BART-so DO-bray
Bigos (stew): VEE-gose
Choinka (Christmas tree): HO-yink-a
Chruschiki (bowtie cookies): croosh-CHEEK-ee
Czy jesteś dobra (Are you all right?): too YES-day DO-bra
Dobry rano (Good morning.): DOE-bray RON-o
Do siego roku (I wish you well): DOE SHAY-go RO-coo
Idiotka (idiot): id-YOTE-ka
Jak są wy (How are you?): yok so vay
Kanapki (sandwiches): can-OP-kee
Kawaler (bachelor): ka-VA-la
Motyle (butterflies): MO-tee-leh
Nowa Huta (Kraków district): NO-va HOO-ta
Olimpijski (Olympics): o-lim-PEE-skee
Oplatek (communion wafer): o-PLA-tik
Paczki (doughnut): POTCH-kee
Pasterka (midnight mass, aka "shepherds' mass"): poss-STIR-ka
Pierogi (dumplings): pair-O-gee
Pozdrawiam (thank you): pose-dra-vee-OM
Przepraszam (I'm sorry): zhi-PRA-zham
Przewalski (wild horse): zhi-VAL-skee
Salwator: SAL-va-tor
Smok Wawelski (dragon of Wawel): smoke va-VEL-skee
Sylwester (New Year's, named for the saint): sil-VEST-er
Szopki (crèches): SHOP-kee
Tadeusz (Theodore): TA-da-oosh
Tokaj (sparkling wine): TOE-koy
Tu przyjść (Come here!): TOO preescht
Ukochana (sweetheart): ook-o-HONN-a
Wawel (regional area of Kraków): VA-vell
Wigilia (Christmas): Vee-GEEL-ya
Zlotys (currency): ZLOT-is

1

"Let's do this."

Polina Kominski snuggled deeper into her down jacket as she strode through the ancient city of Kraków. The wind sliced past the faux fur on her collar, cutting her cheeks with cold. *Why couldn't Mom have been born in Miami Beach?*

The wind howled, whipping powdery snow across her red plaid vinyl boots. Christmas in Poland. Bleak, gray, icy. Like her heart. Thanks to horrendous weather over the Atlantic Ocean, she'd endured two delays, one missed connection, and a sleepless night on the floor of an airport terminal waiting area. As much as she craved a cup of hot coffee right now, she wouldn't give in. The caffeine jolt would only screw up her sleep pattern, already skewed by the travel and the time difference. Instead of her favorite crutch beverage, she breathed in the crisp December air, tangy with the promise of coming snow, and picked up her pace. She had to reach Planty Gardens in the Old Town historical district before dark.

Last time, she vowed. This was the last time Mom could rearrange her daughter's life to suit *her* whims. Pain mingled with her relief. Mom's dying wish, that her ashes be buried in her homeland, had caged Polina into a trip to Europe for Christmas—an expense she could've done without.

"Spend this Christmas in Krakow, *ukochana*, sweetheart," Mom had whispered that last afternoon. "The beauty, the magic, will refresh you. After you do this last thing, you'll be free."

Free. Ha. The past clung to her like stale cigarette smoke—unpleasant and unwelcome. Free. Free to pursue her life at last, without interruption. A *normal* life.

One last task. She could do this. Head down, she propelled herself forward with the single-mindedness of a charging bull.

"O...kay, Mom," she said to the gray sky overhead. "Let's do this."

She hadn't expected the craziness around her. Easy to recognize her mother had once lived here. The city's residents represented everything her mother had loved: chaos, color, and cacophony. Street performers littered the sidewalks like trails of popcorn on the midway. Every corner hosted a singer with a guitar, marionettes, accordion players, or a string quartet playing Beethoven's *Moonlight Sonata*.

When she found the entrance to the closest garden, she sucked in a breath at the sheer beauty. Snow painted the tree limbs in pristine white, sparkling on branches that reached slender fingers to touch the lavender sky. Dusk had fallen, and yellowish light from the nineteenth century oil lamps washed the grounds in liquid gold. On the other side from where she stood, a large castle-like building called the Barbakan reigned proud and fearless over the snowy grounds below.

Taking a seat on a bench facing the imposing structure, she rifled through her backpack—her only luggage—and pulled out Mom's itinerary.

What next? She scanned the list, ignoring the more bizarre instructions like, (5.) *Follow the dog*, and (8.) *Kiss a stranger*. She crossed off (3.) *Visit Planty Gardens* and her finger stopped at (4.) *Have your fortune told.*

Naturally. Because Mom would continue to push her interests in the paranormal, the *abnormal*, even from beyond the grave.

Last time, she reminded herself again. Those two words, now a mantra, kept her moving forward.

Okay, fine. Get her fortune told. Where? As if on cue, a young girl, dressed in scarlet and tangerine scarves dripping with gold medallions, peered out from the closest alcove and crooked her finger in Polina's direction. There, of course.

After replacing the list and zipping up the backpack, she made her way toward the archway where the dark-haired, dark-eyed girl with skin the color of Arizona sand waited. Inside the stone apse, the girl had set up a long wooden shelf littered with hand-painted wooden dolls and sequined trinkets. Polina hated sequins and spangles, hated anything anyone used to make shoddy products shiny. True quality didn't need spotlights or halos, a lesson she learned early in life.

"I tell your future?" the girl asked in stilted but understandable English. "Ten *zlotys*?"

"Yes, please." She passed over the money, roughly three American dollars.

The girl stuffed the brass and black coins into a brightly colored woven box and shoved it under the shelf, then took Polina's hand. The gypsy didn't ask Polina to remove the glove or even attempt to read her palm, she simply riveted her dark gaze into Polina's blue eyes. "You have suffered great loss," she intoned. "But don't weep. Someone very special waits around a corner. Follow the dog."

"Follow the dog," Polina repeated with a sigh. The same instruction her mother had given her. "What does that mean?"

"Sometime this evening, you will hear a dog barking. Walk in the direction of the sound to find your future."

Great, Polina thought. *That sounds exactly like something Mom would say. Did every fortune teller in the world use the same schtick?*

"I am sorry. That is all I can tell you," the gypsy girl said, dropping Polina's hand.

Oh, big surprise. "Thanks."

Polina turned away to hide her disgust. Really, what had she expected? She'd grown up around these charlatans, knew all the gimmicks and cons they used to get marks to ante up more cash. *Follow the dog*. Next, the girl would tell her someone had placed a curse on her, and for ten thousand *zlotys*, the gypsy could wrap an egg in a handkerchief and remove the ill will.

When had she become so naïve? Time to smarten up and remember. Mom didn't invent the con; she'd just perfected it.

Jet lag was probably inhibiting Polina's brain from functioning logically. What time was it? She glanced at the watch again. The simple black face with silver numbers, the only tangible inheritance she gained from her mother's death, read six o'clock. Still too early for check-in.

Good. She needed a chance to regroup before tackling the next item on her mother's To-Do list. The mysterious barking dog would have to go on without her. Or find her tomorrow. Right now, she planned to find a warm place for dinner. After that, she'd grab herself a room at St. Tadeusz, a five or six minute walk away, and collapse for the night. A hot bath and several hours' sleep would rejuvenate and prepare her for whatever Mom's detailed list had planned for tomorrow.

Leaving the gardens, she crossed the thoroughfare and strode past the rows of storybook storefronts, all painted in rainbow hues. Funny. When she first heard she'd be forced to spend December in Kraków, Polina had envisioned a bleak existence of dust and rubble, of poverty and grit. She'd never imagined this fairyland of twinkling lights on a primavera palette, music filling the air, and happy people everywhere. For heaven's sake, the notorious Auschwitz concentration camp lay only forty miles away from this charming city. Then again, that was Mom's true nature. Never see reality, cover up anything sad or unpleasant with garish colors and glitter.

When she turned the next corner, she spotted the now familiar copper spires of the Pulaski Hotel's roof piercing the twilit sky. Soon, she'd be warm and comfortable. She passed a bakery, and the yeasty aromas that scented the air brought sharp reminders from her stomach. She hadn't eaten in hours. Just another few blocks, she told herself and her rumbling empty tummy. Thank God, she still had half a sandwich in her backpack.

Woof! Woof!

She stopped in mid-step on the crowded sidewalk. No. It couldn't be.

Woof! Woof!

Yes, it was. A barking dog. Gloved hands fisted at her sides, she steeled herself to ignore the animal. Her gaze remained pinned on the hotel looming only a few blocks away. Thoughts of a soft bed in a warm room filled her mind, pushed her feet forward. Food, bath, sleep. In that order. No dog.

The barking, however, grew louder and, crazy as it seemed, even more insistent. *Follow the dog. Woof! Woof! Follow the dog.*

Exasperated, she threw up her hands. Okay, okay. Apparently, the dog was in cahoots with Mom and the gypsy girl. A flush of embarrassment warmed her cheeks as she turned around to follow the barking sounds, but she consoled herself with the thought that she'd only walk back one block. After that, if he had something to show her, the dog would have to run up and introduce himself.

Once again, she passed the bakery. God, she was starving! Maybe she should splurge on a real dinner tonight. Grab a cheeseburger deluxe with fries and onion rings. And some fresh apple fritters for dessert.

This time around, she couldn't help but stare longingly at the glass display case where lighter-than-air pastry shared a starring role with loaves of freshly baked bread. Gaze riveted on the goodies in the shop window, she turned the corner.

Wham! Something huge collided with her midsection and knocked her onto the slushy sidewalk. Stars exploded in her skull as the back of her head slammed against the cobblestones. When she finally opened her eyes, a hairy gray face came into view, with sharp teeth inches from her nose. A wolf! She cried out and raised a hand to shield herself from a vicious bite.

A wet black nose snuffled into the space between her elbow and her chin, and she gave a low whine, squeezing her eyes shut, tensed for the attack.

"Kacper, *tu przyjść!*" a brusque voice ordered.

Who was that? She lowered her arm, opened her eyes, and came face to snout with her attacker. Not a wolf. A dog. A tremendous, wiry-haired dog with a toothy grin.

Slurp!

A dog that had just licked her nose. Ick. She wiped a sleeve across her cheeks to swipe at the doggie slime.

"Kacper, *tu przyjść!*" The order, dark as smoke, came again. Lucky for her, the man patted his thigh, and the dog immediately bounded off her to stand beside him.

Polina looked up beyond the not-so ferocious beast that had vacated her chest to check out the owner of both the smoky voice and the overly affectionate animal. He was tall, broad-shouldered, and despite the frown he flashed at her new furry friend, very appealing with a wide face and hazel eyes, framed by thick honey-colored hair. His clothes were expensive, shoes gleamed. Money. He smelled of it, *reeked* of it.

"*Przepraszam. Czy jesteś dobra?*" He held out a hand to assist her to her feet.

With her limited grasp of the Polish language, she had to rely on the man's body language to assume he was apologizing and, maybe, asking if she was hurt. "I'm okay," she replied with a nod she hoped would translate.

"You speak English?" Surprise glazed his words stronger than the very British accent he used, and he gripped her hand a little tighter.

She nodded. "I'm American."

His smile beamed white, lighting up his face, and Polina's heart sat up and took notice. "Oh, thank God. My Polish isn't exactly flawless yet." Reaching into his pocket, he withdrew a leash and clipped it to the dog's collar. "I apologize about the dog. He belongs to the son of a colleague, got away from the kid, and I've been chasing him for the last three blocks. Are you sure you're all right?"

"Uh-huh." Her brain spiraled into free fall as his gaze raked her from disheveled head to booted toe. In an attempt to regain some sense of calm, she turned slightly and hitched up the nylon backpack. "I landed on this. Not exactly a cushion, but it's better than full contact with cobblestones." Of course, the knot blooming on the back of her head said differently, but she opted to keep that a secret. Along with her now crushed and useless sandwich. She didn't want to engage in explanations or additional conversation.

He continued to stare at her, saying nothing.

A rush of heat bathed her, and her throat dried up, leaving her tongue thick in her mouth. All she wanted right now was a juicy cheeseburger, then a soft bed to dive into, where she could escape the crazy thoughts racing through her head. *Follow the dog.* How stupid could she be? "Well, nice meeting you." She glanced down at the hairy beast. "I guess."

Before she could turn, he grasped her jacket sleeve. "No, wait. Where are you headed?"

She craned her neck to point to the copper spires shadowing the quickly darkening sky. "Just over there."

"The Pulaski Hotel?" Confusion clouded his gorgeous eyes. "But..." He looked beyond her and to the left, toward where she'd indicated. "You were going in the wrong direction."

"Yeah, I...umm...made a wrong turn." No way did she intend to correct any of his misconceptions. Her destination and how she got there were nobody's business.

"Ah." Understanding bloomed on his face. "You're new to the city then?"

"Just arrived." She shrugged the sliding backpack up on her shoulders. "Well, two hours ago anyway."

He looked around where they stood on the busy sidewalk, gestured at the dwindling clusters of people rushing by, then at her side where one would normally assume a significant other might hover. "You're alone?"

She sighed. Another explanation she didn't want to share. "Long story."

"Why don't you tell me about it while Kacper and I escort you to your hotel?"

Alarmed, she scanned the emptying street and growing darkness. Talk about stupid. She'd just told a total stranger she was alone in a strange city. If this were a horror movie, she'd be Serial Killer Victim Number One. She held up her gloved hands and took a step back, out of arms' reach. "Oh, you don't have to do that. I'm fine, really."

"It's no trouble."

"I'll be fine on my own."

"I insist. It isn't safe for a lady to be alone after dark. And I know Kacper may seem like a lunk, but he is, usually, a fierce protector." He shot a disgruntled look at the dog, and the beast lowered his head, as if in shame.

A smile twitched Polina's lips. She relaxed her stance. He didn't seem like a serial killer. Not that serial killers had a certain look, but he dressed in expensive clothes and...God, he smelled great! Like lime and sea breezes. When would she ever get another chance to walk beside someone so...clean?

"I'm actually heading in the same direction," he continued. "And since you were already turned topsy-turvy before Kacper knocked you down, the least I can do is see you safely to your destination. I am Rhys, by the way. Rhys Linsey. See?"

He reached inside his coat and pulled out an ID tag on a retracting coil that showed his name and a grainy photo beneath a colorful logo for some kind of international banking organization. Did serial killers carry corporate IDs?

"Originally from the north of London," he said with a careless shrug. "I transplanted to Poland a few months ago."

That explained his very British accent. "Polina Kominski." She held out her hand to him, a gesture of friendship. "From...the United States."

"Welcome to Kraków." He took her hand and lifted it to his lips, placing a kiss on the soft brown leather.

Why hadn't she taken off her gloves? She'd give up a lung to know how his mouth felt against her bare skin.

"Come on." Placing her hand on the sleeve of his cashmere coat, he allowed the dog with the goofy canine smile and guilty conscience to take the lead. "Tell me, Miss Kominski, what brings you here?"

Not Miss Kominski. Even her mother had never answered to that name, legal as it might have been. "Please call me Polina."

"Polina." Her name sounded like a purr when it flowed from his lips. "And I'm Rhys to my friends. Why have you come to Kraków alone?"

How much to share with this stranger? As little as possible. While they crossed the street, she briefly explained her mother's last wish that her daughter come to Poland to inter her ashes in the family crypt and remain through the traditional Polish Christmas celebration. He offered condolences on her loss before giving her a little more info about himself. Rhys Linsey was an investment banker who'd transferred to Kraków with his company, and he'd been in the city since July.

"Does your wife like the city?"

He chuckled. "No wife, no girlfriend. I, too, am alone here. Some might call it fate that we have found each other, Polina."

Oh, cripes. She hadn't expected someone so intelligent- and successful-looking to fall for that crap. "More like coincidence," she stated.

"You don't believe in fate?"

"My mother..." She swallowed the bitterness rising in her throat. "...was...a bit of a bohemian. She believed in magic and destiny and..."

"And so you don't." He made the statement without rancor or censure. "Do you know they call Kraków the 'Magic City'?"

Polina surrendered to the sarcasm brewing on her tongue. "Of course they do."

His chuckles, rich and throaty, spun her insides like a Tilt-a-Whirl. "Your mother didn't tell you that, eh?"

"No, she...umm...neglected to mention that fact."

Or maybe Polina had never listened when Mom brought it up. Lost in a haze of painkillers and booze long before the cancer hollowed her insides, Mom often rambled about magic and fortunes. Those childlike qualities made her a terrific gypsy. But a terrible parent.

Outside the Pulaski Hotel, he stopped and took her hand again. "I would like to show you around the city, if you'd allow me, Polina."

While her heartbeat galloped against her ribs, she deftly pulled out of his grasp. "Thanks, but no. I...umm...my mother has me on a strict schedule. See, she wrote out a list for me—stuff I have to do on a very short timeline."

He held up a gloved index finger near her nose. "Ah, but if you have tasks to complete, wouldn't it be more prudent to have a guide who knows the city? Someone who could save you time in the long run?"

Yes. But not someone like him. "No, really, I appreciate it, but—"

"No buts. I insist. I'll meet you here in the lobby tomorrow. How does ten o'clock sound? Is that late enough for you? I want to make certain you're well rested and you've adjusted to the time difference."

Like she had any hope of sleeping with thoughts of Rhys Linsey and magic littering her head. "Ten should be fine," she managed to say.

"Wonderful." His smile lit up the night. "I'll see you tomorrow then."

Not if she could help it. "Right. Goodnight."

Before he could continue their discussion, she dove into the revolving door and pushed her way into the hotel lobby. Her chest grew tighter, and her head swam. Before full panic set in, she ducked behind a tall ivory pillar and waited for her breathing to return to normal. Around her, well-dressed people milled near the gleaming mahogany reception counter, their soft laughter and murmured conversations creating a soothing hum. Massive sprays of spiky white flowers and heart-shaped greenery sat on graceful pedestals interspersed throughout the lobby. They soaked the air with perfume, tickling her nose, and she stifled a sneeze to avoid drawing attention to herself. Piano music played, a classical piece she didn't recognize. Tchaikovsky maybe? Chopin?

God, what would it be like to walk into a fancy place like this and never question whether you belonged? Never have the staff look at you as if you were as welcome as a cockroach?

Once she'd regained control, she exited the hotel. Back out on the cobblestones, she spotted Rhys's broad back as he strode down the quiet sidewalk, the giant wolfhound loping beside him. When the night swallowed up his outline, Polina strode across the street to the hostel where her room waited. Forget dinner. She'd lost her appetite. With luck, she could grab a quick shower in the communal bathroom before hitting the dormitory bed she'd been assigned.

Last time, Mom.

2

Strolling away from Polina and her hotel, Rhys sensed someone's gaze on his back. He had to fight the urge to turn around to see if Polina had returned to the sidewalk. When the stoplight at the next intersection turned red, he took advantage of the enforced pause to kneel and rub the wolfhound between the ears. "*Pozdrawiam*, Kacper." Who would've guessed he'd have to thank this lumbering dunderhead dog for an early Christmas gift?

Kacper's obvious affection-at-first-sight had only confirmed what the sudden adrenaline coursing through Rhys's veins had indicated. Despite the dirt smeared on her cheek and her terrible sense of direction, Polina Kominski intrigued him.

Two blocks later, they rounded the last corner to the street leading to his office building. Henryk and his son, Feliks, waited at the bottom of the marble steps of the bank's main entrance. The seven-year-old boy sped forward, arms outstretched wide to accommodate his dog's extra-large girth. "Kacper!"

Emitting a happy yip, the wolfhound yanked hard, attempting to reach the boy. Rhys wouldn't be taken in by the dog's exuberance and kept a tight grip on the leash until he was close enough to hand control over to Henryk, his friend and business associate.

"*Pozdrawiam*, Rhys." Henryk took the leash while Feliks knelt to hug the dog.

"Actually," Rhys replied with a grin. "I might owe you

the thanks, Henryk."

Henryk arched a shaggy gray brow. "Oh?"

"Your dog just introduced me to someone special."

"Really?"

Yes, he knew how ridiculous that statement sounded. Under normal circumstances, if someone else had uttered something so ridiculous, he'd be the guy laughing loudest. But not this time. Oh, sure. Henryk could try to make him feel foolish, throw a sarcastic jibe his way, but he would fail miserably. Rhys hadn't lied when he'd told Polina he thought fate had brought them together.

All his life, he had relied on gut instinct to guide his decisions. That certain tingle on the back of the neck, a spark in his blood, or the sudden flip of his stomach as if he rode a roller coaster were all signs he stood on the edge of something new and amazing. Something life-changing. Through that constant faith in himself, he would sense the right moment for anything, which allowed him to gamble almost recklessly, a distinct benefit in his career—and in his personal life. Knowing when to buy and when to trade any commodity made *him* a hot commodity, made his hunt more than a matter of trust with dealers. He'd never lost. Oh, sure, he'd come close a few times, but that subtle shift in the air always led him to the precipice then rocketed him off to soar into the stratosphere.

Now, that very same magic had surrounded his meeting with Polina. Whether she wished to believe it or not.

"Who is she?" Henryk asked with a brow arched in amusement.

"Polina Kominski, a tourist from America."

"America? You couldn't find a local girl?"

Rhys shrugged. Where she came from didn't matter. What mattered was where they went from here. He still had to visit Crete, Syria, Russia, Mexico, and China. If he had his way, wherever he went, she'd be with him.

The minute he saw her, sprawled on the sidewalk with Kacper's paws pinning her, he knew. It was as if he'd been struck by lightning. Every sense jolted to full alert, attuned to her sweet face, her baby blue eyes and strawberry blond hair. "She came around the corner by Hubert's Bakery, and Kacper knocked her down. The thing is, she was walking toward Kacper's bark, *away* from her original destination."

Henryk's face took on a skeptical scowl. "And?"

"And what? You know what that means." So did he.

Despite her statement to the contrary, Polina must believe in magic to turn *away* from the direction of her hotel and walk toward the sound of a barking dog. That fact alone would have charmed Rhys into wanting to spend time with her. Not everyone knew the Old World superstitions, much less paid them heed. He *did* know—from personal experience and lots of research. Henryk's wife, Bianka, had filled in any blanks for him.

According to legend, when a woman walked in the direction of a dog's bark at Christmastime, she would then meet up with her future husband. How fortunate for him that he'd opted to let Henryk stay with Feliks while he chased Kacper when the wolfhound had escaped his leash. *Fate.* No one could fight destiny.

"Rhys." Henryk sighed dramatically, as if explaining the wonders of the universe to Feliks—in ancient Sanskrit. "That particular legend pertains to Christmas Eve. The woman who leaves a home after *Christmas Eve dinner* and follows a dog's bark will meet her future husband along the way."

Rhys dismissed the doubts with a wave of his hand. "Yes, but, since neither Polina nor I are Polish natives, I think we can allow for some leeway in the legend."

Henryk doubled over with laughter. "If you say so, friend. God help you, I don't know who I feel sorrier for— you or your new *ukochana*. Tell me, did she feel the thunderbolt the way you did?"

No. But she was in mourning, jetlagged, and probably too numb to notice the electricity between them. She'd told him her visit to Poland was her mother's deathbed request—to spend the holidays in Kraków. So she'd be here for Christmas.

He turned his attention to Henryk again. "Your wife's still hosting *Wigilia* this year?"

"Did someone revoke your invitation?" Henryk retorted.

"Nope. Just checking." Rhys couldn't fight the smile playing over his lips. He wondered if Polina knew the tradition of the extra plate at *Wigilia*, Christmas Eve.

He'd already agreed to spend the holiday with Henryk and his family. Bianka would, as tradition dictated, set an extra place at the dinner table, in anticipation of an unexpected guest. Thanks to Rhys, Polina would be that unexpected guest, heralding good fortune to Henryk and Bianka for the coming year.

Polina Kominski. He couldn't wait to see her again. Crazy? Maybe. But the tingles on his nape never led him astray. From the day he left home while still a youth, determined to forge his own destiny away from his father's reputation, he'd heeded no instincts but his own. And he'd always won whatever he sought.

Which explained why he wound up outside the hotel at nine-thirty the following morning. Since it was too soon to have the front desk ring her room, he settled in an overstuffed wing chair in the lobby. He managed to sit for all of thirty seconds before he popped up to pace the marble floor. Just thinking about seeing her again had him twitchy. He turned to stare out the bank of windows that opened onto the street. That's when he spotted her. On the sidewalk outside the hotel, walking away from him. Even though her head was down to buffer the strong winds, there was no disguising that cheap, shiny coat or her light red hair. How she had managed to elude him, he couldn't fathom, and he didn't waste time trying to figure out her Houdini act. He shoved his way around the revolving doors and popped up directly in front of her.

On a high-pitched gasp, she jumped back. "Mr. Linsey."

"Rhys." With a wide grin, he stepped closer to her. "If I didn't know any better, I'd think you were trying to run away before I got here this morning."

A rush of pink bloomed in her cheeks. While the cold air might have caused the color, he believed the blush came from guilt that he'd caught her making her escape.

She narrowed her eyes. "What are you doing here so early?"

"Would you believe me if I said I camped out here in the lobby all night?"

Her laughter tickled his spine. "No."

God, he loved a challenge. How would it feel to wake up with this woman every day? Like coming home. Every day, every night. He stared at her face as, in his mind, days turned to months, months to years. He could picture her smiling while they shared meals, laughing at the antics of their children, turning to him for solace in times of grief, consoling him when he sought comfort from her. Theirs would be a love story to share—to be told to their children and their grandchildren—starting now.

"So where were you headed?"

She jerked her head in the direction of the fast food place across the street, gleaming silver in an eternally greasy steam. "I was just going to pick up a cup of coffee to get rid of the last fuzzy clouds of jet lag."

Lie. The hotel had an excellent coffee shop in the lobby. She didn't need to venture outside to find the perfect caffeine jolt.

She'd been trying to duck him. They both knew it. What he didn't know was why. But he could be patient, figure out her secrets one at a time. "I have a better idea. Why don't I take you to my favorite café? They have wonderful flavored coffees and teas and an assortment of pastries. We can share a quick breakfast while we make our plans to tour the city. And lucky for us, the café is close to the Wawel Cathedral and Castle."

"Mr. Linsey, really." She frowned. "You don't have to babysit me."

"Rhys," he corrected again. "And maybe I want you to babysit me."

Shaking her head, she let out an exasperated breath. "Yeah, right."

"Truly. I'm like Kacper. I get into trouble when I'm left to my own devices. Think of it as a public service."

He tried to see emotions play across her face, but she let nothing show. Hers was a countenance made for gambling, all banality and devil-may-care attitude. Scanning her from head to toe, he found her Achilles heel. Literally. Her feet shuffled over the slushy sidewalk, toeing designs in the gray matter. The mute tap-dancing told him what her lack of expression didn't. She was confused, unsure.

Biting back a smug grin, he pushed his advantage. "Spend a few hours with me. If I still make you uncomfortable, say so, and I'll leave you alone."

She said nothing, but her feet picked up tempo, scraping the cobblestones. Finally, she sighed. "O...kay. *Two* hours. And I pay my own way. You're my guide, nothing more. Don't think I won't tell you to shove off if you make me uncomfortable. I'm not some English rose, too delicate to give you what-for."

"Whatever you say." But in his mind, she was definitely a rose: beautiful, yet thorny. A heady combination. He offered her a bow and watched the corners of her lips quirk up. Her very kissable lips.

Let the games begin.

♥

Since she had to leave the hostel every day before ten a.m. and wasn't guaranteed a room upon her return—much less the same room—Polina had stuffed all her belongings, including her mother's itinerary, in her backpack before heading off this morning. She had assumed Mr. Linsey— *Rhys*–would show up long after she'd disappeared for the day.

Talk about bad timing. Seeing him dash out of the Pulaski Hotel's lobby had jolted her. Who knew he'd not only come this morning, but that he'd get here early?

She hadn't really lied to him. The only reason she was still on the block was to get a quick caffeine fix. The last person she expected to run into was Rhys Linsey, sleek as a panther, from the grace of his strides to his black ensemble. Last night, he'd looked suave and sophisticated in a top coat and gray wool trousers with shiny black Oxford shoes. This morning, in a leather jacket, snug dark jeans and black boots, he made her yearn for something hotter than coffee. Something she could never have. Something she had never before wanted so badly.

Still, if she could cross off a few more of Mom's must-do items and enjoy this delicious man's company at the same time, maybe that wasn't such a bad thing. So long as he played by her rules.

The morning chill eased when he took her gloved hand in his and said, "Come on, then. This way."

She allowed him to lead her down the street, past rows of shops, all decorated for the holidays in garlands of silver, green, and red. When it came to hawking wares, the midway couldn't compete with this charming city. A toy store displayed robotic puppies that yipped and wagged their tails, multi-storied dollhouses painted in vivid colors, and vibrant kites with scenes of animals or graphic designs flying on the breeze from lines knotted on a wooden railing.

The dollhouses caught Polina's eye, and she stopped to study them with an interest toward their craftsmanship and appeal. All the walls were straight and flush, and each roof reflected a different style: slate blue, Spanish terracotta, fishscale, and diamond patterns. Pink and blue Victorians with turrets and gingerbread scroll charmed her. She wondered if she'd look like a fairytale character living in such a pretty house. White and gold Georgians impressed her with their pillars—so like the pillars inside the Pulaski Hotel. Too fancy. Much too fancy for her. The last one in the line, a small mint green cottage, boasted a wraparound porch and lots of windows. Yes. That one. That was where she wanted to live when all of this was over. She just had to find it. *After* she finished her tasks here.

"Polina?" Rhys's voice, too close to her ear, elicited a gasp, and he squeezed her hand. "Sorry. Didn't mean to startle you. Do you want to go inside and look around?"

She shook her head and flashed a satisfied grin. "No, I'm done here. Let's go."

In the quaint, warm café, over hazelnut coffee and raspberry *paczki*, Polina struggled to make small talk. Growing up as she had, the art of simple conversation with strangers eluded her. Oh, she could shill money out of anyone, but attempting idle chitchat gave her hives. Someone as normal as Rhys could never understand the type of upbringing she'd lived through. She took a sip of coffee to keep from speaking. Or scratching at her neck. The sweet, nutty aroma helped soothe her anxiety, and holding the cup kept her hands busy.

"Tell me about your mother," he said casually.

She nearly choked as the coffee made a U-turn in her throat. "Why?"

He shrugged. "Because you said she wanted you to

come to Kraków. It might help me understand what I should show you first if I knew a little about why she sent you here."

"To capture the magic." Cripes, did she really blurt that out loud? She took a huge gulp of hot caffeine, looking for a way to snap her brain into functioning mode.

"Hmmm..." Stroking his chin, he practically purred. "Magic, huh? I think I can accommodate that."

"Puh-leez." She snorted. "No one can."

"That's what you think." With a screech of his chair on the tile, he rose. "Come on. Bring your coffee if you're not finished with it yet."

She not only grabbed the coffee, she filched the last *paczki,* as well, before following him out the door of the café. God knew when she'd get another treat like these. It would be a shame to leave any behind. The cold air sliced into her bare hands and goosed her flesh, thanks to her unzipped jacket. After shoving the raspberry doughnut in her pocket, she attempted to gather up both sides of her jacket and attach the zipper tabs with one hand while balancing her unfinished coffee in the other.

"Here, stop." Rhys pulled her closer until her forehead brushed his chin. "Look up," he ordered.

She tilted her head, admiring the way the pale sunlight deepened the green of his eyes. His hands tugged near her waist, and then...

Ziiippppp!

"There you are, all bundled up again," he said with a grin. "Now, give me your coffee so you can put on your gloves."

She handed over her cardboard cup and pulled the gloves out of her pocket, along with the last *paczki.* With her gloves pinned between her torso and her arm, she broke the doughnut in half and offered one of the pieces to him.

Bending, he took it into his mouth, brushing his lips across her hand as he did so. "Mmm...delicious."

A frisson of warmth ribboned through her, and she shivered inside her jacket. Was he flirting with her? God, she hoped not. She'd made it plain she wasn't interested in a Christmas romance—or any other kind of love affair he might have in mind. Why else would she insist on paying her own way?

So his comment must have referred to the doughnut—which she couldn't argue. Once she'd popped the other half into her mouth, she slid her hands into her gloves. "Where to?"

Rhys looked first to the right, then the left side of the street. "We're headed for Old Town," he said and took her hand in his to lead her forward. "I admit, I'm thrilled we don't have to visit the death camp or the Oskar Schindler factory. I really wanted to show you the less horrific places of Kraków. There are a lot of churches and museums, but for starters, you should see more than some dusty old artifacts. I want to show you the beauty and charm of the city, what makes it unique and special, regardless of the heartache that surrounds it. Will that be all right?"

She nodded.

As they walked toward Wawel Cathedral, he told her the history of Kraków's beginnings. "Back in the eighth century, all of this land was a village on the River Vistula, with nothing but mud huts and peace-loving people who traded goods up and down the river. Set into the deep side of Wawel Hill was a cave where a terrible dragon named *Smok Wawelski* slumbered."

She stopped in mid-step on the sidewalk and tilted her head to stare at him with disbelief. "A dragon? Really?"

"Give me a chance to prove it, okay?"

He gave her a pleading look that melted her polar heart. How on earth did he plan to prove a draconian legend? Curiosity overrode common sense, and with a light laugh, she agreed. "Go for it."

Eyes crinkled with a secret smile, he gave one simple nod. "Thank you. Generations were warned against waking the dragon and unleashing its fury upon the poor village, but one day several young boys who, like you, refused to believe the tales, strode bravely up to Wawel Hill to see the dragon for themselves. They crept into the cave and soon came upon the enormous scaly tail of the horrible beast. Well, apparently, one of the boys was so terrified, he screamed, awakening the dragon. The children turned and fled, but the damage was done, and the horrible creature soon began wreaking havoc upon all the townspeople. The dragon would come into their village, day after day, stealing the livestock and carrying off the virgins to be devoured at its leisure.

"The villagers attempted several times to kill the beast, but always failed miserably. Until one day, a shoemaker's apprentice named Krakus mixed up a huge vat of sulfur and coated dozens of sheep with the mixture. When the sheep were ready, he led them to a grassy spot where the dragon was sure to see them. The dragon, naturally, spotted the sheep and swallowed them just as quickly. Soon the sulfur began to take its toll, and the dragon could not contain his thirst. He raced to the River Vistula and drank, but no matter how much water he swallowed, the thirst continued to burn inside him. He nearly drank the river dry until, at last, he swelled so much, he burst like a balloon. *Boom!*"

As Rhys's hands flew in front of her face, Polina jumped back with a squeal of surprise.

Chuckling, he pulled her closer and wrapped an arm around her shoulders. Nothing had ever felt so right as this man's arm holding her close to his heart. She tilted her head at a slight angle, studying his lips, wondering how they'd taste against hers. All he had to do was bend his head forward a few inches...

"Well, of course," he continued, apparently oblivious to her thoughts, "the village rejoiced at the dragon's demise."

She shook off the romantic silliness and refroze her heart. What had she been thinking? A kiss? Good God, she was behaving like her mother, acting on impulse, rather than logic. The last thing she needed was a love affair. Furrowing her brow, she took a step away from him to increase their distance then tried to refocus on his story.

"Krakus was named king and built a castle at the top of Wawel Hill where the dragon's lair once sat. The village prospered into a city and was named Kraków in honor of their hero."

Outside Wawel Cathedral, he stopped in front of a large stone wall where a strange collection of bones sat chained against the rock. An odd-looking snout rode above a rib cage about the size of a giant whale's, some kind of bizarre cloven feet at the base.

"Behold," Rhys whispered against her ear, sending delicious ripples of warm breath across her neck. "Proof. The dragon's bones."

Soft laughter escaped her lips. "Right. Good thing you brought me here. I wouldn't want to waste my time on dusty old artifacts when I could see something as authentic as a dragon skeleton."

"You doubt my sincerity?" He pulled her to another wall and pointed to a plaque. "Here. Look."

Shaking her head at his nonsense, she read the inscription:

KRAKUS, A POLISH PRINCE RULED AD 730-750. HERE IS THE CAVE IN WHICH HAVING KILLED THE WILD DRAGON HE SETTLED AT WAWEL, AND FOUNDED THE CITY OF CRACOW. THIS INSCRIPTION WAS MADE BY STANISLAS JABLONOWSKI, PRINCE OF PRUSSIA AND CAPTAIN OF THE POLISH ARMY ARTILLERY

"Told you so," he said with a wry grin. "One last thing you need to see here." He took her hand to lead her around to the entrance of the closed caves. On a large flat whitish-gray rock, a steel, seven-headed dragon stood sentry, towering over the people milling below. "Watch this." Pulling out his phone, he punched in a series of numbers, then handed the phone to her. The screen read, SMOK. "You do the honors."

She took the phone, confused. "What do I do?"

He pointed to a green arrow. "Press here."

Curiosity riding high, she hit the Send button on his phone. Fire burst from the snout of the steel dragon. She jumped back with a squeal of delight. "Ohmigod, how did you do that?"

"Magic." Wrapping his arm around her again, he escorted her inside the cathedral.

3

She was magic. The more time he spent in her company, the more he wanted to stay with her. Her confusion, her laughter, her frowns, the way she regarded him when she didn't think he noticed—open and vulnerable—all of her charms enthralled him.

Wawel Cathedral was a combination of stunning Gothic and Renaissance architecture, centuries of classical art, and ornate mausoleums for Polish notables. They passed through the arched entrance, and once his eyes adjusted to the dimness compared to the much brighter outdoors, he watched Polina's wide-eyed gaze travel from the golden columns, to the giant crucifix and black marble canopy over the silver coffin flanked by four silver angels, then scan the colorful religious icons lining the walls.

"Whoa," she whispered and stretched her hand toward the ivory-colored ceiling with its Gothic-style molding.

Pleased, he drew her to the right of the nave where, between two massive columns, sat a pair of sarcophagi, one in front of the other. The first was made of red marble, but he bypassed that one for the less fancy tomb.

"Here's something you might find interesting. This is a symbolic resting place, not an actual burial spot, dedicated to King Vladislav III who ruled Poland in the fifteenth century. He was believed to have died at the Battle of Varna in 1444. But his body was never recovered at the site. This tomb was ceremoniously erected in his memory. These days, though, at least one historian claims the king survived and fled to Madeira Island to live in exile, eventually marrying a Portuguese noblewoman. According to this particular historian, the king and his wife had a son who, as an adult, became known to the world as Christopher Columbus."

Polina snapped up her head to stare at him, agape. "Wait. *The* Christopher Columbus?"

"That's his theory. But this historian is a noted expert on Columbus's life. He's spent decades studying the man, doing his research carefully, tracing bloodlines and documents. And he has some valid reasoning that have other scholars agreeing with him. Even I have to admit, it's an interesting possibility."

"So you're saying Christopher Columbus, the man credited with discovering the New World; the guy who sailed the *Nina, Pinta,* and *Santa Maria*; the Genoese explorer who made a deal with Queen Isabella and King Ferdinand of Spain was actually an exiled Polish prince?"

He shrugged, but his nerves quivered with resentment. "His father wouldn't be the first man to create a whole new life, a new identity for himself, to avoid a dangerous situation. And to expect his family to continue perpetuating the lie, even long after he was dead. Not the first, and certainly, not the last, either."

Once inside the cathedral, it took him only a few minutes to conclude that, lovely as some of the tombs and sarcophagi were, Polina had no interest in the various chapels or their attractions. She barely glanced at the intricate stained glass, and completely ignored the delicate effigies of deceased royals.

All to the better, in his estimation, since he didn't really want their day together to focus on death. Her mother had requested she see the magic of this city, and Rhys was happy to accommodate that wish. Without pausing to point out the stunning altar, he led her past the Zebrzydowski chapel and the miraculous portrait of the Virgin Mary, which, according to legend, cried bloody tears in the seventeenth century. Somehow, he doubted she'd be impressed with weeping paintings. He stopped when they reached the sacristy. Dozens of other tourists—most from an American university, judging by their red and white jackets embroidered with the name of the same college—

gathered near the staircase, waiting to ascend the bell tower. He drew her into the group where they waited for an English-speaking tour guide to take them up.

He allowed her to go first, which turned into a bad miscalculation on his part. As she climbed her way to the top via several flights of stairs, her hips and bottom swayed in a provocative manner he couldn't help but appreciate. Several times, he had to fist his hands to keep from gliding a palm over her thigh or clasping her waist to pull her closer. At last, they reached the belfry where the thirteen-ton ceremonial gray steel bell hung from a simple wooden frame that looked almost incomplete, jutting out from walls of ornate red brickwork.

"These days, the Royal Sigismund Bell is only rung on religious holidays and state occasions," the guide told them. "It takes ten men to sound the chime, which can be heard for fifty miles around. You can see the reliefs of Saint Stanislav and Saint Sigismund etched into the bronze. Legend says, the ringing bell banishes clouds and welcomes the sun."

Rather like her smile, Rhys thought.

One by one, the students stepped beneath to touch the clapper that dangled long past the rim of the bell itself.

Her gaze locked on him, head cocked toward one shoulder. "What are they doing?"

"If you make a wish," he explained, "and then touch the clapper, legend says your wish will come true." She frowned, a silent rebuke at his constant allusions to magic, he supposed. "Hey, it's not my idea. That's the legend, which has been around for centuries. If you don't believe me, ask the guide. She'll tell you."

Her gaze shot to the guide who stood in one corner of the tower, arms folded over her chest as she waited for the guests to finish with their wishes. He wasn't sure why Polina fought so hard to deny the possibility of fate, luck, and magic, although he understood her need to forge a path away from parental influence.

In the last fourteen years, he'd never gone home. He'd limited his family contact to sporadic phone calls and internet chats—all to avoid facing off with his father. Always restless, he continually volunteered for the ex-pat jobs.

After a year-long stint in Athens, he spent eighteen months in Hong Kong, almost three years in India, fourteen months in Toronto, and now, Kraków. This particular job would probably last another year or two before he packed up and headed out to another city in another country. Where to next? Who could tell? So far, he had his eye on Dubrovnik, Rome, and Mexico City. Three vastly different locales with different challenges to tackle.

Did Polina share his adventurous spirit? Was that why he'd been so drawn to her from the start? He studied her carefully, mentally picturing her in each city. She still stood near the bell, indecisive, while dozens of other tourists waited their turn to make a wish and touch the clapper.

"Go on," he nudged her with a head jerk.

Clouds of doubt shielded any wonder he might have seen in her eyes, but she paused, exhaled as she made her wish, then turned to take hold of the rod-shaped center.

"Now your wish will come true."

Her blue eyes sparked neon in the dim tower. "Gee, ya think so?" Sarcasm dripped from every word. Turning, she faced the window that overlooked the rooftops of Kraków.

"It's beautiful, isn't it?" He kept his voice low and soothing as he drew nearer, not wanting to rouse her impatience any more than he already had. The entire city sat sprawled beneath them in splendor—snow-coated and sparkling in the early afternoon sun. "There's something special about every city at Christmastime. But, Kraków... Kraków is one of the most beautiful places I've ever seen. Wouldn't you say so?"

On a loud sigh, she faced him with a frown. "Enough already. Are we done here?"

The edge in her tone didn't escape him, but he opted to stay on the soothing tack, hoping to draw out the childish delight she'd displayed when he showed her the smoking dragon trick. "At the cathedral, yes. But we still have to see Wawel Castle."

Her posture stiffened, and she folded her arms over her chest, shooting her weight to one hip. "Why? What's there?"

"The only remaining crown jewels of Poland, the coronation sword, artwork..."

She feigned an enormous yawn that her hand didn't

attempt to cover. "No, thanks. I'll pass."

Her reaction should have surprised him, but while they'd strolled through the cathedral, he'd drawn a few new conclusions about her. Crown jewels, sparkling tiaras, and even elaborate stained glass held no sway with Polina. The crowd, however, drew her attention again and again with more than idle curiosity.

Once he'd figured out what interested her, he watched her watch the people around them. He didn't need a doctorate in psychology to understand why she gravitated toward the interaction between parents and children. After all, she'd only recently lost her sole family member. But then, she displayed an equal interest in the smooching college youths near the bell.

"No more fantasy." Her open impatience shook him from thought to action. "How about we check out something *real* now?"

He couldn't help himself. In two long strides, he stood a breath from her, so close he could see the tiny vein pulsing in her slender throat. "How's this for real?" He dipped his head and pressed his lips to hers. She stiffened for the briefest moment before giving herself over to him. Her arms wound around his neck, fingers playing with the edge of his hairline. Tongues danced, hearts pounded, and the world melted away.

She tasted sweeter than cotton candy. Her soft curves pressed to the hard planes of his chest and flat stomach. His hands settled on her waist, and he intensified the kiss. A low moan from deep inside her mouth landed on his tongue. She melted into him, her legs between his.

As suddenly as she'd accepted him, her hands pushed against his chest, breaking the kiss. When he finally came down from the incredible high, the first thing he saw was her frown.

"Your two hours are up," she said with lethal quiet. "Goodbye, Rhys."

He didn't have time to form an argument before she fled down the stairs.

♥

He'd kissed her! In front of everybody in the tower. She should have known. She might be in another country, but when it came to men, only their accents changed.

Really, it was her own fault. She'd practically thrown herself at him with that challenge about him showing her something real. Stupid. Hadn't Eddie's behavior taught her what all men wanted from her? The way they saw her as easy pickings?

As she stomped down the narrow wooden steps, she tried to find the humor in the situation. At least, she could cross number eight off her mother's list. *Kiss a stranger.* She made a giant checkmark in the air at the same time her feet hit the ground floor of the cathedral. Been there, done that.

Even before the wind outside bit into her face, her eyes stung and tears shimmered. Dammit! She wasn't her mother and wouldn't become her mother. She had plans, plans she would finally be able to accomplish. So long as nothing and no one distracted her. All she had to do was get through the next five weeks. *Last time, Mom.*

"Polina!"

Hearing him call her name, she took off at a run across the busy street, ignoring the car horns that blared at her. Nearly blind from tears, she headed for the square. She hit the sidewalk, dodging Saturday afternoon tourists left and right. Her boots, a little too big, clumped awkwardly, impeding her pace. She dared a quick peek over her shoulder and found him racing toward her, closing the distance between them.

"Polina, stop!"

Fat chance. She needed to get far away from Rhys Linsey and whatever he wanted from her now. She reached the square and immediately realized her mistake. Too open. Nowhere to hide. No cafés or museums here. Just barren, snow-covered gardens, steel fencing, and a fountain. Where on earth could she go to shake him off her tail? The hostel wouldn't allow her into a room until seven p.m.—six hours from now.

She pushed herself harder, cutting across the square, hoping to become invisible in the crowd. People she zipped past turned to watch, but no one offered help of any kind.

Her heart thudded against her chest, and once again, she found breathing difficult. She veered around a tight corner toward an alley between two buildings, hoping for an outlet on the other end.

Frantic, heart pounding, and out of breath, she scanned the crowd, searching for someone—anyone—to help her.

And suddenly, there she was: the gypsy girl from last night, still garbed in her fiery scarves, beckoning from a new alcove in a different square than yesterday's. "Hurry! This way!"

With no other choice, Polina hobbled toward the fortune teller. "Thank you," she huffed out as the girl slid sideways to create a hiding place between the wall and her shelves of glittery geegaws. Protected by the gypsy's voluminous skirt, she sank to the frigid ground and watched Rhys stop short in the middle of the square.

He turned a slow circle, scanning the throngs of people who loitered to take pictures or point out items of interest. When he didn't find her among the crowds, he sped off in the opposite direction from where she hid.

Still struggling to catch her breath, Polina clambered to her shaky feet. "Thanks," she told the gypsy again.

The dark-haired girl shrugged. "It was just a kiss, you know."

Polina sucked in a sharp breath. "What?"

Her eyes took on an other-worldly luster. "He only kissed you. Why did you run?"

"Because...it's...he...I..." she sputtered. How could she possibly explain her past to this child? Then anger took over. Why did she have to explain anything? To anyone? "If you know so much," she retorted, "*you* tell *me* why I ran."

"Because the last man who kissed you thought you were like your mother," she replied without hesitation or emotion.

"H-how did you...?"

"This one doesn't know your mother. He kissed you because you're you."

Polina didn't want to hear this, wasn't sure how some rogue gypsy girl guessed the truth, but she didn't have to entertain her lunacy. "Well, thank you for your help, but I have to go now."

"Of course." The girl stepped out of the alcove to allow Polina room to pass. When she did, the gypsy grabbed her hand. "If you weren't ready for your future, you shouldn't have followed the dog last night."

"Yeah, great, thanks," she grumbled and yanked away. At least she could walk through Old Town at a more leisurely pace for a while now, until she decided where to go next.

"Don't forget to seek out the cemetery," the gypsy called after her. "Your mother wants her ashes interred with her parents."

Polina never turned around again, never questioned how the girl knew what she knew. Maybe her experience with Eddie Reznick remained stamped on her features or the bruises he'd left behind hadn't fully faded, even all these years later.

Jablonski Enterprises had picked up Eddie outside Enid, Oklahoma when she was fifteen. At first, he'd charmed her, though Tiny hated the new cowboy on sight.

"Something isn't right with that bronco-buster," the old professor warned her. "You steer clear of him."

She should have heeded that advice, but Eddie's good looks spoke louder than any dire prediction. Years of loneliness had roused a need in her—a hunger for a friend close to her own age. And Eddie *seemed* so nice. Until that night after the show in Wildflower...

The brisk wind howled a mournful tune and, shivering, she huddled deeper into her coat before slinking into the shadows, hoping Rhys wouldn't find her, yet wishing he could.

♥

Rhys had no idea what had set her off, but the second he realized Polina had flown, he chased after her. On the top step outside the cathedral, he spotted her as she zigzagged through the crowd across the street. What the hell?

"Polina!" he shouted.

She didn't even turn around. Instead, she shot like a

deer who'd sensed a hunter, except the ridiculous boots she wore made her a lot less graceful in flight. He scaled the steps two at a time and caught a break in the traffic to cross the street.

When she looked over her shoulder, he pleaded, "Polina, stop!"

She ducked her head and bolted into the center of a crowd of tourists who snapped photos near a fountain. He sped in that direction and nearly barreled over an elderly couple strolling in front of him, their focus pinned on the fountain. Skidding to a halt inches from the old man's belly, he murmured a quick apology and waited for them to pass. As soon as he had enough room to maneuver around them, he wended his way toward where he'd last seen Polina.

Gone. He stopped, turned a full three-hundred-sixty degrees. No sign of her, her telltale hair, or ridiculous boots. She'd disappeared.

Dammit. Now what? She could've gone in any direction. He'd lost her. Possibly for good.

No. Hope glimmered inside his brain. He might not know where she headed now, but he knew where she'd be tonight. The Pulaski Hotel.

Destination in mind, he left the square and raced the few blocks to her hotel. He pushed into the lobby and strode straight to the reservations area. A pretty brunette behind the counter greeted him in Polish. "Good afternoon, sir, can I help you?"

"English please?" He didn't dare trust his rusty knowledge of the native language to such an important matter.

"Of course, sir," she replied. "Are you checking in?"

"No. You have a guest staying here. I'd like to leave her a message."

"Do you know what room she's in?" She lifted a telephone receiver.

"No."

Replacing the receiver, she frowned at him, eyes narrowed with open suspicion. "I'm sorry. I can't release that information to you."

He smiled and held his hands up, hoping to relieve the tension and the woman's dark suspicions. She probably thought he was deranged. "No, that's fine. I just want to leave her a message she can pick up later. Would that be all right?"

Her expression softened. "I think so. Do you want to leave a voice message or a written message?"

"Which is better?"

She shrugged. "I would imagine it depends on what you want to say."

"I want to say I'm sorry."

A brilliant smile illuminated her face. Figured. A groveling man could make the snootiest woman amenable. "Well, personally, I would prefer flowers in that case, but a voice message is probably the next best thing. I'll dial her room and hand you the phone, and you can leave your apology. Yes?"

"Yes." He breathed a sigh of relief. This would work. He just needed a minute or two to figure out what he'd say. He still didn't understand why she'd run off, which made coming up with the right apology difficult, but if he had to grovel, he'd crawl on the ground for her.

"What's her name?"

"Polina Kominski."

The clerk turned to her computer to search for Polina's room number. After a minute or two, she looked up, a confused expression on her face. "Would you spell the last name, please?"

He didn't know how. He assumed it was obvious. But he couldn't admit that to her or she might go back to thinking he was a dangerous stalker. "Is there a problem?"

"I don't have a guest with that name."

Ridiculous. "She checked in yesterday."

The woman returned to the computer and did a little more typing, then shook her head. "No, sir, I'm sorry. Nothing under that first name or last name. Are you sure she checked in here? Perhaps she's at the Polska Hotel?"

No. He'd left her here yesterday, and met her outside this hotel four hours ago. Was she registered under a different name?

"Can you tell me if any single women checked in here yesterday? She's about this tall..." He held his hand level with the top of his chest. "...strawberry blond hair, blue eyes. American."

"We only had two Americans check in yesterday while I was on duty, and neither of them comes close to that description."

He scratched his scalp, revitalizing his brain cells. So maybe she checked in when someone else was behind the desk? On second thought, he'd never actually seen her check in. She'd gone into the lobby last night and then...

Didn't he sense she watched him walk away? At the time, he'd chalked it up to attraction. Because his ego wouldn't permit him to think anything else.

But what if she'd exited the lobby immediately after he'd gone because she didn't want him to know where she was really staying? Disappointment sank fangs into his heart. She could be anywhere in the city. What could he do now? Traipse around Kraków, asking every desk clerk in every hotel in the area if she'd checked in there?

The reservations clerk stared at him, her eyes alight with curiosity, and he forced a bland expression. "You're probably right," he said at last. "I must have screwed up the Pulaski with the Polska. I'm sorry to trouble you."

She offered him a tired smile that suggested such a mix-up was a common occurrence. "No trouble at all, sir. Have a nice day. And good luck."

Good luck. He'd need it to find her now. He turned away from the reservations desk, his mind reeling. Polina had tried to ditch him this morning by leaving before the time they'd set up to meet. That was no accident and no simple run for coffee.

What did he know about her anyway? That her name was Polina Kominski—if she hadn't lied about her identity. Unlike him, she hadn't shown any identification when they met. Who would've thought to ask? She claimed to be from the United States. Those were the only facts he had, and he couldn't be sure they were true. She hadn't even told him *where* in the States she hailed from.

She'd ditched him this time, for certain. For one brief day, less than twenty-four hours, he'd held a treasure in his hand. Now, it seemed that treasure was simply fools' gold.

4

Hours of stomping in her too-big vinyl boots caused an inordinate amount of agony. Blisters abraded her heels, her toes ached, and her legs silently screamed with every step. By five o'clock, Polina had no choice but to head back to the hostel in the hopes she could talk someone into taking pity on her and giving her a place to warm up and prop up her feet for the night. Around the corner from her destination, she found a pharmacy and picked up a bottle of pain relief pills and some adhesive bandages.

After paying for the purchase, she checked her wallet and frowned at the outlay of cash in her first forty-eight hours in this city. Maybe she shouldn't have fought so rabidly to go Dutch, particularly since Rhys had kissed her anyway. In paying her own way, she'd established a boundary. At least, she *thought* she'd established a boundary. Either Rhys thought differently, or he hadn't cared. Still, it had been a wild kiss, full of electric promise— the kind of kiss that her mom would have followed through to its inevitable end: in bed with a handsome stranger. But not Polina. She would not become her mother just because the same passionate blood pumped in her veins. She had control over her emotions; they didn't control her.

The fast food place near the hostel wafted the smell of old grease into the evening air. Dinner called. Too exhausted and aching to voice her disgust, she limped into the scorching light of the restaurant. While her eyes adjusted to the brightness, she only discerned shadows, customers huddled in booths or standing on line, waiting to order.

"You're hurt."

The two words came from behind her, and she whirled. Voice and physical outline confirmed what her tired eyes refused to believe. Rhys sat in the corner booth, a cup of sludgy coffee in front of him.

"I'm fine," she bit out.

"It's those boots," he replied as he slid out of his seat. "You should know better than to run in boots like those."

Drained, her feet throbbing, she snapped, "I left my track shoes behind in my other backpack."

"That's not all you left behind."

Cripes, she didn't have the energy for a verbal sparring match. Shifting her weight, she folded her arms over her chest. It was too warm in the restaurant to leave her jacket zipped, but she needed to shield herself from his barbs and anger. Although the pain in her feet kept her from standing up straight, she fisted her hands and forced a harsh tone. "What do you want, Rhys?"

"Quite a lot actually." He pointed to the booth. "Sit. Get your weight off your feet."

"No, thanks."

He leaned close, eyes narrowed to feral slits, and hissed, "Sit."

She sat. As she slid onto the hard plastic seat, he knelt beside her and lifted her legs until they were parallel with the bench. "Hey!"

"Quiet!" He yanked off her boots, one at a time, spraying pain across her arches. She winced and swerved away, but he pulled her back and slid off the socks. She didn't have to look; his sharp intake of breath said it all. "Wow. If your goal today was to blister your feet, you succeeded admirably."

She folded into herself, hugging her knees against her chest. "I'm fine!" The shout erupted loud enough to cause other customers to turn toward them. For an agonizing moment, no one moved while all eyes stared at her until she wanted to squirm out of her skin.

Rhys didn't even look up. "No, you're not fine," he growled. "Now knock off the martyr act and sit still so I can help you."

Her stomach grumbled loudly, and his gaze traveled from her feet to her face. "When was the last time you ate?"

Cheeks aflame, she twisted her lips into a sneer and attempted to change the subject. "What are you doing here, Rhys? Don't you have a home to go to?"

"I asked you first," he retorted.

Typical caveman response.

"Tough," she snapped back, then turned her attention to the glowing board near the counter. Her mouth watered at the pictures of juicy burgers piled high with ripe tomato slices and crisp green lettuce.

"Answer me. When was the last time you had something to eat?"

"This morning." She knew the real product would look nothing like the photo. The burger would taste like lint from a dryer, with soggy lettuce and flavorless tomatoes. Her empty stomach didn't care.

"What the hell have you been up to since you ran off?"

Oh, well, now that was unfair. She wasn't exactly a felon or an international spy. "Nothing."

The fight seemed to flow out of him in one giant flood. The stiffness left his posture, and he sank onto the opposite bench, folding his arms on the table. His hazel gaze fixed on her with concern. "Are you in some kind of trouble, Polina?"

"What?" Was he insane? "Of course not."

He rubbed his fingers over his eyes. "Then, what's going on with you?"

"Nothing." She removed her gloves and stared at the thin nylon lining, stared at the thick black coffee, anywhere but at him.

He reached out and placed his hand over hers, squeezed gently. "I'm a patient man, sweetheart. I can sit here for hours. In fact..." He gestured to the half-filled coffee cup. "...I already have. So if you want me gone, you're going to have to answer a few questions for me first."

Her head snapped up. "Like what?"

"What's your real name?"

She blinked. "You already know that."

"Humor me."

What, like she was hooked up to a lie detector or

something? Wow. He really did think she was a criminal. Or a spy. Okay, fine. The sooner she cooperated, the sooner he'd disappear. "Polina Kominski."

"And where are you staying in Kraków?" His voice was low but an undercurrent of anger laced his words. "Because you sure as hell aren't registered at the Pulaski. Why'd you lie about that, Polina?"

"I never told you I was staying at the Pulaski. You just assumed it."

"You *lied* to me."

"No, I didn't." She pulled her hand away from his. "Think about it. I don't know Kraków, and I don't speak Polish. That makes it kind of difficult to get around if I can't ask people for directions or tell a cabdriver where to take me. So I chose the nearest landmark to where I'm staying. You can see the Pulaski's spires from just about anywhere in this area. No matter where I go, I always look for the copper spires, and I can find my way back. Last night when we met, you asked me where I was headed, and I pointed to the spires. That's where I was headed. *You* assumed that meant I planned to go to the Pulaski."

Deep frown lines etched his forehead. "That still doesn't tell me where you *are* staying."

"What does that matter?"

"It matters to me. What are you hiding? Are you married? Or staying with a lover?"

"No, of course not!" Did he think she was like her mother? The idea turned her stomach. "*Definitely* not!"

"Then, why the secrecy? Why can't you tell me where you're staying?"

"Okay, fine." She let him see her annoyance by rolling her eyes and heaving a sigh that sounded like air brakes on a Mack truck. "St. Tadeusz Youth Hostel."

His jaw dropped. "That rathole down the block?"

"It's not a rathole."

"Oh, I beg your pardon. Gentlemen overdose on heroin and ladies are beaten and raped in all the finest Kraków establishments."

She winced but refused to apologize for her accommodations choice. "I keep my door barricaded at night."

"Jesus." He raked a trembling hand through his hair. "You're serious."

"It's not a big deal. I know how to be careful. Besides, I've been in worse places."

"Really? Where? Afghanistan?"

She clamped her lips together and reached for her sock. She'd had enough. Enough of his censure and his judgment and his unsubstantiated anger. "It's been fun, Rhys. Have a nice life." The pain in her feet could cripple an elephant, but she fought back tears and managed to fumble the socks over her toes with some effort.

"You are the most stubborn, exasperating woman."

Her gaze shot up level with his. "You don't have to stay with me. Go home."

"I'm here because I want to be here. I care about you."

"You don't even know me."

He slapped his palms on the tabletop. "Whose fault is that? If you trusted me and told me the truth, maybe I could help." Reaching across, he clasped her hand again. "Talk to me, please."

She hated to admit how much warmth and security he communicated with that simple contact. Could she trust him? Did she dare? What had the gypsy girl said? *He kissed you because you're you.* He didn't know her mother—didn't know her, either, for that matter. So, if she took the chance, told him the truth, would he be able to separate who she was from the specter of her mother's actions? Only one way to find out.

On a defeated sigh, she rolled her shoulders, braced for the coming storm. "What do you want to know?"

"For starters, explain how this hostel works."

She shrugged. "Nothing to it. I check in every night at seven and check out every morning by ten."

"And where do you go when you check out?"

"Wherever I need to go. I told you, my mother left me an itinerary with stuff she wants me to take care of while I'm here. I keep busy."

"Maybe you kept busy yesterday and probably today." He jerked his head at her foot. "But by tomorrow, if you keep wearing those boots, you won't be moving much."

"I'll be okay. I bought some aspirin and a box of Band-

Aids. I'll take care of the blisters when I get into a room tonight." *If* she got into a room tonight.

"I've got a better idea." He pulled his cell phone from his pocket and punched in a number. "Henryk? I need your help with something."

She leaned across the table to listen in, but he immediately switched to Polish to finish the conversation.

After several frustrating minutes, he tucked the phone back into his pocket. "Let's go get your luggage out of that place. I'm taking you somewhere else."

Since she had no intention of going anywhere with him, she didn't bother to argue. "I don't have any luggage."

"Where's all your stuff?"

She fingered the straps of the backpack on her shoulder. "I keep it with me."

His eyes widened. "You have five weeks' worth of luggage in that little rucksack?"

"I pack light."

"How light?"

"Three pairs of jeans, five shirts, a weeks' worth of underwear and socks, an extra pair of gloves, my tablet, and my passport."

"That's it?" he demanded. "That's all you brought with you for a trip halfway around the world that will last more than a month?"

"What else do I need?" She sat up when she remembered something else. "Oh! I also have my mother's ashes. But that's temporary until I can arrange for her to be placed in her family crypt. I have an appointment with someone at the cemetery on Monday."

"We can talk about all that later. Right now, you're coming with me—"

"No. I'm not going anywhere with you. I'm staying right here, having something to eat, and then checking into my room for the night. At Saint Tadeusz. Whatever other plans you just made, cancel."

A superior, smug smile crept onto his lips. "I called my friend, Henryk. He and his wife, Bianka, are expecting you. They have a spare bedroom that's yours for the duration of your stay. Bianka is a nurse so she'll be able to properly care for those blisters. She's also a great cook. And if we hurry, you can have *bigos* tonight instead of this slop. Do you know what *bigos* is?"

She nodded, her stomach begging her to accept this generous offer, but pride still overruling hunger. "Hunter's stew. Uncle Leo used to make it sometimes."

"Uncle Leo?"

"Mom's godfather. I grew up with him." Her mood, already near the basement, plummeted.

"Where exactly did you grow up? Where are you from in the States?"

"Everywhere and nowhere. We moved around a lot." Like every week.

Clearly, he didn't believe her. If his expelled breath didn't communicate impatience, the slow shake of his head did the trick. "Dammit, Polina, I wish you'd be honest with me."

She thumped a fist on the table. "I *am* being honest with you. I've never really had a home. My family wasn't the stick-around type."

His eyes glinted like marbles, disbelief gleaming. "Where did you live?" he retorted. "In a tent?"

"Nope. A trailer." Satisfaction rippled through her. Time to go in for the kill. "And not in a trailer park, either. I'm talking about a true *mobile* home."

He didn't even wince, just sat there, expression bland, waiting for her to say more. He wanted the truth, thought he could deal with whatever she told him. But he didn't know the real dirt. Okay. Let's see how fast he ran when she revealed all. Most people couldn't wait to distance themselves from her when they heard a fraction of her past. Except for Eddie. Eddie, who'd only stuck around for the "fringe benefits" he assumed she'd be giving him. On a deep breath, she leaned forward to whisper, "Do you know what a 'carny' is?"

"A what?"

"A carny."

"Can't say I do."

"It's a person who works in a traveling carnival."

"You traveled with a carnival?!" His voice rose several decibels, and she clamped her thighs together to keep from diving under the table.

GINA ARDITO

"Yeah." She grimaced and let the sarcasm fly. "Trust me. It's not as glamorous as you think."

He clasped his hands on the table. "What *was* it like?"

"Lonely and back-breaking," she replied.

"Oh, come on. There must have been fun times, too."

"Not many," she murmured, then shook her head to clear the bitter memories. She needed a pleasant distraction. "What about you? What's your family like?"

"Not worth talking about." He shrugged. "I've lived a very dull life, compared to you. I'm the only son with four sisters. There were times I would've liked to join a carnival. Being with my family isn't much different; it's noisy, chaotic, and crowded."

"It sounds wonderful," she murmured, unable to stifle the wistful air in her tone.

Sure, her life had been noisy, chaotic, and crowded too. The difference was, for him, all those inconveniences came from *family,* people who knew him and loved him twenty-four hours a day, seven days a week, fifty-two weeks a year. In her case, the noise, chaos, and crowds were due to strangers. In her personal life, no one took an interest in her, knew how she took her coffee, cared if she were sick or hurting. Not even her mother, who spent her offstage time drunk or high.

"Most of the time," she continued, her mind going back to all those years with Jablonski Entertainments, "I handled ride maintenance and repair. Mom was in charge of dukkering. You'd call her a gypsy, telling fortunes and predicting futures with cards or a crystal ball. But we all pitched in wherever we were needed. If you've seen anyone working at a carnival, chances are, I've done that same job at least once in my life. I sold tickets, manned the rides, lifted steel."

"Lifted steel?"

"Basically, it's what it sounds like. Assembling the rides and outbuildings. I also dropped awnings, which is what we call closing up shop for the night. I played the gypsy role when Mom was too blotto to do her job."

"Was your mother a real gypsy? A Rom, I mean."

"No. She just sort of looked like what most people consider a gypsy to look like. Actually, she made herself

40

look like what people consider gypsy-like. She dyed her hair black, which looked 'mystical' with her pale blue eyes. Almost otherworldly, I guess. And she wore heavy makeup. Uncle Leo—he owns the carnival we traveled with—he brought my mother to the States from Kraków a long time ago, when my grandparents died. She practically grew up around the carnival."

"And you? When did you get involved?"

"I was born in the bunkhouse."

"What about your father? Do you look like him? Was he part of the carnival too?"

"Dunno. I never met him. By the time my mother realized she was pregnant with me, she was six towns ahead with a different lover she'd left behind in each one. Even if she'd heard his name the night I was conceived, she would've been too incoherent to remember it. Mom went through men like most people go through toothpicks."

And just like that, there they were. All her sins laid out flat on the table, a deck of playing cards stacked against her. She struggled to rise from the bench. Better to say goodbye, rather than watch someone else walk away from her in disgust. "I should go. Get some sleep."

"Absolutely."

A sharp pang of regret pierced her heart when he followed her lead and got to his feet. She knew it. As soon as anyone learned the truth about her, they couldn't wait to get as far away from her as possible.

But Rhys wrapped his arm around her waist, bent to catch her knees, and then scooped her up. "Come on. Henryk and Bianka are waiting."

5

"Hey!" she exclaimed.

He ignored her protest as he scooped her against his chest, grabbed her gloves and dangled her boots from his fingertips, then carried her out of the grease pit. The icy December air refreshed his face and allowed him to breathe freely after four miserable hours stuck inside the overheated fast food place.

Fate.

She'd been planning to get coffee in this dump this morning so he took a chance she'd come back here for lunch. Lunch had nearly turned to dinner, and he'd almost given up, but she'd finally appeared. Hurt and hurting, but safe.

And now, after he'd learned about her unusual upbringing, so many pieces of her puzzle fit together. Oh, he still had plenty of questions, but they could wait.

"Put me down please," she said, her breath warm against his neck.

He tightened his hold. "No. If I put you down, I have no guarantee you won't try to run away again."

"You've got my boots. I'm not running anywhere in my stocking feet."

"Sorry, I'm not taking any chances so make yourself comfortable. You're stuck with me holding you 'til we get to the car. And then I'm going to drive you to the Nowaks' house and put you directly into Bianka's hands."

"How far away is your car?"

"Four blocks up in my company's employee garage." He

jerked his head toward the thirty-story steel structure, incongruous in this part of Kraków.

"Why didn't you drive when we were touring the cathedral this morning?"

"Because parking in town is a bear. It's easier to leave the car and walk—if you're wearing decent shoes. Henryk lives about five miles from here, and while you may be a lightweight, I don't think I have the energy to carry you that far."

She said nothing for about a block or two before she announced in a strong and loud voice, "I'm not going to sleep with you, Rhys. I'm not my mother."

Jesus. Did she really think that was all he cared about? What kind of louts was she accustomed to dealing with? His thoughts traveled back to her comment about her room at Saint Thadeusz. *I've stayed in worse places.* Where? What had it been like for her, growing up among carnival folk?

Later. He'd find time to get additional info out of her, but she'd already given him so much of herself, how could he possibly ask for more?

"I never met your mother," he remarked in a bland tone, "which means I'll have to take your word on the contrast between you two."

"I'm serious."

"So am I. I already told you, Polina, I'm a patient man. I just hope you didn't take a lifetime vow of celibacy because that would really suck."

She actually laughed, but only for a moment before her smile flipped to a frown. "Are you sure your friends won't mind us just showing up?" A tremor of fear rattled her words.

"We're not 'just showing up.' I already called them. They're expecting us. Don't you know anything about Polish hospitality? They have an old proverb here: 'When you welcome a guest, you're welcoming God into your home.'"

"Don't tell them what I told you," she said in an urgent whisper. "About where I'm from. They won't be so happy to see me if they know the truth."

He could've argued with her. The Nowaks wouldn't give a whit about where she came from. She was in trouble and they could help. That was all that would matter to them. For now, he let her stew, promising nothing. Soon enough, she'd see for herself.

He made it to the parking lot and found his car in his assigned slot. "I'm going to put you down for a moment to unlock the doors. Stand on the tops of my feet to keep your socks dry, all right? Promise not to take off?"

She gave him a quelling look. "How far could I get?"

"Smart girl." He leaned forward and kissed her on the forehead. She drew back, surprise in her eyes and a frown on her lips. "Don't worry. I don't consider that foreplay."

"Funny."

After gently placing her on top of his booted feet, he reached into his jacket pocket for his keys. Once he unlocked the car doors, he opened the passenger door. "Get in."

To his amusement, she didn't take a step onto the cement at their feet. Instead, she folded her body so her backside hit the edge of the seat, then she slid backwards until she could pull her legs in, unscathed. "All set. Hand me my boots."

"Over my dead body." He slammed the passenger door, then strode around the front of the car before climbing into the driver's seat and tossing her boots in the back.

Ten minutes later, she was sound asleep, her head bouncing slightly as he took the curves. He drove the rest of the way to the Nowaks' house, listening to her even breathing.

I'm not going to sleep with you, Rhys.

Casting a quick glance at her slumbering form in his back seat, he smiled to himself. She'd definitely need more time before she'd admit it, but she was already sleeping with him. Not in the way she meant the statement, and certainly not in the way he hoped their relationship would eventually proceed, but this was a start. She trusted him. Considering her background, he sensed she didn't offer that gift lightly.

He arrived at their destination a short time later, and pulled into the driveway of a cozy two-story home on a quiet street. Before he turned off the car's headlights, the front door opened, and Henryk stepped out onto the stoop. Rhys cut the engine.

Polina stirred and slowly sat up. "Pretty house. Too pretty. I can't stay here."

"Don't move," Rhys said, unclasping his seat belt. "I'll come get you."

"No." She climbed over the car seat to grab her boots. "Take me back to St. Thadeusz. I can't stay here."

He blew out an exasperated breath. "Polina, look on the porch." He jabbed a finger at the windshield. "That's Henryk standing there. You're welcome here. They're expecting you. Trust me."

"That's because they don't know who I am." The uncertainty in her expression pierced him with sympathy. "Maybe you should tell them. I'll wait here." She folded her arms over her chest, as if protecting her heart.

Enough nonsense. She had no reason to feel inferior. The sooner she realized that, the better for both of them. "You're coming with me. Right now. Even if I have to carry you over my shoulder."

"No! You're not carrying me inside like an invalid."

"Oh, for God's sake."

"I mean it, Rhys. I don't want your friends thinking I'm some helpless orphan you found roaming the streets of Kraków, a Polish version of the Little Match Girl."

Pride. And shame. Whereas she started this trek too ashamed to stay, now she would let whatever iota of pride she possessed overrule her common sense. He gauged the distance from the driveway to the front door. A good forty-five meters. Maybe she was right. The damage was already done.

"I can walk it," she insisted.

Stepping out of the car, he muttered to himself about stubborn women who didn't know what was good for them. When he opened her door, she had her feet back in the ridiculous boots. Even in the darkness, he noted the glimmer in her eyes from unshed tears. She hadn't taken her first step yet, and already had to stifle the urge to cry from the pain.

On one deep sniff, she looked up at him, and forced a wan smile. "Let's do this."

He leaned into the car and looped an arm around her

waist to pull her forward. The minute she stood on her own, she sucked in a wince.

From the top of the stairs, Henryk shouted out, "Bianka!"

"Come on," Rhys said, straightening. "Before they grab the stretcher to carry you into the house."

"God, no. You're kidding, aren't you?"

"You want to test that theory?"

"No," she said with a shiver that rippled through him.

"Okay, then. Lean on me to keep most of the weight off your feet." He flung her arm over his neck and wrapped her waist, drawing her slowly up the driveway and toward the stairs. Once there, he didn't offer her a choice. He scooped her up and carried her the rest of the way.

"Hey!" This time, she made her displeasure known by pounding her fist on his shoulder. It had as much impact as hitting him with cotton balls. "Put me down. I told you not to carry me."

"Sit tight, and I'll have you back down on solid ground in a minute." By the time he reached the top, Henryk and Bianka both waited, concern etched on their faces.

"Bring her inside, Rhys," Bianka ordered in her brook-no-nonsense tone as she swept the door open. "Put her on the sofa, legs propped up on the pillows please."

He sidled past his hosts, strode directly into the living room, and set her on the prearranged couch. Several pillows piled on the opposite end would elevate her legs.

Bianka, right on his heels, switched on the lamp at Polina's feet. "Hello," she said in very thickly accented English, her reassuring smile aimed directly at Polina. "I am Bianka, Rhys's friend. I am going to take very good care of you." Bianka pointed to the boots. "I can remove these, yes?" At Polina's nod, Bianka slid the plastic boots from her feet with deliberate care. Still, Polina winced and sucked in a sharp breath. Bianka took one look at the blisters and abraded skin, then clucked her tongue.

Henryk and Bianka spoke in rapid Polish, then Henryk translated for Rhys and Polina. "My wife says you're lucky the damage isn't worse. She'll treat the blisters, but you'll need a pair of good, comfortable shoes, and you'll have to give your feet a chance to heal before you do any more extended walking."

"How long?" Polina asked, alarm in each word.

He spoke to his wife, then turned to Polina with an apologetic shrug. "A day or two. Not to worry. You're welcome to stay as our guest for the next few weeks until you return home."

While Henryk spoke to Polina, his wife spread some kind of salve to her feet and applied small open bandages to the affected areas.

Sucking in a sharp breath, Polina flinched, nearly leaping off the couch again. "No, thank you," she said. "That's very kind of you, but it's not necessary. Rhys, tell them. I can't stay here for five weeks."

"Why not?" He arched a brow at her. "Are you in a rush to go back to that hostel?"

"I have stuff I have to do." She spoke through her teeth, eyes wide. He didn't know whether she wanted to convey some secret message to him or to knock Bianka's probing fingers away from her poor, battered feet. "Remember? The list from my mother?"

"I know," he assured her. "And from what you told me, that list included celebrating a traditional Kraków Christmas. You'll do that here. With the Nowaks and with me. If there's anything else on the list you need to see to, I'll help."

"But...you can't...I mean..." she sputtered. "You don't have the time."

"We have the rest of the weekend right now. Come Monday, I'll call the office and rearrange my schedule so I can handle some of my work off-site. That will give me more time to be with you."

Polina folded her arms over her chest. "No. This is ridiculous. I barely know you." She pointed at the Nowaks. "And I don't know them at all. I can't stay here."

Rhys perched on the edge of the couch and cupped her fingers inside his palm. "Relax. You're in good hands here. Better hands than you'd be in at St. Thadeusz."

"Rhys!" Feliks raced into the room, eyes alight with excitement, an equally enthusiastic Kacper barking at his side. The dog seemed overjoyed to see Polina and bounded toward where she lay on the couch.

"Kacper. *Tu przyjść!*" Bianka immediately chastised the wolfhound, grabbed his collar, and handed him off to Henryk. "Take him out of here before he scares our guest. I need to see to dinner." She shuffled out of the living room, Henryk and Kacper right behind her.

Alone with Polina and the boy, Rhys ruffled Feliks's hair. "Feliks. *Jak są wy?*" The boy replied he was well, and Rhys switched to English for Polina's benefit. "This is my friend, Polina. She and I are staying for dinner, if that's all right with you. She doesn't speak Polish. Perhaps you'd like to practice your English with her?"

The child stepped forward, hand outstretched. "Hello, Polina. You are the one Mama needs to help, yes?"

She cast a curious glance at Rhys, who shrugged. "I guess so."

"How did you hurt your feet?" the boy asked.

"Walking around in boots that don't fit right."

"Oh." He looked from Polina to Rhys, and switching to Polish, remarked, "She doesn't say English words like you do."

"She's American," he explained.

"Ahem!" Polina interjected. "Care to share with those of us who know you're talking about us, but don't understand the language?"

"Sorry," Rhys told her. "His English is about as decipherable as my Polish so we tend to meet in the middle. For what it's worth, he said he thinks you're very pretty even if your feet are uglier than a troll's."

Feliks giggled, and Polina's cheeks flushed bright pink. "He did not."

"Enough teasing." Bianka reappeared in the living room, a tray full of steaming dishes in her hands. "You two." She jerked her head at Rhys and Feliks. "In the dining room. Before your dinner gets cold."

Rhys sent a glance Polina's way, and her panicked expression nearly broke his heart. "I'm in the next room, sweetheart. Relax."

♥

Relax. Yeah, right. While her feet grew numb from whatever that stinky stuff was Bianka had spread on the blisters, her brain went into full panic mode, urging her to run away. This was insane. She couldn't stay here. With people she didn't know. People who didn't know her. And she certainly couldn't stay here for five whole weeks.

Bianka and Henryk Nowak were not what she'd expected. They weren't much older than she, maybe early thirties. Henryk was a handsome man, tall and barrel-chested, with fair hair and lovely light green eyes. His wife had a figure like a roller coaster, full of lush curves, reddish-brown hair and brown eyes. Both smiled and nodded and fussed over her as if she were a royal princess. Which was so far from the facts of the matter.

Before she could make a move, though, Bianka sat beside her and placed the tray on the coffee table. "Rhys said you like *bigos*."

"Yes. My uncle used to make it. But you don't have to bring my meal in here. I can sit in the dining room with everyone else."

"No, you cannot." She tucked a napkin under Polina's chin then picked up the bowl of hearty stew made with several meats, root vegetables, and a thick gravy. After dipping a spoon into the bowl, the older woman gestured for Polina to open her mouth.

"Really," she argued softly, "I can feed myself."

"No. You too skinny for Polish girl. I make sure you eat more. Open, please."

The ridiculousness of the situation struck Polina as she did what Bianka demanded, and her thoughts flew to Mom's list. *Note to self: be sure to add (26.) Pretend you're a baby bird.*

At first taste, Polina fell in love. Sure, Uncle Leo made *bigos*, but *never* like this. His *bigos* always had a greasy film on top. The older guys often complained that Uncle Leo could use leftovers to keep the cogs spinning on some of the rides. The meat was usually stringy and tough, not tender enough to melt-in-the-mouth like Bianka's. Uncle Leo's gravy, while thick, had lumps of flour often mistaken for bits of potato. This, though...this was heavenly. The best meal Polina had ever eaten.

"You tell me about you?" Bianka said. "You American?"

"Yes." The spoon appeared near her mouth, and she automatically took the stew, chewed the tender meat and vegetables then swallowed.

"Your mother, she was from Kraków?"

With her mouth full of another spoon of delicious stew, she couldn't speak, so she settled for a nod.

"How old when she left Poland?"

She swallowed and smacked her lips. "I'm not sure. Six or seven, I think."

"Like my Feliks."

Unsure whether Bianka compared Mom's age or Polina's lip-smacking to Feliks, she nodded. "Her parents died, and her godfather took Mom to live with him in America."

"And now *she* died, so you came home, eh?"

"Not really. I mean, yes, my mother died, but I'm only here for the holiday. This isn't home for me. Mom thought the magic of the city would refresh me."

"It will. You'll see. There is nothing like Kraków during Christmas. The *szopki, choinka, Wigilia,* so much fun and beauty. Your mama, she was right. It is a magic time. You'll stay here 'til it's time for you to go home. Rhys told us where you planned to sleep." She didn't elaborate further, but her pursed lips and knitted brows made her displeasure obvious.

"It wasn't so bad." Polina dipped her head to hide her embarrassment. Not that she had any reason to be ashamed. What did these people with their warm, cozy home and abundant meals know about living hand-to-mouth, never having enough money or food or safety?

Bianka tipped up Polina's chin. The older woman's solemn expression darkened as she shook her head. "Not good. Not safe. Not your fault, but you deserve better. It's better here. We'll take good care of you."

Throughout the conversation, Bianka spoon fed her stew then sopped up the last of the gravy with pieces of bread. At last, she handed her what looked like a toddler's first cup, covered with a plastic lid and built-in straw.

"Tea," she said, "with honey and lemon." She opened a small, white bottle and tapped two tablets into her palm.

"For pain." She passed them to Polina, then watched, eagle-eyed, until Polina swallowed the pills with sips of warm, sweet tea. "*Bardzo dobry.* Very good. I'll check on the men now."

While Bianka bustled the tray and empty dishes back into the kitchen, Polina let her gaze travel the room. Compared to her trailer with Mom, this place was a mansion. Despite the cold outside, the whole house felt warm and cozy. No icy drafts blew in from misaligned window frames or cracks in the glass panes.

The wallpaper, with tiny red and gold flowers dancing on an ivory background, enhanced the warm and cozy feeling. Aside from the couch where she lay, several other cushioned chairs clustered around the fireplace. Another pair of matching chairs gave occupants a lovely view through a very large window that overlooked the street outside, and some kind of miniature cushioned chair with no back, which might belong to Feliks, sat between them. The living room had five tables: one on each side of the sofa, plus a long wooden oblong one in front, where Bianka had set the dinner tray. Two more framed the chairs by the fireplace.

Built-in shelves framed in dark wood housed rows of books. Polina loved that idea. When she finally found a house of her own, she would insist on a similar setup. Always forced to leave most books behind due to space constraints, she would appreciate a permanent spot for all the imaginary friends of her childhood and the lessons she'd learned as an adult.

In the far corner, a magnificent Christmas tree, the *choinka,* unlit but fully decorated with silver ribbon and delicate glass ornaments, brought the holiday spirit into the house. Even the air held that magical scent of fresh pine and gingerbread.

What struck her hardest were the framed photographs. Henryk and Bianka's wedding picture took center stage on the mantel above the stone wall fireplace. On either side sat half a dozen photos of Feliks from red-faced bawling newborn to a more formal snapshot taken recently where he wore his dark blond hair slicked back and a striped blue and yellow shirt that made his blue eyes glow with electricity. Other photos decorated the walls and the three tables. In every shot, the family smiled out at the living room's occupants: happy, loving, joyous.

Polina's limited experience with families came from watching the various guests at the thousands of fairs she'd worked in her childhood. Most of them laughed too loudly, ate too much, got dizzy on the rides, and forked over more money in one night than she and her mother made in a year. Then, of course, there were the places Social Services sent her after what happened with Eddie. Between the ages of sixteen and eighteen, she'd lived in four different foster homes. Trust wasn't easily earned in those situations. *Two* of the foster homes locked the kitchen at night to keep her and the other kids from getting food "after hours." Hard to imagine such activities happened in a normal family. Sipping her tea, she wondered. How could she ever hope to live a normal life if she didn't have a frame of reference? She didn't really know what was considered normal or average.

Spending the holidays here, with this happy family, could give her insight for her future that she could never gain at Saint Tadeusz and ease some of the pressure on her wallet. Yes, she would stay with the Nowaks, but not as a burden. She would find ways to be useful to them. And she would learn from them. Learn how to be the same as everyone else.

She closed her eyes, envisioning that special home of her own. The mint green cottage from the toy store floated through her imagination. When she found it, she would plant a huge garden with flowers and fresh vegetables. She could picture herself in the side yard, a large floppy hat shielding her skin from the sun, crouched among the greenery. Orange and black butterflies flitted from blossom to blossom. The scent of honeysuckle—her favorite— sweetened the air. In the background, her cozy little cottage with the wraparound porch, a real *home*, welcomed friends and family to come inside and spend time with her. A gray- striped tabby cat sunned himself in the sunniest spot on the porch.

The picture in her head became a dream as she drifted off to sleep.

♥

After dinner, Rhys rose from his seat at the dining room table.

"Leave her be." Bianka bounced her hand to propel him back into his chair. "Your *ukochana* needs sleep."

He should have been embarrassed she knew so much about his thoughts, but his concern for Polina and the fears she'd already revealed to him, overrode his dignity. Lying in a strange house in a strange country, surrounded by strangers, she probably needed reassurance before she'd sleep.

"I'll just take a quick peek," he said.

Bianka exchanged a bemused look with Henryk before waving him off. "Go. No matter what I say, you won't think straight until you see for yourself. You have her suitcases in your car?"

"No suitcases. Just a backpack." He shrugged. "I know. It's crazy."

"Not crazy. She a good girl. No fussy. You go check on her now. If she's asleep, like I think, you bring her to guest room. Don't wake her. Then fetch her rucksack."

"Yes, ma'am." He offered her a quick salute and sped away before she could smack him. Sure enough, he found Polina sound asleep on the couch. "Come on, sweetheart," he crooned. "You've had quite a day. But you're safe now. No need to barricade the doors here."

The idea she'd ever lived that way made his skin clammy. What kind of childhood had she survived? What sordid acts had she been involved in that made her so distrustful of men—of strangers? And what would become of her once she left Poland? Only one way to be sure she'd be all right. He'd have to find a reason to make her stay here. With him.

"Well?" Bianka's prompt broke through his musings. "Don't just stand there looking at her like Feliks stares at the puppies at the pet store. Pick her up. Bring her into the guest room."

Complying with Bianka's demand—like he had any

choice in the matter—he scooped up Polina and carried her down the hall. After placing her on the bed, he kissed her forehead. In response, she sighed and curled up into the size of a child. "You should've stayed awake for dessert. Bianka makes the best *sernik*. After I gorge myself on her cheesecake, I'm going to bring in your backpack. And I'll be here first thing tomorrow morning. That's a promise."

6

Once back in his own apartment, sleep wouldn't come for Rhys. Not with pieces of the Polina puzzle tumbling around his brain. *Don't tell them what I told you. About where I'm from. They won't be so happy to see me if they know the truth.*

Had she really believed he and the Nowaks would think less of her if they learned about her past? He considered the fear in her eyes and the way she tugged her lower lip with her teeth before she'd uttered the phrase, "Do you know what a carny is?"

Yes, she really did think her secret would change their opinions. She obviously didn't know about his knack for spotting quality beneath the ashes—a benefit of years spent at the knee of an archaeologist and historian.

In Polina's case, he had some research to do. After brewing a cup of strong coffee, he settled at his desk, powered up his laptop, and typed the word, "carny" in his search engine. Several movies with that title popped up first, all of them featuring a dark and sinister motif. Hackles rose on his nape. Ridiculous, he chided himself. Carnivals had always seemed places of happiness when he was a child. This was just Hollywood, making the child-like fantasy into adult horror.

He scrolled past the films to glossaries of "carny slang" and a dozen online diaries that supposedly reflected the carnival workers' life. For more than an hour, he immersed himself in the garish, harsh world where Polina had grown

up, becoming more sympathetic and horrified with each
video clip, each image, and each description of the seedy
living conditions. These were tales of abject poverty with
employees surviving on extremely low wages, sleeping in
trailers or in tents behind the trailers, performing back-
breaking work under the hot sun for long hours. They were
malnourished, aged before their time, and risking injury
with every set-up or breakdown of equipment.

At last, he pushed away from the desk, his mind
buzzing with facts and recriminations, and checked the
time. Nine p.m. here meant ten o'clock there. Not too late to
phone. He owed her that much.

While the connection went through, he counted the
rings and practiced the words he'd use to explain this
stunning turn of events. She'd be surprised to hear from
him—especially when he conveyed the reason for his call.

She picked up on the fourth ring, and he went straight
into his rehearsed opening. "Hello, Mother. I hope I didn't
wake you."

"Rhys?" Alarm tinged her tone and rushed her words.
"Is something wrong?"

"No." He sipped his coffee for a jolt of courage before
continuing the conversation. "I…umm…just wanted to say
thank you."

"What on earth for?"

"For giving me a good life," he said.

Silence greeted his pronouncement, and he swore his
heartbeat sped up. Finally, she expelled a long breath that
whistled through his receiver. "Rhys, have you been
drinking?"

He laughed. "No. I just realized that I'm grateful. That's
all. I know we haven't always seen eye-to-eye, but I do
appreciate all you did for me. And for the girls."

"Well, now," she replied, her tone a contented purr,
"you're very welcome. May I ask what brought about this
sudden awakening?"

"I met someone who reminded me how lucky I was."

"Hmmm… Be sure to thank him for me."

"Her," he corrected.

"Her?" No denying the interest that pronoun sparked.
"Even better. Who is she?"

"A friend."

"Then, be sure to thank *her* for me."

The silence returned between them, not a comfortable sensation, yet not as awkward as he'd expected. He drained his coffee and placed the cup in the sink, waited for her to say something more.

"Would you like to convey some gratitude to your father, as well?"

At the mention of his father, the air grew heavy, but he forced himself to keep his tone light and breezy. "I better not. I doubt the old man's heart could stand the shock."

"Hmmm..." she repeated. "You're probably right. Does this mean you're coming home soon? For a visit, perhaps? We'd love to see you..."

Despite the yearning lilt in her questions, he shook his head. Not yet. This phone call was a huge step. A visit home was impossible. Still, he didn't want to dash his mother's hopes entirely. "I'll see what I can arrange after New Year's," he promised.

"Let me know," she said.

"Will do."

"It was...nice...to hear from you," she murmured. "Maybe you'll call me again?"

"Maybe." He'd done his good deed for the evening. Time to call an end to the cease-fire. "Goodnight, Mother. Say hello to Father for me."

"Will do. Goodnight, Rhys."

Golden sunlight warmed Polina's face, and she opened her eyes to find herself lying on a cloud in the middle of a floral wonderland. She scrubbed a hand over her face, blinked, and looked again. A bedroom. She was in a bedroom, but the prettiest darn room she'd ever seen. Painted red roses adorned the walls, some only buds, others in full bloom. Yellow daisies and bumble bees scattered over soft linens on the bed, and she snuggled deep into the thick mattress with a contented sigh. Stretching her limbs as far as her muscles would extend, she still didn't hit any mattress edge. This was what she wanted for her life: a comfortable place to lay her head.

But not here. She wanted something uniquely hers. All hers. Soon. She was so close to reaching her goal. After ten years of scrimping, of watching every penny while she peddled her designs to every amusement park in the country, soon, she'd realize her dream. Another few months, if she watched what she spent here in Poland, if her latest proposal was picked up, she'd have a home of her own—free and clear. No mortgage. No one would ever get the chance to take what was hers away from her.

Sitting up, her gaze focused on her backpack perched on a chair in the corner of the room. Through a sleepy haze, she vaguely remembered Rhys carrying her in here after dinner and his mild teasing that she shouldn't have fallen asleep before dessert.

On the table beside the bed sat an old-fashioned bell with a teak handle and a folded card, her name printed in block letters on the outside. Curiosity overwhelmed comfort, and she took the card, flipping it open.

Good morning, Sleeping Beauty.

Rhys. This had to be from Rhys.

Since you barely skipped a snore when I carried you to bed last night, I assume you slept well.

Ha. She didn't snore.

Did she?

No. She shook her head and returned her attention to the card and Rhys's bold scrawl.

Bianka insists you stay in bed this morning until she's had a chance to look at your feet.

He must have sensed she'd argue with that because the next line was in parentheses.

(Don't fight with me; it's not my demand.) Ring this bell when you're awake. DO NOT GET OUT OF BED. Seriously. She'll punish us both.

She giggled. For such a big man, he sure was a wuss. Bianka didn't scare her. But once again, he anticipated her reaction.

Don't underestimate Bianka because she seems like such a nice lady. Take a look at your backpack. Notice it doesn't appear as full as it was last night. That's because Bianka took your clothes. She said she wants to check them

*in case they need mending or laundering. Don't kid yourself.
She's holding your garments hostage. You defy her, and
you'll never see your jeans again.*

Hmmm…he might have a point. Currently, she wore a
billowy pink flannel nightgown, lent to her by Bianka who'd
been shocked to discover Polina normally slept in a t-shirt
and sweat pants. Never knowing when she might have to
bolt out of bed in the middle of the night, she'd grown up
prepared for an emergency at any time. When Bianka
mentioned her lack of nightgowns or pajamas, dopey from
the painkillers and exhausted due to jet lag, she'd agreed to
wear the borrowed garment to please such a giving,
generous woman. Now, she wondered if that generosity
actually hid an ulterior motive. Time would tell, since she
knew for a fact her clothing was clean and in excellent
condition. With so few belongings to call her own, she took
extreme care with what she had.

*If Bianka gives you the okay, we'll tackle another item
on your mother's list. Something small and not too taxing.
You won't be running today. That, I promise. So while you're
waiting for Bianka to come to you, review your list and
choose one or two items we can do.*

From here? Only one item came to mind. Number eight.
Kiss a stranger. No, they'd already gone there. No big deal.

Oh, who was she kidding? She'd loved the way his lips
fit against hers, how he managed to penetrate her fierce
barriers without a fight. Yes, she'd panicked. In hindsight
and based on what she'd seen of Rhys since that kiss, she
realized he was nothing like Eddie, nothing like the
multitudes of men who'd spent a few hours romping with
her mom and then gone home to wives or girlfriends
without a second thought. She, unlike her mother, was not
someone who found vicarious thrills in flings and one-
night-stands. Polina wanted forever. Temps need not apply.

Okay. Enough brooding. Time to get this show on the
road. Picking up the bell, she rang for Bianka and snorted
back a laugh. When had she become the heroine in a Jane
Austen novel? Seriously. Was this what rich people did?
Lazed around in bed, ringing bells until servants showed up
to take care of simple tasks? God, how dull! She'd been
awake ten minutes, and her feet already itched to hit the

floor. At least, she didn't have to wait long.

After a quick rap of knuckles on the door, Bianka bustled into the room with another tray. "*Dobry rano.*"

"Good morning." Polina gave the same greeting in English, a gentle reminder to the older woman about her lack of foreign language skill, before folding the sheet and quilt to her chest. Time for the baby bird routine again. Oh, she could argue, but she figured she'd be better off choosing her battles with care and wisdom. As lovely as she found this room, she had no intention of spending her vacation imprisoned here.

"You slept well, yes?" Bianka said with a cherubic smile on her round face.

"Yes, thank you. I can't remember when I slept so deeply."

Bianka clucked her tongue. "I told Rhys you needed rest. Rest and lots of food in your belly. You too skinny for Polish girl."

"Yeah, you mentioned that last night."

"So that means it's true." She set the tray on Polina's lap and, moving the backpack to the floor, pulled the chair across the hardwood floor to sit beside the bed. "We fix that now."

Fix it? Polina stared down at the ginormous egg dish crammed with chopped sausage, cheese, and diced peppers. Thick planks of golden bread beneath a blanket of white cheese sat catty-corner to the omelet, along with a small bowl of oatmeal topped by a lake of cream. If she continued to eat all the food Bianka put in front of her, she'd have to fly home in a cargo plane.

Once Bianka tucked the napkin into the collar of Polina's nightgown, the feeding ritual began. Rhys's warning to not take the older woman at face value prickled the hair on her nape and forearms. She needed an ally. Craning her neck around Bianka's bulk to peer in the doorway, she asked as casually as she could, "Is Rhys here?"

"In the dining room with my boys. He can wait. So can you." Using the side of the fork, she cut a huge slab of omelet, folded it into a cube, and pierced it with the tines.

"That's too big a piece," Polina protested. *Grrmph.* Too

late.

Bianka shoved the egg cube in her mouth. "How you hurt your feet so badly?"

She had to chew around the edges of the glob in her mouth just to breathe, let alone speak. When she finally had the morsel down to a manageable size, she said, "I thought Rhys told you, my boots are too big for my feet."

"Blisters like yours, you didn't hurt yourself walking on a path. You do...?" She put the fork down on the plate and rolled her hands. "What is word? Like those skinny little girls do in *Olimpijski*?"

Olimpijski. Olympics? "Do you mean gymnastics?"

The older woman nodded. "That's it. *Jeem-nas-tiks.* You do flips on sidewalk?"

"Of course not. I was running from—" She stopped, picked up the fork, and shoved the next block of egg into her mouth. Better to fill her mouth than to spill her secrets from it. But once again, she was too late.

"You were running from Rhys," Bianka finished for her.

"This is delicious, Bianka," she said, pointing to the omelet. "I'd love to have the recipe if you'd be willing to share it."

"You were running from *Rhys*," Bianka repeated, this time with more emphasis on the man's name. "Why?"

"Don't be silly. I wasn't running from Rhys."

Bianka frowned. "Ah, so then the *Smok Wawelski* was chasing you?"

"No, of course not."

"You were with Rhys, who would have scared off anyone who might mean you harm. If the dragon no chase you, you must have run from Rhys. You tell me why."

No sense fighting. Bianka could break down a rock in an argument. "Because he scared me."

"Rhys?" Her laughter could shatter the mirror on the dresser. "That man is big pussycat. What he do to make you afraid?"

Polina dropped her gaze to the egg dish, the cheese congealing as the meal grew cold. Suddenly, she'd lost her appetite. How on earth could she possibly explain why she'd run from Rhys yesterday? Even she knew she'd overreacted. She couldn't make Bianka understand her dread. Not without a long, drawn-out discussion about Eddie's assault and the direction her life took afterwards. "Nothing," she murmured. "He didn't do anything."

"You look me in the eye when you tell me that," Bianka insisted and chucked her under the chin, tilting her face up. "You a good girl, Polina. I knew that *before* I read your mama's letter."

She stiffened. "Wait." Had this woman just admitted to invading her privacy? "You read my mother's letter to me? The letter in my backpack?"

Rather than apologize for such a breach in etiquette, Bianka waved her off. "Ah, sure. You a guest in my house. I have right to know if you could hurt my family. While you sleep, I go through your things last night. And I read your mama's letter."

So much for Rhys not telling the Nowaks about her past. Why couldn't he, at least, have told them not to go through her things?

Oh, the sins that missive contained! Most of them her mother's, but what was that old saying? "The apple doesn't fall far from the tree." No matter how hard she protested, strangers would always see her as her mother's daughter. Hadn't Eddie hammered that fact home? Now, with all her truths revealed, only one question remained. How soon would Bianka throw her out to protect her family's reputation?

"You a good girl," Bianka said, jerking Polina out of her thoughts.

She blinked. "I am?"

Bianka's wide brow furrowed. "You are not?"

"No. I mean," she hastened to add, "I *am*. Really. I'm nothing like my mother. I swear. She was—" She stopped there, family loyalty clashing with her need to deny the genetic traits. Time to change the subject. "This is such a pretty room. Thank you for letting me stay here."

"You need help, we help." The older lady wagged a finger at Polina's nose. "But you wouldn't need help if you weren't running in big boots. So, you tell me. What did Rhys do to make you run?"

She shook her head. "It's stupid. I shouldn't have. He really didn't do anything wrong."

"What did he do?"

"He kissed me."

"And you no like?"

"No, I liked it fine. I mean, it was really nice. Rhys made me feel..." Words failed her, and she let the sentence trail off.

Bianka patted her hand. "That's how Henryk made me feel when he first kissed me. Like *motyle*, butterflies, flew in my belly. You feel that for Rhys, yes?"

Yes.

No.

"I'm not sure. I've only known him two days."

"Bah. Means nothing. I know Henryk five minutes, I tell my mama, he's the one for me. We had big wedding the next summer. You know, too, *ukochana*." She tapped two fingers on Polina's chest. "In here, you know." The fingers moved to her forehead. "In here, not sure. But you will be."

No. She couldn't be in love with Rhys. Aside from the fact they barely knew each other, she had plans. Plans that did not include staying in Kraków.

Bianka rose from the chair. "You eat. I check your blisters." She flipped the quilt and sheet off Polina's feet.

Cold air blasted her, and she shivered.

"Sit still, please." Bianka took her by the ankles and lifted her legs toward the sunlight streaming through the window. You need more rest for these."

Oh, God. Rhys was right. The woman planned to keep her locked in this room!

"No, please. I don't want to be a burden. You and your husband have been so kind. I'm stronger than I look. Really, I am. I'm a hard worker. I can help you—I don't have to stand. I could..." Her brain went into frantic overdrive to come up with something. "I could read to Feliks. Or I could sew if you have anything that needs mending. I can fix things. I'm good with tools. Please?"

On a sigh, Bianka lowered her leg and replaced the covers. "All right." She wagged her index finger. "But you stay in living room, with feet on pillows. Keep bandages clean and dry. No sewing, no fixing things. You need rest."

"Deal!"

7

Polina seemed in much better spirits when Rhys knocked on her bedroom door and stepped inside.

"Thank God it's you!" Her smile zinged straight to his heart, sending his blood pumping faster through his veins. "I was afraid you might be Bianka, coming back in here to tell me she changed her mind."

He chuckled. "She likes you. So much that she gave you a reprieve today. Bianka said I can bring you into the living room where you'll have people around you, but you have to stay off your feet. Which means..." He bowed, one arm wrapped at his waist. "...I am your personal conveyance, madam."

"Oh, good," she said and picked at the lace collar of the flannel nightgown. "Though I wish she'd let me wear my jeans. Apparently, Bianka won't give me back my own wardrobe until I've proven I'm not a flight risk."

"I warned you she's a toughie."

"Yeah, thanks for that." She pushed the quilt and sheet to one side. "And thanks for bringing in my backpack. And for taking me here when I was too stubborn to realize I needed help that I wouldn't get in the hostel. And for all the sightseeing yesterday."

Well, well. Had he broken through her defenses already? Doubtful. But he'd definitely chipped her wall. "You are quite welcome." He approached the bed and stretched out his arms. "You ready?" On her nod, he slid his arms underneath her thighs and lifted her off the mattress.

She clasped her hands around his neck, and he couldn't remember when an action felt so perfect. "God, you must be tired of schlepping me around."

"Hardly. I've carried grocery sacks that weigh more than you."

"Bianka keeps telling me I'm too skinny for a Polish girl. She's determined to get me fattened up before I go home." As he strode past her backpack on the chair near the door, she reached out an arm and hooked it onto her wrist. "I need my mother's list."

"Did you come up with something we can do from here?"

"I haven't looked, to be honest. I mean, most of the stuff requires legwork. Like, visiting the cemetery where my grandparents are buried and gaining permission to have Mom's ashes interred in their crypt. That's scheduled for tomorrow."

"You know which cemetery?"

"Not off the top of my head, but it's on the list."

"What else?"

"I'm supposed to see some kind of shopping stuff at the Historical Museum."

"The *szopki*, no doubt. Handmade nativity scenes. That's legwork, scheduled for another day. Next?"

"I don't know. I can't remember. That's why I need to get the list out of my backpack."

He strode into the living room. The house was empty, and Polina noticed.

"Where is everyone?"

"Church. They'll be back later this afternoon. Bianka thought you might want a little privacy while we work on your mother's list."

"*Now* she wants to give me privacy? Last night, she had no problem going through my backpack. She even read my mother's letter, the last message my mother ever gave me." Tears shone in her eyes. "All the personal stuff about our life together, what she wanted for me and why. My whole life was opened up and examined while I slept last night."

Aha. That explained why Bianka became Mother Hen. "She told you she read it?"

"Yes. Said she knew I was a good girl even before she read my mother's letter."

"Try not to take it personally. She really cares about you, and I'm guessing whatever she found out only confirmed how she was already feeling." There seemed to be a lot of that going around.

He settled her on the couch while she fussed in her backpack for her mother's list. Taking advantage of her distraction, he retrieved the shopping bag he'd brought in earlier. "Here. I picked up a few things for you this morning." He pulled out a thick fleece zippered sweatshirt in an emerald green hue. "That thin parka you're wearing isn't enough protection from the elements. You can put this on under your jacket as an extra lining."

"My jacket's fine. I don't need that."

Once again, he realized her pride warred with her common sense. "Yes, you do," he insisted and placed it over the voluminous nightgown. "Feel it."

She rubbed the fabric between her fingers then brushed it across her cheek. "Ooh, it's so soft. Like cotton candy."

"Maybe. But it's a lot warmer. You'll need it for insulation when we're out walking, especially near the cemetery. The winds here can be fierce. On a cloudy day, the temperature can drop drastically."

"How much?"

"I'm not sure," Rhys said. "At least five to seven degrees."

"No, silly." She pointed at the fleece. "How much did the under-thingie cost?"

He blinked in confusion. "What's the difference?"

"I want to pay for it."

"Not necessary. Consider it a gift."

She frowned. "I don't accept gifts."

"Never? Not even from family members or friends? At Christmastime?"

"A.," she said, planting her hands on her hips, "we barely know each other so the term, 'friend' applies in only the loosest way. And B., what's left of the only family member who matters to me is in a box in my backpack. When she *was* alive, Mom and I never exchanged gifts. Not at Christmas or any other time."

"How about your birthday?"

"Forget it. It doesn't matter. The important thing is I'll pay for this jacket-liner-thingie myself. Just tell me how much I owe you."

"I insist you let me pay for it. After all, it was my idea." What woman didn't like getting gifts? One unaccustomed to receiving them, he supposed.

"Okay, fine. We can figure out a way for me to pay you back later." She refocused on her list, effectively ending the debate.

Good God, she was stubborn. "I have something else for you," he said.

She slammed a fist against the couch cushion in obvious exasperation. "Oh, for God's sake, what else did you bring me?"

He pulled out the white shoe box, flipped off the lid, and showed her the top-of-the-line cushioned walking shoes he'd picked up in town. "Ta da! What do you say? Let's try them on, shall we?"

Her complexion blanched, and she shook her head. "I can't accept those."

"Why not? You agreed to take the fleece."

"Not by choice. The fleece I know I can pay you back for. Those shoes?" She shook her head again, this time more emphatically. "They cost waaaay too much."

"No, they didn't," he lied. "There's a second-hand store near my apartment. I paid fifteen *zlotys* for them."

"You did not."

"Did too. I hope they're the right size. They don't have a large selection, and I had to guess, based on the size of your boots. As soon as Bianka gives you the okay, we'll try them on."

"Thank you. I know you're not telling the truth, and I will find a way to pay you back for them, as well."

She looked up at him, and the wonder shining in her eyes became his undoing. "If I try to kiss you," he crooned, drawing a finger down her cheek toward her lower lip, "are you going to run away again?"

Her smile was the sweetest surrender. "Only one way to find out."

Snaking an arm around her shoulder, he trapped her

against him—just in case she attempted to flee. But she didn't.

♥

At the first touch of his lips on hers, bravado fled. Panic set in. From the recesses of her memory, Eddie's voice sneered. "Come on, Polly. You can do better than that. Your mother must have taught you *some*thing..."

Tremors took over her body, and she focused on trying to stay calm. Rhys, she told herself. This was Rhys. Not Eddie. Rhys wouldn't hurt her. He wouldn't use her mother against her. He didn't even know her mother. Besides, she wasn't that same naïve girl anymore—thanks to Eddie.

Rhys's mouth was different than Eddie's: gentler, not harsh or pushy. He tasted different, too. Better. Cleaner. Sweet.

His fingers skimmed her nape, whisper-soft. Her heartbeat galloped inside her chest, and a fine sheen of sweat broke out on her arms. She liked it, this sensation of floating, of connecting with someone who drifted along with her. A fluttering erupted in her belly—like...what had Bianka said? Butterflies. Yes. Butterflies.

When he deepened the kiss and his tongue swept into her mouth, her tremors increased to shivers.

At that point, he must have sensed her nervousness because he broke the kiss and studied her face with concern. "Let's take a break," he announced with no rancor or upset whatsoever. The easy smile he wore was in direct contrast to the way Eddie had reacted all those years ago when she'd tried to stop him from going farther than a kiss.

A trick? She didn't know. "Are you angry?"

"Angry? No." He skimmed his knuckles down her cheek. "You stayed. That's all I hoped for right now."

She shook her head in disbelief. He must have been at least a little disappointed in her reaction or he wouldn't have stopped. "I panicked—only for a minute. I'm sorry. It's not you. It's..." She dipped her head, hiding her face behind her hair. "It's something that happened a long time ago."

"Do you want to tell me?"

"No."

"All right, then. Tell me this instead. Did you like kissing me?"

"Yes. It was..." What word could she possibly use to describe what she felt? "It was beautiful."

"Beautiful?" He chuckled. "I've never heard it put that way before. But I'm glad to hear you say it. Because I intend to do that a lot. Eventually, I'm hoping you'll feel free to kiss me back."

Eventually, she believed she would. She'd already given him more of herself than she'd dared to show anyone else, ever. And while that thought should frighten her, she felt pretty good about it. He made it easy: his casual reactions, the way he took care of her, made her feel comfortable. Normal. For the first time in her life.

"What else is on your list?" he asked.

She considered her mother's childish scrawl on the itinerary. "Ice skating?"

He pointed to her bare feet. "Pass. For now. Next." He leaned over her to read the list with her. "Most of the rest of the items on here deal with celebrating Christmas and New Year's. You can take those up with Bianka. She knows *all* the traditions. She might even help you with the ones your mom forgot to mention." After placing the papers on the table in front of the sofa, he gathered her close. "Don't worry. We'll figure it all out. I promise. In the meantime..."

His lips came down on hers again, sweet and beautiful. She felt no panic this time, only the scent of him, the taste of him, surrounding her.

Yes, she could easily see a time where she'd ask *him* to kiss *her*, rather than waiting for him to initiate. This was life, in all its glory, with all its highs and lows. She'd craved the experience for over a decade now. She intended to milk it dry.

8

Once again, Rhys stayed for dinner, leaving Polina with a tremendous amount of guilt to swallow, along with the evening's roasted chicken. "As soon as I'm able," she promised Bianka between feedings, "I'll be out of your hair and I'll take him with me. Bad enough you're feeding me, but you're feeding him, too. All because he insists on being here with me. That's a lot more than you signed up for."

"Bah. Rhys eats here all the time, when you're here and when you're not." She scooped up another forkful of chicken and potato dumplings and waited for Polina to take a bite. "What does a *kawaler,* a man without a wife, know about a good meal? He needs a woman to cook for him. Before you leave, I give you recipes to take home with you. Keep Rhys fat and healthy."

"Rhys isn't going with me when I leave."

The reminder left her bereft, which surprised her. She'd only known him a few days and yet, she'd come to enjoy seeing him, spending time with him, talking to him, laughing with him. Kissing him.

Unlike her mother, she wouldn't find another man the minute she and Rhys parted ways. She liked him because he was decent and honest and interested in her welfare without ulterior motives. Unlike all the men who spent a night or two in their cramped trailer and were never heard from again. She liked the butterflies in her stomach his nearness sent into flight, the sound of his laughter, and the way his eyes lit up when he smiled at her. But, there was so much more to the man than what he did to her.

He didn't pressure her to do anything she wasn't comfortable doing, like Eddie had. He seemed to sense her hesitancy, yet never chided her or insulted her for not wanting a temporary liaison. Because she wanted real love. A forever kind of love. She wouldn't settle for less. She'd do without before she gave her heart—or her body—to someone unworthy.

"Maybe you stay here. He's only in Kraków for six more months," Bianka said, redirecting Polina's thoughts. "You could leave when he leaves."

Wait. What? "I don't understand." Puzzlement furrowed her brow. "Rhys doesn't plan to live here?"

"Bah. That one has wings on his feet. He never stays anywhere very long. He travels from country to country, always restless."

"Rhys?" A fly-by-night? Her heart cracked in half. Had she misjudged him? "I thought he only came here from London."

"I don't know where he was last, but my Henryk said Poland is Rhys's third country in four years. He needs a wife, needs to settle down. Maybe, you stay, he stay. Or when he finish here, he come to you. Marry you. You make him stay put in one place."

"Wh-what if I'm not interested in marrying him?"

Not if it meant she'd have to tie him down to make him "stay put." Caged birds didn't do well in captivity. Her mother was proof of that. Too many nights when she was a child, she'd curl up in her narrow bed, covering her ears to drown out the drunken tears, the hushed Polish words she didn't really understand. Despite her best efforts, the misery, though, resonated loud and clear.

"Polina?" Feliks's voice piped in from the doorway between the living and dining rooms.

Grateful for the distraction, she turned her attention to the child. "Hmmm...?"

He rattled off some question, but his thick accent made his words hard for her to comprehend, and she quirked a brow at Henryk, standing behind his son.

"He wants to know if you really lived at a fair," Henryk said.

Under ordinary circumstances, their avid curiosity would make her squirm, but these people had shown her nothing but kindness. She doubted their questioning glances now were meant to embarrass her. No, they were genuinely fascinated. Feliks, in fact, looked star struck, his eyes wide and jaw agape.

"A carnival," she told her rapt audience. "Yes."

Again, the boy said something she couldn't decipher.

"I'm sorry." She shook her head, conveying her confusion.

"Forgive him," Henryk said with a frown that had Feliks dropping his gaze to his feet. "He asks too many questions."

"That's all right," she assured him. "If you'll translate for me, I'll answer as many as I can. I don't mind." She gestured Feliks to come closer and waved off Bianka's next forkful of food. "Honestly, I couldn't eat another bite. Thank you. Everything was delicious."

"You still too skinny," Bianka grumbled. "But all right. I clean up. You talk."

Polina turned back to Feliks who sat at her feet on the sofa. "What did you want to know?"

"Where did you sleep?" Henryk took a seat near the windows on the other side of the room and asked Feliks's question in English.

"My mother and I lived in a trailer. A mobile home." She glanced at Henryk and shrugged. "I don't know how else to say it."

He nodded his understanding and translated—she hoped, accurately.

"Did you have your own room? With lots of toys?" Feliks asked.

"No. There was no room for toys. My mother slept in the one bedroom..." Because she often had men in there with her, but Polina didn't elaborate on that fact. Innocent young Feliks would never understand, and she'd rather not inform Henryk that her mother was the carnival's lot lizard. Some secrets were best left buried. "I slept on a rollout bed in the living area."

"How about a dog?" Feliks pointed to his wolfhound curled up near the fireplace. "Did you have a dog, like Kacper?"

"No dogs. No pets at all. Sometimes, a stray dog or cat would wander onto the grounds because of all the food lying around. When I was about your age, I'd feed them, play with some of them. But I wasn't allowed to take any of them with me when we pulled up stakes and left for the next town. It was easier to avoid them altogether, rather than always have to say goodbye."

"That's sad."

"It was sadder for the animals, I think. Once we were gone, I don't know what happened to any of them. I hope they all found homes somewhere. Living on the road isn't easy for people *or* dogs."

♥

Rhys lingered in the hallway, listening to her hushed tone as she answered all Feliks's questions with brutal—and heartbreaking—honesty.

"I bet you didn't have to eat all your vegetables, like Mama makes me. You probably got to eat cotton candy and lemonade all the time."

She laughed. "I ate my vegetables too. But they came out of cans most of the time. Not fresh, like your mama makes you. You're lucky she's such a good cook! We'd have campfires a lot, and that makes most of the food taste like smoke. Plus, it's hard to know when meat is cooked to perfection. Sometimes my meal was burnt, sometimes still raw in the middle."

"So you didn't get to have cotton candy and lemonade?"

"If the boss wasn't looking..." She shrugged. "...sometimes the food vendors would give us their extras. But that wasn't always such a good idea, either. Cotton candy and lemonade isn't much of a dinner. It doesn't fill you up when you've been working hard."

"What she say?" Bianka's voice hissed in Rhys's ear.

He turned to find her right beside him, listening just as intently to the conversation. "In a nutshell," he whispered back, "she didn't eat well."

She smirked. "Knew it. Too skinny."

"Sssh!" He waved a hand at her. "Later. I want to hear what else she tells him."

Feliks pressed her further. "Why didn't you just go to a restaurant if you were hungry from working so hard?"

"No time. We worked from noon until after midnight, so most restaurants were closed long before we were finished."

Probably true. But Rhys suspected another reason. In his research, he had discovered that most carnival workers didn't make much money. Most of their earnings went right back into the owners' pockets for room and board. Carnies used public restrooms for hygiene, shared space to conserve body heat in colder climes, and rarely saw a doctor. He sincerely doubted restaurants would be a regular part of their budget.

"What about school?" Feliks's question drew him back into the discussion. "How could you go to school when you worked like that?"

Easy, boy. Don't act too eager.

"I didn't really go to school—not like you do. We had a professor with us. When everyone else was too busy to spend time with me, Tiny taught me how to read and write. He taught me math and history and music and geography. All the things you learn in school, I bet."

"Were there other kids? Kids like you?"

"Not with our particular carnival group." Her features pinched. "Every once in a while, we'd work with a townie family. That's a family that doesn't travel with the carnival but works all the fairs and carnivals that come to one area. But making friends with them was the same as becoming attached to the dogs. Whenever we left that town, I wouldn't see those kids again until the next time we visited that town. Sometimes, we never went back. It was easier to stick with the people I knew, the ones who were with the carnival, even if they were all much older than me."

"Forgive me," Henryk said, his brow furrowed, "but it sounds to me like a rather harsh life. Weren't you lonely?"

"I suppose, compared to a normal life, it would seem harsh."

Normal life. Rhys honed in on those two words and the impact they must have had on Polina. No wonder she worried what people might think of her.

"But," she continued, glancing at Feliks, "I had some fun times, too."

"I know." He bounced on the sofa cushion. "I bet you got to ride all the rides whenever you wanted."

"Even better. I got to test out the new rides. Whenever Uncle Leo thought about buying one, he'd strap me in and let me be the guinea pig. It was my job to make sure they were safe and fun."

Rhys's imagination went into overdrive, picturing a precious little girl with her strawberry blond hair in pigtails, flung out of some shoddy amusement car and landing in a heap of broken, bloody bones on a strip of hot asphalt. He shuddered.

Bianka joined him, muttering in Polish about God and heaven before making the sign of the cross on her chest. "Enough. I can't hear no more." She strode into the living room, a big fake smile on her flushed face, and told Feliks to prepare for bed. "School tomorrow."

Feliks scampered into the hallway and stopped in front of Rhys. "How was I?" he whispered.

"Perfect," he replied in the same soft tone. "*Pozdrawiam, Feliks.*"

♥

"Ready for dessert?" Rhys's voice came from behind her, and she gasped, dropping her fork against the plate.

She whirled to face him. "Don't sneak up on me like that!"

"Sorry." His easy grin hit her right between the eyes and traveled through her, leaving tingles in its wake. Not good ones.

"And don't smirk at me," she added.

He cocked his head and held up his hands in surrender. "Easy, sweetheart. I meant no harm."

"I just don't like when people sneak up on me. And then you made it worse by laughing about my reaction like it's some great big joke." To her intense embarrassment, tears sprang to her eyes. And of course, he noticed.

"Hey. Wait." His voice was soft, and his expression sobered. "I'm sorry. I didn't mean anything."

Cripes, she was going to cry. She never cried. Not anymore. She shot up from the chair. "Excuse me. I forgot something." She took off down the hall as the first hot tear slid down her cheek. The shivering began within seconds of her reaching her bedroom. She locked the door and sank onto the bed, hugging herself while the chills racked her.

Find the good, she coached herself. *Come on. You can do this. Find the good.*

The good. Okay. She was safe. She'd just enjoyed a delicious meal. She had a thriving business, and a bit of money put aside—not enough yet, but all she needed was one good turn of luck. The shivers eased.

Good. Now breathe. In, out. In, out.

Her heartbeat slowed to normal. She counted her breathing pattern. *In, one. Out, one. In, two. Out, two...*

Nice, slow, easy, until she had herself under control again.

Stupid panic attack. They sneaked up on her at the worst times—most often, when someone sneaked up on *her*.

A tentative knock sounded, followed by Bianka's muffled, concerned tone. "Polina? Are you all right?"

She sniffed, took one last deep inhale and exhale, then strode to the closed door. "I'm fine," she said through the barrier. "I'll be right out." Throwing back her shoulders, she pasted a smile on her face, and opened the door.

Bianka stood in the hallway, her eyes narrowing as she scanned Polina from head to toe. "Everything good now?"

She pushed the smile wider. "Absolutely. Why wouldn't it be?"

"You seemed..." Again, the full scrutiny gaze. "...*upset* a few minutes ago."

"No, don't be silly! I...umm..." She scanned the room, found the medicinal bottle on her nightstand where Bianka had left it for convenience. "I forgot to take my pain pills."

Bianka nodded. "Take a few more minutes. Maybe splash some cool water on your face. That way, you won't look like you've been crying when Rhys sees you again. We'll have dessert when you're ready." With a wink, she strolled away, humming.

Rather than continue the argument in vain, she closed the door and took Bianka's advice. The last thing she wanted was for Rhys to think he'd affected her in any way.

Later that evening, back in her pretty bedroom, Polina turned on her tablet and accessed her business email. As she waited for the inbox to load, she held her breath. *Please, oh, please. Please tell me you're interested. I need this one.*

Sure enough, after a quick scroll through the list of names in her replies, she spotted the name, FunTime Enterprises, the company behind three of the biggest amusement parks in the southwest. On a deep inhale, with fingers crossed, she awkwardly clicked the message to open it.

Dear Ms. Kominski,
Thank you for your interest in designing our new coaster for our Wild Rides Adventure Park. We received many unique proposals and had a difficult time narrowing down our decision...

Her heart fell. She knew the next words by heart.

...Unfortunately, your design was not chosen for this project.

Yup. The standard rejection letter. Well, okay then. She released the air she'd held in her lungs and rolled her shoulders. Three down with one swing. Awesome.

But she wouldn't let it get her down. Instead, she closed the email, opened the sketch of her latest idea and played with the formulas and schematics until well past midnight. One more. She just needed one more deal to put her next goal in motion.

9

Monday morning brought another jumbo breakfast. This time, Bianka prepared *kanapki,* open-faced sandwiches with layers of tomatoes and cucumbers, thinly sliced hard boiled eggs, and cold cuts, all slathered with mayonnaise. Still full from the previous evening's chicken and potato dumplings, Polina nibbled.

"You'll never plump up if you don't eat," Bianka admonished.

"I can't," she replied. "Honestly. I'm not used to this much food."

"Hmmph! I heard all about what you're 'used to' last night. Campfires, lemonade, cotton candy. No wonder you so skinny. Lucky you still have good teeth and decent bones. Someone should've beat your mama for not taking better care of you."

"Bianka." Rhys's soft chastisement disrupted the conversation.

Still, Polina's family loyalty rose to the surface, and she clasped the face of her mother's watch. "She did the best she could. She really didn't know any better." Tears of outrage filled her eyes, hot and stinging, and she blinked them back before they fell. "Some of us aren't lucky enough to live a life of luxury. That doesn't mean you have the right to insult us or belittle us. We're people too, you know."

"I said my peace," Bianka said, rising from her chair. "I say no more."

No one spoke again while she gathered up the dishes.

Polina sniffed back the tears, bitterness brewing like hot coffee inside her stomach.

Only after she left the room did Rhys say, "She's angry *for* you, not *at* you."

"She has no right to talk about my mother that way. Yes, I'm a guest in her house, but that doesn't give her permission to insult my mother." Behind her eyes, the dam broke, and as the tears streamed, she swiped her cheeks with curled fists. "My mother wasn't perfect. Believe me. No one knows that better than I do. I lived with all her shortcomings. I don't need a reminder."

"Easy, sweetheart," he crooned. "Bianka means no harm. What can I say? You've cast a spell on her—on all of us. She loves you now, she's practically adopted you, and she wishes you might have had a better upbringing, that you had known more love and happiness in your childhood."

She folded her arms over her chest. "Welcome to the club. But trust me. Wishing doesn't change squat. Face it, Rhys. There's no such thing as making your wish come true. Or magic. Or fate. Life is all just one big hunter's stew. Sometimes the white lump is a nice piece of potato. Sometimes it's nothing but flour."

Confusion shadowed his eyes, but he didn't argue. His silence disturbed her, warned her she'd gone too far.

"Are you finished now?" he said at last.

She could only nod, horrified. What on earth had possessed her? "I'm sorry. I don't know what came over me." The possible repercussions of her tirade registered, and she gasped. "Bianka's going to throw me out now, isn't she?"

"I'm guessing that during your impassioned speech, you missed the part where I said Bianka loves you."

"No, I heard you."

"Then, sweetheart, you should know Bianka won't throw you out for a minor temper tantrum. If you truly love someone, you forgive them when they err."

"It wasn't a minor temper tantrum. I raised my voice to her." Shame weighed her down, and she dropped her head. "That's unforgiveable, considering how good she's been to me." His aftershave tickled her nose, and she lost herself for a moment in the lime and sea breeze scent. "Maybe I should apologize to Bianka before we leave today. Just to be sure she doesn't want me gone."

"You good girl," Bianka interjected from behind them, eliciting a gasp from Polina. "Loyal to your mama. Loyal to your friends. No apology."

♥

"Are you cold?" Rhys asked as they walked hand-in-hand down Royal Road.

"No. As a matter of fact, I'm surprisingly warm." She beamed at him and tugged at the neckline of her jacket until a pop of emerald peeked out. "Buying this fleece for me was genius." She kicked out a leg. "And the shoes are perfect. I feel like I could run a marathon."

"Let's just settle for a brisk walk right now."

She laughed. "I know. Thank you for thinking of me."

"It was nothing."

"If it were nothing, I would be shivering from cold and hobbling along in those awful boots right now. It was a kindness I won't soon forget. I'll remember you for this, long after I've gone back home. Thank you."

Her gratitude seemed a bit over the top for something so simple, and he barely managed to mumble, "You're welcome."

Once again, she stopped in front of the toy store. Her gaze fixed on the array of colorful hand-carved dollhouses on the table out front.

"You sure you don't want to go inside and take a look?" he suggested.

Her head swerved to him, eyes wide with alarm, but soon, her lids came down, hooding her first reaction. "Nope," she said blandly. "No reason." Without another word, she strolled away, leaving him to pick up his jaw and follow. When he caught up to her, she tossed over her shoulder, "How much farther?"

"Another few blocks." This morning, they were headed to Salwator Cemetery, where they had an appointment with manager Walter Sawicki, to arrange for the interment of her mother's ashes.

They crossed two more streets before turning left and climbing uphill toward Waszyngtona Avenue. The original red brick church still stood on the grounds, but their destination was the newer, more modern building of white stone and narrow rectangular windows. Around them lay a virtual city of graves and crypts. Headstones were simple or elaborate, some vertical, some horizontal, some with ornate carvings, others holding ceramic pots filled with Christmas bouquets of pine and holly berries.

"This is it?" She pointed at a nearby copper-colored stone crypt etched with images of angels. "This is the cemetery where my grandparents are?"

"I guess so."

She spun slowly, head tilted toward the dim sunlight, taking it all in. "It's so pretty, so peaceful."

"Mmm-hmm." He opened the door to the building. "Come on. Mr. Sawicki is waiting."

With one last glance, she headed inside, Rhys following behind her. After checking in with the receptionist, they waited in the quiet lobby until a tall, beefy man with salt and pepper hair and a compassionate face, his apple cheeks rosy, gestured them forward. He introduced himself as Walter Sawicki and ushered them into a warm office with hunter green carpet, dark wood paneling, and golden lamplight. Within minutes, they were discussing the business at hand, with Rhys translating for Polina's benefit.

"He said they can do a small service on Sunday morning, if you'd like."

"A service?" She looked befuddled, blinking at rapid speed, unfocused.

"A religious service," he clarified.

"For *my* mother?!" To his surprise, she burst into laughter. "I'm sorry, but the idea of Serafina Kominski sitting through a religious service..." She shook her head as her mirth subsided into a more fatalistic attitude. "Mom wasn't much of a church person. On Sundays, she refused to get up before the crack of noon. I sincerely doubt just because she's dead now, she's changed her ways. Please tell Mr. Sawicki I appreciate the offer of a service, but it won't be necessary."

At Rhys's translation, the man nodded and proceeded

to tell him about the next step.

"You have to choose an urn," Rhys said to Polina.

"Oh." Her bewilderment returned. "I didn't think of that. I should've brought one with me, shouldn't I? Instead of keeping her in a box?"

Mr. Sawicki must have understood the look on her face, because he interjected to tell them he had urn samples in their showroom.

"Oh," she repeated. "That's good. O...kay." She rose from her chair, and both men did the same. Running her hands down the thighs of her jeans, she took a deep breath, exhaled slowly and said, "Let's do this."

The director led them through the carpeted hallway to a side room, away from the chapel area. Glass cases, illuminated by mini spotlights, held dozens of styles of funereal urns. There were urns made of ceramic, bronze, metal, glass, marble and wood. Some were shaped like Grecian works of art, others fashioned into crosses, racecars, animals, or, Jeez...baby shoes. He looked away from that particular vessel, couldn't fathom how painful that choice might be for some unfortunate parent.

"How am I supposed to pick one?" Polina whispered. "I've never done this before."

"Neither have I. What were her interests? Besides you, of course."

"Ha." The syllable, flat and emotionless, filled the small room and echoed back. She strolled from case to case, staring at the various containers, saying nothing more. At last, she pointed. "That one."

"Ah." Mr. Sawicki approached the case, inserted a key, and put his hand on a slender brass urn with ornate carved handles. He turned to her, questioning the choice.

"No." With a swish of her hand, she indicated the item behind and to the left of the one Mr. Sawicki touched.

Nodding, Mr. Sawicki lifted a black enamel box with a simple carved design of lilies inset with mother-of-pearl and handed it to her. The piece she'd opted for looked more like an old-fashioned jewelry box than a funeral urn. An odd choice, but what did Rhys know?

Polina traced the front of the box from the horn of one lily to a simple brass plaque, blank but ready to be engraved. Handing the box back to the cemetery director, she nodded. "Yes. This one."

He spoke in rapid Polish.

"What'd he say?"

"He wants to know what you want engraved on the brass tag."

"Oh, umm...I guess her name."

"Anything else?" Rhys asked. "Her date of birth and death? 'Beloved Mother,' maybe?"

"No. Just her name."

♥

Just her name.

She'd seen the way Mr. Sawicki looked at her, the disbelief in Rhys's widened eyes and slack jaw. But, honestly, what else could she say? She had a tough enough time choosing from the vast array of urns in that room. The only reason she picked that box was because she found it pretty. Her mother hadn't known much pretty in her life and Polina wanted her to have something pretty in death. Had she known she had to engrave details in the tag, she would've picked a different one. She had no idea when Serafina was born and certainly had never considered the woman as a "Beloved Mother." Guilt stabbed her at the admission, but theirs had always been a tumultuous relationship with each of them throwing barbs and verbal missiles at the other.

"You want to see the crypt?" Rhys asked, and she jolted back to the present. He waved the paper map with its big, black X mark that Mr. Sawicki had given them.

"Yes." She didn't know why. These people—or bones, she supposed—meant nothing to her. Nevertheless, some ghoulish need to see where they lay spurred her onward.

"All right then. Let's go." They headed out of the building, and a sudden burst of wind nearly knocked her backwards. Rhys caught her before she stumbled. "Easy."

His arms wrapped around her, pulling her tight against him. His brawn buffeted her from the cold, from the wind, from the harshness around and inside her. She thought she could melt into him, lose herself in him. The idea terrified her, and she yanked away before she could become accustomed to the sensation. "I'm okay."

She trudged forward, passing hundreds of headstones, many decorated with holiday bric-a-brac, until a chilling thought stopped her in her tracks. "Oh, God. Should I have brought flowers?"

"You brought them their family member. I think they'll appreciate the importance of the gesture without expecting flowers, too."

She walked ahead of him, pondering his words, perhaps a bit too seriously. Why should they expect anything? They were dead. "Do you believe in ghosts, Rhys?"

"No. Not really. You?"

"What do *you* think?" She planted her hands on her hips.

"I think Mom believed in the mystical, so you don't. That, I assume, would include ghosts."

She tapped an index finger to her nose. "You paid attention. Good boy."

"I'm a stickler for details."

The crypt where they stopped was gray marble with a carved, winged angel hovering over the door, etched with "Kominski" in large block letters at her feet. In smaller upper and lower case letters were the names and dates of the crypt's...residents. One name, in particular, stuck out.

"I must have been named for my grandmother." She read the last name on the list. "Polina Dziuba Kominski. I never knew that. I wonder what she was like."

"Your mother never told you about her?"

"She died when Mom was a kid. My grandfather, too." She shrugged. "Maybe she didn't want to remember her parents because the memories were too painful."

"How old was your mother when her mother died?"

"Six, I think. Maybe seven. Mom rarely talked about her life in Poland." She grimaced. Mom rarely talked—period. Not to her daughter, that was for sure. She mumbled incoherently a lot, occasionally shouted obscenities. Polina never knew how to handle the outbursts, the shrieks, and rocky mood swings.

Did that make her a bad daughter? Was that why her mother had abandoned her? Because she hadn't comforted her in those awful nights?

She touched the etched name of her grandmother once again. "I'm sorry," she told the cold marble. "I was just a kid. What was I supposed to do?" She placed her forehead to the stone and murmured again, "I'm sorry."

She probably would have stayed there until she became part of the crypt if Rhys hadn't taken her arm and pulled her away. "Come on. Let's take you back to the Nowaks'. I think you've had enough for one day."

As they walked, a thousand recriminations echoed in Polina's skull. She could envision her grandmother standing in front of her, wagging her finger and chastising, "You should have done more! Why didn't you try harder?"

Polina had no answer, no excuse. Yes, her mother was difficult—she always had been. Why hadn't she insisted her mother come live with her once she was settled after college? If she'd had proper care and decent living conditions in the last few years, would she still be dead now? If Polina had tried one last time before Leo had called her, maybe Serafina would have lived a bit longer. Why didn't she try harder?

Her limbs grew heavy, and her footsteps slowed as the years of guilt weighed her down. "I'm sorry," she mumbled.

"What was that?" Rhys asked from beside her. "Did you say something?"

Tightening her lips, she shook her head. The wind howled, slicing into her cheeks, and she shivered—not from cold but the hail of bullets her conscience hurled.

10

Rhys sat at his desk and struggled to focus on the most recent email from his agent in Brazil. *Per Jon Adamiak's instructions, due to these issues, we've settled the agent's fees into Interbank's account..."*

The issues, according to details provided in a previous email, included some regulatory problems with their usual transfer agent. Adamiak, chief financial officer of Volker-Kellogg Bank and part-time miracle worker, had managed to use his considerable influence and business ties in the financial markets to open interim accounts with Interbank until they could revert to their usual business practices.

Another crisis averted. An especially lucky scenario at year-end.

If only coming up with a Christmas gift for Polina was as easily solved. At lunchtime, he and Henryk strolled Old Town and the Cloth Market. The cream-and-rust-colored Renaissance-style building, with a wall of graceful arches, gothic turrets, gingerbread scrollwork, and the massive statue of Polish poet Adam Mickiewicz in front was, in actuality, the world's oldest shopping mall. Hundreds of vendors crowded outside the building with their wooden stands, and one by one, they approached the two men to show off their handicrafts. There were toys and ornaments, baked goods and candies, musical instruments. Nothing seemed right for Polina.

At the toy kiosk, he caught sight of a line of ornate dollhouses and remembered how she always studied them when they passed by. Why? Did she want one? Knowing she'd grown up with so little, he wondered if giving her the toys she'd only dreamed of in her childhood was the right option. But, no. He shook his head. Ridiculous. Besides, how would she get such an enormous contraption on the plane to take home?

"I need to find something portable," he murmured.

"Jewelry's portable," Henry suggested. "That's what I'm getting Bianka. A necklace with all our birthstones in a heart-shaped pendant."

"Jewelry's too personal," Rhys replied.

"Then I guess underwear's out, too." Rhys shot him a disgusted look, and Henryk snickered. "A joke, friend." He clapped a hand on Rhys's shoulder. "Relax. During dinner tonight, I'll have Bianka steer the conversation toward gifts. Maybe she'll give you a hint about what would make her happy. And if she doesn't, what does it matter? She'll be gone in a few weeks' time anyway. At least, if you screw this up, she won't be around here to remind you every day."

But he wanted her around. God help him, he wanted her to stay.

A bulldozer's roar cut through the icy wind and captured Rhys's attention. As if hypnotized, he turned toward the sound and walked in that direction.

"Rhys?" Despite the fact the man stood beside him, Henryk's voice seemed to come from some deep hole in the ground. "Where are you going?"

He didn't answer. Nothing else mattered but the sound.

"Rhys?"

"I have to see..." he murmured, speeding away. When Henryk fell into step beside him, Rhys waved him off. "Go to the office. I'll meet you there."

Henryk grabbed his elbow. "Come on. You come with me. You have to let this go."

"No." Rhys shook him off. "I have to see." He crossed the street, aimed for the site.

The increased noise level made civil discussion impossible. When he reached the edge of the demolition area, he stopped on the sidewalk and checked out the sign. A Polish company. He expelled a tense breath. According to the before and after photos, the razed building would be replaced with a shiny new department store.

"Rhys," Henryk prompted again. "It's all right."

He pointed to the pile of rubble behind the barricade. "Did you know about that building?"

"No, but—"

Ignoring the rest of that statement, Rhys strode to the barrier where a squat, middle-aged man wearing a bright yellow hardhat stood watching the massive machine dig up the earth. "Hey!" he shouted.

The man looked up at him. "Step back, sir," the man ordered in Polish, one gloved hand upheld. "Please."

Rhys turned to Henryk. "Ask him."

"Rhys..."

"Ask him."

Henryk shook his head, but did as Rhys demanded and engaged the construction worker in a shouted conversation while the bulldozer droned on. After a minute or two of back and forth, Henryk returned his attention to Rhys. "It *was* an old store, built in 1982, that went out of business in 2010. The site's been vacant and abandoned ever since. Lots of safety issues. Drug dealers moved in about a year or two ago, started using the place as a warehouse-cum-meeting site. Oh! And the city's Preservation Society is a hundred percent behind the project." He planted his hands on his hips. "Are you satisfied? Did I miss anything?"

Rhys veered his gaze from the befuddled construction worker to Henryk's smug expression. Relaxing his rigid stance, he nodded. "Thanks."

"Can we go to work now?"

"Yes." He returned to the other side of the street and muttered, "Sorry about that."

"That's the third time this month you've gone rabbiting off to a demolition site. Do you want to tell me why you care so passionately about some old buildings in a city you'll live in for a year or two?"

"Habit," he said and clamped his mouth shut for the rest of their walk.

♥

As expected, Bianka and Feliks returned home by four,

Henryk at five, and family dinner began promptly at six. Polina, who'd never experienced an average family lifestyle, found comfort in the ritual as the days melded one into the other. Dinner hour became her favorite part of the day. She loved how the Nowaks reviewed the day's events, shared a meal with her and Rhys, and reconnected after hours spent apart.

After dinner that evening, the conversation turned to the upcoming Christmas Eve celebration, *Wigilia*.

"You like fish, yes?" Bianka asked her.

"Yes." She'd never eaten much fish except for the occasional fried clams or shrimp at fairs, but how bad could it be?

"Good." Bianka nodded. "No meat at *Wigilia*. You are our very special unexpected guest, and it is my responsibility to make sure you are happy. We'll eat and sing and share gifts, eh?"

Gifts. Polina's mind raced. Of course there would be gifts. She'd totally forgotten that aspect of Christmas. When she was a child, Tiny and Sasha would sometimes reminisce about holidays they'd celebrated when they were children and detail the gifts of warm clothing and shoes and fruit and candy left by Saint Nicholas. But, from what Polina glimpsed in her time here, the Nowaks had plenty of clothing and sweets. What on earth could she give to these generous people that would show how fond she'd grown of them? And Feliks?

"Polina?"

Rhys's prompt centered her puzzlement on him, this man who'd literally plucked her from the icy sidewalks of Kraków. She had to give the fortune teller credit. In following the dog on her first night here, she'd gained a true friend. No. More than a friend, someone she cared for deeply. If she had more time here, who knew where their friendship might go?

What kind of gift would communicate how much Rhys had come to mean to her? Heat flooded her cheeks, and she stared down at the tablecloth.

"Polina?" Rhys asked again. "Are you all right?"

"I'm fine." She looked up into his concerned face, smiling to reassure him. "Really."

"Good. I thought you might like to go see the *szopki* tonight. What do you say?"

The *szopki*. Number ten on Mom's list. "That would be great."

♥

Unlike the usual stable full of hay and animals seen in most crèches, *szopki* more closely resembled miniature Russian palaces.

"Every year," Rhys told her, "on the first Thursday in December, Kraków holds a competition in the market square. Afterwards, all the entries are moved inside the History Museum, but only those who win receive a permanent home on display here."

She scanned the cavernous room, filled with people and miniature palaces, though the term, "miniature" was an anomaly in this case. The entrants were separated by size. Sure, some of these pieces were small enough to fit in a shoebox, but others looked like they were carried in by forklifts.

Each crèche was more elaborate than the one before with multi-colored spires of gold and vibrant foil, some with Polish eagles and flags, all featuring the Nativity scene on the upper level. Lower levels displayed the arrival of the three kings, shepherds and their flocks, or even modern people celebrating the season with ice skaters, carolers, or families gathered together.

As they strode from one to the other, Polina took little more than a passing interest. Yes, they were pretty, but in that glitzy way she'd come to hate. "Why do they all look like that place in Moscow with the swirly ice cream tops? What's it called?"

"St. Basil's Cathedral," he replied and gestured to the *szopka* in front of them. This one had some kind of ballroom scene with dozens of dancing couples on the second tier and swans on a lake at the bottom. "Centuries ago, the harsh winter months were a time of little to no work for local craftsmen. No work equaled no money, which meant a life-or-death struggle to eat and keep warm. They started creating *szopki* for the wealthy residents as a way to survive. The more elaborate the piece, the more they could charge for the work, guaranteeing them they'd get through the winter. Let's face it. Even in those days, no one would pay exorbitant amounts of money for a typical stable-style Nativity scene."

"I get it. So they'd build these fancy-looking things with lots of glitter and shine, and all the cake eaters would clamor to out-glamour each other." Shaking her head, she clucked her tongue. "I always thought people outside the carnival world weren't what the showmen said they were."

"What do you mean?"

Dang. She'd just insulted the man and everyone he knew. "Nothing."

"No. You were about to say something. What do showmen say about cake eaters?"

She snorted. "You don't even know what cake eaters are."

With one hand on her sleeve, he stopped her before she could slip away to the next garish palace. "No, but I can guess. I'm adept at picking up languages."

Of course he was. Just her luck...

While Polina's cheeks burned with embarrassment, Feliks, with the wonder and glee of a child, raced from one display to the next, oohing and aahing at the colorful foils that glamorized the spires. "Mama, why don't we have a *szopka* at home?"

"Maybe someday," Bianka said as they moved on to the next display, "we will."

The boy's question sparked a new interest in Polina. She touched Rhys's hand and offered an apologetic smile. "I'll be back."

Before he could ask what she meant, she strode back to the very first creation and reviewed every crèche in the museum, this time to study each of the structures with a critical eye, determining what materials were used to make the pieces and how they were put together.

"What exactly are you looking for?" Rhys asked her.

Unready to share her idea just yet, she shrugged. "I'm not sure. My mother insisted I see these. She knew me, knew my interests. If she sent me here, she had a reason."

"All right then," he said. "Take your time."

♥

He might have rephrased that had he known how much time she would actually take. Every *szopka*, no matter its size or level of difficulty in construction, received the same scrutiny. He shifted his weight from foot to foot and waited. Checked the time on his phone and waited. Exchanged bemused glances with Henryk and Bianka, waited some more. The crowds thinned. Still, she crouched and stretched and stared while he waited and watched, his curiosity growing.

After what seemed like hours, she looked up from the very last piece and nodded. "Okay. I'm done."

"Did you figure out why your mother insisted you come here?"

"Sort of."

"Care to share?"

"You'll find out soon enough."

When they left the museum, Henryk and Bianka took Feliks to a local café for hot chocolate while Rhys escorted Polina toward his car. "Now you get to check another item off your mother's list."

She mimed a giant checkmark in the air. "Tick."

Unlocking the car, he opened the passenger door. "What's left at this point?"

"Off the top of my head, the only one I can remember that's not part of the holiday celebrations is ice skating." She frowned. "I wonder if I'm ready to slap a pair of blades on my feet yet."

"Is there a certain order or schedule you have to follow for these tasks?"

As she buckled her seatbelt, she sighed. "The only schedule I have to follow is to be finished by the day after New Year's. When I go home."

Home. The casual way she said it felt like hot lead in his gut. He didn't want to see her go yet. He had so much more to show her, to teach her. He had to find a way to make her stay. But first, he had to know what he was up against.

"What waits for you when you get there?" Maybe he

could offer her a better deal.

She sighed. "Tying up my mother's loose ends, then back to the plans I've let lapse while I took care of her."

"What kind of plans?"

She shrugged. "The usual. I'll go home and return to work, pick up the projects I should've finished a year ago."

He frowned. "Where *is* home anyway?"

"Right now? Texas. But I don't know if I'll stay there. I'm not sure I want to live in a state that only boasts two seasons: hot and hotter."

Leaving the car door open, he crouched on the sidewalk beside the passenger seat. "Where do you intend to go?"

"I'm not sure yet. It depends on where I find what I'm looking for."

Was she being deliberately obtuse? "Which is...?"

All he got in return was another sigh. "I'm not sure I can explain it."

"Try," he bit out. His patience hung on a dandelion puff, one whiff from flying off into the stratosphere.

After a deep breath, she leveled a steely gaze his way. "I've never really lived a normal life. My mother wasn't exactly parental material, and my upbringing was far from the idyllic childhood you had."

"You obviously never met my father," he remarked dryly.

Fire blazed in her eyes. "Oh? You want to compare miseries, Rhys? Because, from where I'm sitting, you didn't seem to have it so bad. You're successful, educated. You've been free to live your life and make your way without any hindrances. Tell me what you missed, what you didn't get from your parents that you had a right to expect. Did you get your three square meals a day? I'm guessing you did. You don't look undernourished to me. I didn't. I was often lucky to get one meal a day, good or bad. In fact, I never got any of the basics you take for granted: clothing, shoes, love. The *one time* I came to my mother damaged and bleeding, afraid and looking for comfort, she abandoned me to the courts and turned me over to strangers to raise, wanting nothing more to do with me. For ten years, I struggled to figure out what I did, how she could turn her back on me. Then one day, after I'd finally started living a normal life, I got a call that my mother needed me. I could've done what she did. I could've turned my back on her, but I didn't. I dropped everything to take care of her for the last ten months, going right back to the poverty and hard work and hunger I'd thought I'd left behind. I was with her 'til the day she died. Now, all I have for my efforts is a box of ashes, a lifetime of regrets and lost opportunities, and this beat-up watch." She thrust her arm in the air to display her wrist.

When she spoke again, her tone was heavy with sorrow. "You have no idea how lucky you are, to have a family that loved you enough to give you the opportunities and support you needed to become who you wished to be. I had to find that on my own, and I'm not done looking yet."

Silence reigned between them, and her ragged breathing suggested she fought back tears.

He wanted to speak, to comfort her, but he couldn't find the words. He couldn't imagine how harsh her life had really been, but he sensed she would refuse sympathy or pity, even if he tried. "Easy, sweetheart. I get it."

"No," she retorted with an angry swipe across her eyes. "I don't think you can understand. I didn't come to Kraków willingly. Mom just had to pull my strings one last time. Right now, I'm only half a person, still straddling two worlds and struggling to find my place in either one. I won't settle down now until I discover the real me."

Despite her protestations, he really did understand. Hadn't he left his home in England to find himself, to get far away from his family reputation? To find the treasures stolen from him? He'd had ten years abroad to come to terms with his two sides: the independent ex-pat nursing a grudge and the man tethered to family in England. He had to allow her the opportunity to do the same.

"Okay, then. So I'll wait for you." He quirked a brow at her, hoping to lighten the mood. "About how long do you think it'll take to find the real you?"

She snorted, a shaky smile on her lips. "I have no clue, but I'm eager to find out."

11

Polina didn't sleep much Tuesday night. Her conversation with Rhys ran over and over in her head: forward, reverse, forward, reverse. She shouldn't have rambled on and on about her unhappy childhood. After all, her life wasn't Oliver Twist-awful. She did have some fond memories. For some reason, though, whenever she was with Rhys, she tended to focus on the more sordid details of her past. Why? Was she deliberately pushing him away? Was she afraid she might grow to depend on his presence in her life? Somehow, wind up as needy as her mother?

Probably. Or maybe she recalled the harsher parts to remind herself that for people like her, joy was elusive and fleeting. No sense in becoming accustomed to cotton candy and lemonade when they would never sustain her in the years to come.

For now, though, she opted to live in the moment and enjoy happiness while she could. Put a smile in your heart, she told herself as she made her way into the kitchen.

"*Dobry rano,* Polina," Bianka greeted her. "How you sleep?"

"Fine," she lied.

"You slept late today. I make you breakfast now before I go to work."

Polina stopped in front of the refrigerator. "You don't have to do that. I'll take care of myself."

"You no do good job taking care of yourself." Bianka clucked her tongue and gripped Polina's shoulder in her meaty hand. "You too skinny for Polish girl."

Surrendering on a sigh, Polina headed to the dining

room. "All right. Thank you."

"You like the *szopki* last night?" Bianka called after her.

She paused in the foyer between the two rooms and turned back to Bianka. "Goodness, yes! I couldn't believe the intricate detail in some of them. They looked so delicate, like buildings out of some beautiful fairyland."

"I liked them too," Feliks said from his seat at the table. "Mama says someday we'll have one here."

"And we will." Bianka waved him off. "Go. Get your books. We leave soon."

The boy rose. "Yes, Mama." With a quick wave at Polina, he sped down the hall toward his bedroom.

That little exchange inspired Polina as much as the displays had awakened her artistic heart last night. She now knew what she wanted to give the Nowaks for Christmas. After the house emptied out, she picked up her tablet and spent several hours drawing a plan, sketching designs, and creating a list of items she'd need. In the afternoon, when Rhys showed up, she handed him a list, along with plenty of Polish currency.

Still in his overcoat and hovering in the doorway, he looked at the items in his hand, then back down at Polina. "What's this?"

"A shopping list. Is that enough money to get everything I have on there?"

He scanned the list and counted out the *zlotys*. "Yes, of course. More than enough."

"Good. Can you pick up that stuff for me?" When he didn't immediately move, she added, "Now?"

"What for?" He glanced at the list and read off several of the items. "Wood, cardboard, colored foil? Is this part of your list of tasks for your mother?" He leaned toward her, his lips a breath from the crook of her neck. "Want to let me in on what you've got planned with this?"

Delicious shivers raced down her back, but she silently lectured herself to stay strong. *Don't melt. Remember the old carny saying. Eyes on the prize.* "Not yet," she told him, then placed her hands on his shoulders and pushed. "Now go buy those things for me. I need to get started if I want to finish on time."

"On time for what?"

She flashed him a tight-lipped smile. "You'll see."

Once he left on her errand, she raced downstairs to the basement. If anyone caught her, she'd probably wind up tied to a chair for the remainder of her stay, but she needed a place to work *and* hide her project while in progress.

Dampness weighted the air, and mildew stung her nostrils. There was no natural light, due mostly to the snow piled higher than the ground level windows. Boxes lined the walls, along with a vertical stack of folding chairs. A spider web the size of Kansas, its fuzzy gray occupant loitering in the center, hung from one corner of the room. Not exactly ideal working conditions, but she'd dealt with plenty of worse situations over the years.

A bare bulb dangled from the ceiling, and when she flipped the switch, the room flooded with harsh white light. Yes, this would do fine. She created a makeshift workbench from a sheet of plywood and two sawhorses. For another few minutes, she took stock of Henryk's tool box, making sure he had everything she'd need and cursing herself for not considering that aspect earlier. She would hate to have to send Rhys back out for something she couldn't easily explain—like a blow torch—the minute he returned.

Rhys. He wasn't going to be as easy to figure out. Especially since the one gift they both wanted—for her to stay here in Kraków—she couldn't give him. So what *could* she give him? She still didn't have an idea when he came back with two bags of supplies. "Where do you want these?"

"In the basement please."

He stopped, turned to look at her, eyes narrowed in suspicion. "What's going on? What are you up to now?"

"It's a special Christmas present for the Nowaks."

He looked at the filled bags in his hands, then up into her face. "What are you making?"

"A *szopka*."

His expression softened, and she could almost read his thoughts: *Aww, how cute! She thinks she can recreate magnificent works of art with a glue stick and aluminum foil.*

"You don't have to do that, Polina."

She opted to meet his doubts head-on. "You don't think I can build one, do you?" Self-confidence lent her tone bravado. She could do this; she knew she could. She'd studied the seams and lines at the museum, done her research online all morning. After all that scrutiny, she knew she could build a *szopka* with one hand tied behind her back.

His eyes widened, and his smile quirked up on one side. "In ten days? Sorry, sweetheart, but no. Artisans in the city spend months working on their pieces."

"Well, you're wrong. I *can* do it. And I will. The Nowaks have been very good to me these last few days. I have to give them *something* for Christmas, or *Wigilia,* or whatever they call it."

"Look," he said on a heavy sigh, "if it's an issue of money, why don't I take you Christmas shopping this weekend? You can pick out anything you want and I'll—"

"No! You will *not* pay for the gift I plan to give them. Even *I* know that's cheating. Besides, gifts aren't about money; they're to show you're thinking of the recipient. Since I've been staying here, I haven't had to pay for my room and meals so I have some money squirreled away. I can do this on my own."

"All right. Fine. If you say so, I'll take you at your word. But if you're planning this gift as a surprise, do you think you can keep Bianka out of the basement until it's done?"

"Let me worry about the particulars," she said with a dismissive wave.

♥

Rhys shuffled through the meager influx of mail he'd retrieved from the post. Bill, bill, advertisement, bill, advertisement, advertisement...all the typical Christmastime flotsam and jetsam. Advertisement, ad—

Hell-o. The last missive in the pile was an embossed heavy-weight envelope with familiar flowery writing on the outside. He lifted the envelope to his nose, sniffed. She still used the same scented paper. Or was he the only lucky recipient of this particular perfume because she wanted him to remember all the memories entrenched inside? He wouldn't put it past her to resort to emotional blackmail to get a rise out of him. That had always been one of Eliza's most devious tricks.

Already knowing what he'd find inside, he tore open the flap. Sure enough, an invitation greeted him. A very personal invitation, including the added postscript, *It would mean a lot to your family if you came.*

Well, he supposed he should RSVP since she went to all this trouble for him. Mailing back the response card wouldn't do. Neither would a phone call. Maybe she was online? He'd love to see her face, even via cyberspace. It would be good to revisit, to tease her about her overbite for old times' sake.

He powered on his laptop and accessed his chat function. Lo and behold, her name appeared in his list of "online now" associates. Naturally. Eliza was the ultimate night owl. He typed a quick, "Ahoy, E!" to her and waited. It didn't take long before her pretty face—with the adorable, but prominent overbite—appeared on his screen.

"Well, well," she purred. "Look who decided to be sociable this year. And to think I thought I'd have to wait until the end of the decade to hear from you. To what do I owe the pleasure?"

He waved the ivory envelope near his screen. "I got your invitation."

"And you didn't immediately chuck it in the nearest dust bin? Progress. I'm honored."

"How are you, Eliza?"

"I'm well, Rhys. But, what's going on with you? Mum said you called her the other night, and now, here you are, tagging me to chat? Are you dying or something?"

He chuckled. "Sorry to disappoint. I've met somebody. She's got me rethinking my priorities."

A smug smile split her apple cheeks. "Would this be the same somebody who had you thanking our parents for your idyllic upbringing?"

"Mother told you about that, huh?"

She snorted. "You're lucky she didn't alert the media." She curled her fingers in air quotes. "The Prodigal Son is returning to the fold."

"It wasn't that big a deal."

"It was to her. She broke down crying when she told me."

Oh, for heaven's sake. "Happy tears or angry tears?"

Their mother was known to cry both. Delighted when a chipmunk scampered across their lawn, she could fall into a full-on weepfest if that same chipmunk got attacked by the neighbor's cat.

"Happy," Eliza told him. "Most definitely, happy." She leaned closer to the camera, her face filling his screen and warming his heart. "Tell me about your somebody."

"Why? You need to hear the gossip before Sara does?"

She clucked her tongue. "Couldn't I just be concerned about my wayward brother?"

"Since when?"

"Since always. We love you, Rhys. Even Sara. You have no idea how much your phone call the other night meant to all of us."

"Including our father?"

She sighed. "Still nursing that grudge?" His lips tightened into a grimace, but the groan escaped anyway, and she pointed a finger at him, laughing. "My God. You're still afraid of him?"

"I've never been afraid of him. I just don't want to be tainted by association."

"You've been running away from him since you could walk."

"Wrong. How can you all just forget what he did? To Mom? To us?" His voice rose in anger—as it always did when the subject of his father's shenanigans came up, and he shook his head to give himself time to calm down again. "Trust me," he said in a much softer tone. "I'm better off being far away from Father for a decade or two."

"I'd say that, after fourteen years away from home, you've made your point." When he didn't reply, she added, "Oh, for heaven's sake! Come home, Rhys. Bring your somebody with you. I'm betting Mum would love the chance to meet the woman. By the by, what *is* her real name?"

"None of your business."

She tapped a finger on her chin. "Hmm. A trifle long for the place card, but I'll do my best to fit it. I don't suppose she'd let me abbreviate it to 'None,' do you?"

"Write what you want. It won't matter to us."

"So, I'm right, then? You tagged me tonight to say you're bringing her to the anniversary party? Maybe *I* should contact the media. 'The Prodigal Son returning to the fold and bringing a somebody along with him.' That should make all the major news outlets."

"Don't even jest about that."

She bounced up and down, hands waving madly. "Ooh! I have a great idea. Let's surprise Mum and Dad. I'll say you couldn't make it to their party, and then, after everyone's seated, you can suddenly appear and make the first toast to them. That'd be only fair anyway since you're the eldest. And it'll put Sara's nose out of joint—especially if I don't tell her you're coming. Let her find out when you're up at the podium. We might even render her speechless. Win-win-win. What do you think?"

"I think you're getting ahead of yourself. Who said I was coming to the party?"

Reverting to a more sedate pose, she gave him a sour look. "If you weren't, you would have simply dropped the response card in the post and gone on with your life the way you have with every invitation we've sent, including Sara's wedding."

He didn't reply. How could he? She'd nailed him with one sentence.

"You haven't even seen your new niece," she added.

He waved a hand in dismissal. "I've seen pictures."

"I've seen pictures of Queen Victoria. It doesn't mean I know her."

"For God's sake, Eliza, she's a year old. What does anybody know about her? How often she needs her nappies changed?"

"She's almost three now. Do you even know her name?"

"Sure I do. It's..." Rowena? Regina? Roberta? Something with an R. He knew that much.

"It's Rhiannon. She's named for you and James's sister, Shannon."

"Really?" How did he not know that?

"You're pathetic." Eliza sighed. "Come home, Rhys. Even if it's just for the party. Make peace with Dad. Give Mum a real hug instead of some empty words in a midnight phone call. Tell us all to go to the devil, if you want. Just say you'll come."

Waffling in indecision, he glanced at the invitation

again, at the early March date. Plenty of notice. He could make the trip doable with little inconvenience to his workload. His gut clenched at the thought of facing the old man.

Polina's words echoed in his head. *You have no idea how lucky you are, to have a family that loved you enough to give you the opportunities and support you needed to become who you wished to be.*

"I'll think about it. But I won't be bringing my somebody. She'll be..." Where? He didn't even know. Texas? Or would she have already driven off to some other destination by then? He shook off the dismal thoughts and focused on his sister's interested expression.

"It's time you and Dad cleared the air, don't you think?"

Long past time, in fact. "Maybe," was the best he could say.

12

By Friday afternoon, Polina had an excellent start on her *szopka*. She made some adjustments to her original design, which would streamline her timeframe considerably. Only one shadow darkened her sunny mood: what to give Rhys. Before she could devise an answer, he arrived at the Nowak house to take her on another outing.

"Where are we going?"

"I want to show you something your mother probably didn't know about. The Father Bernatek Bridge." He held up a padlock with a key dangling from the bottom. "You'll need this."

"What for?"

"You'll see. Come on. Let's get you bundled up. It's chilly out there." He fetched her coat and helped her into it, zipping her in all the way to her chin. "Let's go."

Outside the house, a pale distant sun glowed, and she lifted her face to the natural light she'd denied herself for days. By some mute agreement, they hadn't revisited the conversation they'd shared outside the History Museum since that night. Nor did they discuss the fact that she would be returning to America immediately after the holidays.

In silence, they drove past the familiar Pulaski Hotel spires and the gothic architecture of Wawel Castle. Memories flooded through her—their first meeting on the icy sidewalk outside the bakery, their first date when he helped her with her mother's list, their first kiss...

A sudden blaze of fire lit up the gray sky, and she bit

back a laugh. The dragon. Rhys and his magic. Silly, silly man. Silly, delightful, wonderful man.

Magic? No. She'd bet anything the fire came from some kind of electronic starter and a gas flame. He must have known that, too. But, for him, the folklore meant more than the facts. Sort of like her mother. And yet, unlike her mother, Rhys had his feet firmly planted on solid ground.

An idea burst inside her brain with the suddenness and luminance of that dragon's fire. Maybe, just maybe, she might know the perfect Christmas gift for him after all.

She'd need to talk to Bianka and Henryk. Such a project would require extra assistance.

They drove on for a short while, and she struggled to come up with a safe topic, one that might help her plan the perfect Christmas surprise for him. "How come you know all the traditions and history here?"

He stole a quick glance at her then swerved his gaze back to the road. "I make it a point to learn the customs and folklore of every place I visit."

"Why?"

"I'll tell you at the bridge."

At the bridge. On a sigh, she returned her attention to the highway zipping by outside the window. Her mind raced faster than the car. So much to do, so little time. Could the Nowaks keep a secret? That would be crucial. She wouldn't want Rhys to suspect anything—or worse—discover what she wanted to give him. As she'd already told him, the true meaning of a Christmas gift was something *from the heart*. With plans bouncing around her skull and her excitement building, this excursion to the bridge now became an inconvenience. How much longer?

He finally stopped in front of a graceful arc of steel, wood and stone, spanning the Vistula River. "Here we are. Welcome to the Father Bernatek Bridge."

"How pretty." Sort of. As bridges went, it wasn't very remarkable. Not big, not fancy, not imposing at all. Maybe there was another significance she'd missed? "Where does it lead?"

"It's a footbridge that links this side of town with the tourist sites like the Schindler factory."

She frowned. "I thought we agreed we wouldn't focus on

death and tragedy when you showed me the sights."

"This place isn't about death or tragedy. This place is about life—the best part of life. I promise."

"What is it?"

"I'll show you." She unclipped her seat belt, and he placed a hand on her wrist. "Stay there. I'll be right with you. Meanwhile, look in the console. There should be a thick black permanent marker inside. Grab that. We might need it."

"For what?"

"You'll see. Don't forget the lock." He climbed out of the car while she found the marker and placed it in her lap with the padlock. When he opened her door, she showed him the items. "Now, do you want to tell me what this is for?"

"Nope. Come on."

They strolled along the walkway until they passed below the curved arch. Bordering the bike path, a chain link fence ran the bridge's length. Other couples milled about the area, securing padlocks on the metal diamonds. Thousands of locks hung from the fence, a variety of colors, shapes, and sizes. One woman, after attaching a lock, kissed the key, gave it to the man with her to do the same, and then tossed the key over the rail, into the river.

"This is also known as Lovers' Bridge," Rhys said from behind her.

The husky quality of his voice warmed her cheeks. "And the padlocks?"

"Lovers write their names and the date on the locks, lock them on the fence, and then throw the key into the river."

Looking up at him, she quirked a brow. "What on earth for?"

"It's romantic."

"It is?"

"You don't think so?"

He sounded disappointed in her reaction, and regret nibbled at her conscience. Maybe she should pretend to be thrilled with this place. No. She couldn't do that. Not only because she wouldn't lie to him, but because this was all wrong.

"I guess it's nice," she said with hesitation. "I never thought about it."

"What's there to think about?"

"I don't know, really. It just seems to me that if two people are in love, they wouldn't want to hide that love from the world—or lock it up on a fence. You bury things that are dead. Or things you're ashamed of. And you lock up stuff that's harmful. Dead, shameful, or dangerous hardly sounds like adjectives for love to me." She paused, unsure, as she studied the smiling, flushed faces of the strangers around them. Clearly, she was wrong. Otherwise, why would all of these couples look so happy to participate in such a silly activity? Embarrassed, she glanced at the lock in her hand. "I'm sorry. Pay no attention to me. I don't know much about love. Or bridges, for that matter."

In the carnival world, happily-ever-afters were as rare as millionaires. Couples might hook up for a season or two, but if they actually decided to marry, the procedure was as simple as a ride once around on the carousel. No big church wedding or legal ceremony needed. Divorce was even easier—just call it quits and move on. No courts, no lawyers. She'd seen it dozens of times over the years.

From the time she was old enough to understand about love and marriage, she wanted more. Someday, she wanted enough fuss and love to last a lifetime, not a season.

"No, I think you know more about love than anyone else I've ever met."

She shook her head. Now he was just placating her. "You don't have to say that."

"I mean it. You're absolutely right. If two people are in love, they should be so excited they want to tell everyone they meet. And if you have to lock up love to keep it, it's not real love at all." He took the padlock from her. "You make me feel rather foolish for bringing this along, as a matter of fact."

Gee, talk about ruining the moment. The last thing she wanted to do was to insult him or make feel stupid. One fact her mother had taught her, there was nothing more fragile than a man's ego.

"You know what?" she said brightly. "I have a better idea. Tell me a secret. Then we can write our names on the lock and the date to show we're keeping the secret between us. That makes sense, right?"

He cocked his head. "Tell you a secret?"

"Yes. You promised to tell me here on the bridge why you like to learn the old traditions when you go to a new country. Go for it. Now."

"What makes you think that's a secret?"

She flipped her hair off her shoulder and winked. "My mother was a fortune teller." She laced her tone with the old gypsy accent and waved her hands as if clearing the fog from a crystal ball. "We see all..."

"It's not much of a secret. You're going to be disappointed when I tell you the truth."

"No, I won't. You know all about me. I know very little about you. Share this with me. Please."

♥

She thought he knew all about her? Not true. He could spend a lifetime learning every detail about Polina Kominski. She always kept him guessing. Just when he thought he had her figured out, she surprised him again. He'd continue to enjoy trying to guess where her mind would take them next. If only they had more time. Oh, he understood her reasons. That didn't mean he liked the situation.

"Well?" she said with a grin. "Do we have a deal?"

"Are you sure?" He shot his weight to one hip, arms folded over his chest. "You're going to be vastly disappointed."

"Quit stalling and talk."

"Fine, but don't say I didn't warn you. It's about my grandfather."

"Your grandfather?"

He nodded. "My grandfather was a history don at Cambridge—what you'd call a professor, I suppose. More than that, he was a true *aficionado* of all things historical. Whenever he went on holiday, he'd travel to archaeological digs and ancient sites for unique finds. His home and his office at the university were filled with hundreds of artifacts he'd acquired from around the world."

"Sounds like an interesting guy."

"He was more than that. He was my safe haven. My father and I...well, let's just say we butted heads often. Grandfather was my refuge. Every time I visited, he'd take out a few of his trinkets and tell me about them: where they came from, what significance they held. He'd provide so much detail I always felt like he brought their stories to life right there. He was the single most influential man in my life until the day he died. So now, whenever I travel to a new place, I learn as much as I can about the place's history. It's my way of keeping the old man's memory alive."

"When did he die?"

"Years ago. Heart attack."

"And all his wonderful artifacts?"

"Were left to me since I was the only family member who appreciated them."

"That must be quite a collection."

He nodded. It would have been. If his father hadn't sold off every damn piece. Casting off the bitter memories, he pointed at the padlock. "See? I warned you it wasn't much of a secret."

"Hmm."

She cocked her head, studied him until he wanted to squirm in his boots. Instead, he looked away suddenly—as if some strange movement had captured his attention.

"Actually," she continued in the same breezy tone, "I think there's more to the story than you're telling me."

His gaze veered back to her, to her knowing smile and piercing blue eyes. Surprise, surprise. She'd guessed the truth.

"You just wish there was more because it's not much of a secret," he lied. "Now you're disappointed. I hate to say I told you so, but..."

She smiled. "No. You're choosing to keep your secret as close as you can, but still let me in."

"You're imagining things, sweetheart."

"No, I'm not. You elaborated where you felt it was safe to do so, but avoided details too painful to review." When he stared at her agog, she shrugged. "Told ya. Fortune telling. It's in my blood." He started to argue again, but she cut him off with a dismissive wave. "That's okay. I'll cut you some slack for now." Offering him the pen, she added, "Here. You do the honors."

He uncapped the marker, and she handed him the lock. In tiny print, he fit "Rhys & Polina" on the barrel, adding the date underneath. "Since I wrote it, you get to lock it. Deal?"

She took back the lock, twisted the key to open the shank and approached the fence. After choosing an open link, she attached the lock, clicked it into place, and pulled out the key. "Do you want to kiss it for luck?"

"I'd rather kiss you," he replied and captured her mouth with his.

By God, he'd never get enough of her. She was sunlight, laughter, all that was good in the world, and he needed that more than he cared to admit. "Come on. Let's have lunch at my flat."

Once inside his flat, he helped her remove her jacket and tossed it on the arm of his sofa. Meanwhile, she walked straight to the étagère in the living room—the source of most of his grievances. Her gaze started at the top shelf, at the broken figurine of a cat's head with a woman's body created from ancient black limestone, and descended slowly, studying each piece from afar.

"Your grandfather's artifacts," she said in a hushed tone. "How beautiful."

He didn't bother to correct her.

"Tell me about them. What's that one?" She pointed to the cat.

"Ah. That particular piece is from Egypt. A dig near Cairo. Probably from about 300 BC, give or take a century. That's Bastet, the goddess of cats, home and hearth, and fire."

She whirled to stare at him, agog. "There's a goddess for cats?"

"The Egyptians valued cats above all other animals."

A flurry of emotions crossed her face in the blink of an eye, from disbelief to consideration to acceptance. "Oh, right. I forgot about that."

"Did you? Or do you believe I'll think less of you if I discover you didn't know about something?"

She neither confirmed nor denied his subtle charge, and although the words never left her lips, her blush and sudden interest in his windows spoke volumes.

"Polina." He knelt beside her chair so they were eye-to-eye. "Don't ever pretend to be something you're not. Not with me. I know your upbringing was...*unconventional,* and I don't think any less of you because of it. If you don't know about something, say so. Ask me any question you want."

"Anything?"

"Anything."

Chewing on her lip, she pointed at the terracotta piece on the middle shelf. "What's that?"

"A Byzantine oil lamp. Seventh century, AD. Do you know about the Byzantium Empire?"

She shook her head.

For the next two hours, he shared details for every piece in his collection and the history of the peoples who used them. She sopped up the information and asked for more. If she reacted this way over the few artifacts he had on display, he could imagine what she was like as a child. Someday, he'd like to meet this professor from her carnival, hear the stories of young Polina, the student.

After reviewing all the pieces and their histories, she said, "One more question."

"Go on."

"What are you hiding from me about these?"

"Nothing."

Heaving a deep sigh, she shook her head. "You know, Rhys, you say I should tell you everything and you won't judge me. I don't worry you'll judge me. I've been judged my whole life. Being found lacking is normal for me."

"I already told you I could never find you lacking."

She gave him a mirthless smile. "That's the problem, Rhys. I don't care if you find me lacking. I care that I find *you* lacking. I think you want to treat me like one of your precious artifacts. You'll research and examine me until you've unearthed all my secrets, but always keep me at arms' length from what matters to you. If you can't share your sins, you'll never really let me into your life." She strode away from the étagère and grabbed her jacket off the couch. "I think you should take me back to Bianka now."

"Don't say that, sweetheart."

Neon fire flashed in her eyes. "Then tell me what the big deal is. Why do you get all defensive and protective whenever we discuss anything about your family?"

"Because some things don't concern you."

"You told me I could ask you anything."

"Anything about history," he clarified.

"Right. So long as it's not *your* history. You know what? Forget this. Forget you."

"Hey, now." He reached out a hand to stop her, but she jerked away from him. "Stop. Don't. Sit. Please."

"I'm not your dog, Rhys. I'm not your student, and I'm not some little match girl who needs your protection." She stormed away from him. "I'm outta here."

"Polina." His tone was soft, cajoling. He didn't want to increase her animosity with his reminder, but the words had to be said. "It's sleeting outside, you don't know where you are, you have no money and no way to get home. I have to drive you wherever you want to go."

Once again, she surprised him with her reaction. Her eyes narrowed to slits beneath winged brows. "No, you don't. I was doing fine before I met you, I'll do fine now, too."

Oh, for God's sake! Apparently, he'd have to spell it all out for her. "You're at least three miles from the Nowaks'. And that's if you travel the highway. Going by foot will take you twice as long, particularly dealing with the weather and your shoddy boots, which I might remind you, will give you new blisters. If you come home in sorry condition, Bianka will lock you in the house to keep you from further injury— *after* she carves my heart out of my chest and serves it for dinner." The distrust in her expression slipped, still there, but not as deep, and he pressed his advantage. "Look, I'm sorry. Truly. If you really want to know about me, my family, and my treasures, I'll tell you. But not now."

"Why not now?"

"Because we have so little time together before you leave. I don't want to spend a minute angry." Her expression sharpened, and he added, "Not that I'd be angry

111

with you. Talking about my family always raises my ire. The day you leave. I'll tell you everything you want to know on the day you leave."

"Two weeks from now. Why so far away?" Understanding lit her eyes, and she wagged a finger at him. "Don't think I'm going to forget. I'm going to hold you to this."

"You won't have to. I'll hold myself to it." The last vestiges of distrust eased from her face. "I want our time here to be filled with happiness. With magic. That's what your mother wanted for you. Not heartache and grief. There'll be plenty of time for anger and regret when you get on that plane to head out of here. All right? Can you forgive me? Give me all your smiles and joy right now? And let me share all my smiles and joy with you?"

She said nothing, simply stood near his door, one hand stretched out toward the knob. At last, she dropped her arm. "I want more than your smiles and joy. I want you to be honest with me. I want to know all of you, not just the good stuff. But, I can respect your request for now."

13

"Wake up, *ukochana*. Much to do today. It's *Wigilia*."

Wigilia. Christmas Eve, the most important day in the Polish calendar.

Polina rolled over to find Bianka looming over her pillow, a wide smile on her face.

"Up. Up." At the woman's continual urging, she pushed off the covers and slid her legs to the floor. "Come. Wash."

She stiffened. "I washed last night." Seriously, how dirty could she possibly get while sleeping between clean sheets?

"Last night, you washed from the day's work. Now, you wash for *Wigilia*. You start the day clean, you live clean all year."

Like the house, she supposed with a sigh. Throughout the prior weekend, Bianka had prepared the house for tonight's feast. Windows sparkled, and not a speck of dust remained indoors. According to Poland's version of Mrs. Clean, legend said a dirty house on Christmas Eve foretold a dirty house all year long. Apparently, everything a person did or didn't do on *Wigilia* held a deep significance for the coming year.

Polina followed Bianka into the bathroom where the vanity basin was already filled with water and, in the bottom, sat a *zloty*.

"Wash. Touch the coin. No pick up. Just touch. Many times. You touch the coin many times, good fortune will come to you in new year."

Under Bianka's watchful eye, she washed her face and hands, remembering to touch the coin often. Once she was satisfactorily scrubbed, she dressed and headed to the kitchen for breakfast, a light repast of almond soup and apple pancakes in anticipation of the night's bountiful feast. After the dishes were washed, the hectic preparations began in earnest.

Bianka bustled through the house like a whirlwind, scrubbing, dusting, and making sure every item sparkled. Polina was put to work in the kitchen, chopping vegetables, stuffing *pierogi*, and polishing the silver. There would be eleven dishes served tonight, including pickled beets, mushroom barley soup, *pierogi*, four different fish entrees, cabbage with split peas, fruit compote, and home-baked cookies. Meanwhile, because of the placid blanket of fluffy snow which had fallen overnight, Henryk had taken Feliks sledding in the nearby park.

Rhys was God-knew-where, since he wasn't expected at *Wigilia* until the evening, along with all the other guests. Not that she minded. She'd need the time to put the finishing touches on her gift for him.

"Why do women always get stuck with the work while the men have fun?" she grumbled at Bianka.

"Because men are big children," Bianka said as she stirred the soup on the stove. "You no trust them with something as important as *Wigilia.*" Leaving the pots to simmer, she sat beside Polina at the kitchen table and clutched her hand. "You make peace with your mama?"

She nodded.

"Good girl." The clutch transformed to a sympathetic patting. "No hate in your heart today. Only love. *Wigilia* is all about love. Love and forgiveness. Start the day clean in body and spirit. Happiness all year. Beautiful girl. Inside and out."

Tears stung Polina's eyes. In the weeks she'd spent in this house, she'd received more love and acceptance than she'd known in twenty-eight years of life. "Bianka?"

"Hmm?"

Her throat ached. "Could I...could I...could I have a hug?"

"Och, sure." She stood and gestured with her hands for Polina to do the same.

The second the woman's arms enfolded her, Polina burst into tears.

"Hush, *ukochana*. It's all right. Be happy. No tears."
While she crooned, she ran a hand down Polina's hair.

The comforting gesture only unnerved her more. Tears
fell faster, and she shivered with overwrought emotion.

"Okay. You cry," Bianka said. "I wait."

And she did. Polina had no idea how long they stood in
the doorway between the kitchen and dining room while she
wept a lifetime of tears, but Bianka never rushed her or
tried to unwind herself from the embrace. At last, the
deluge slowed, and equilibrium returned.

Pulling away, Polina sniffed and wiped her exhausted
eyes. "I'm sorry."

Bianka kissed her forehead. "No sorry. You carry too
much. Too skinny. Too sad. Too lonely. You stay here past
New Years. Get strong."

Looking at the older woman carefully, she asked, "Did
Rhys tell you to make me stay?"

"No." She shook her head and repeated with more force,
"No." She thumped her chest with two fingers. "*I* say. You
stay. You need us."

Warmth surrounded Polina. How could she turn down
such an offer? But she had to. And she knew why. "Thank
you. Your generosity to me has been overwhelming, and I'll
never forget it. But I need to finish what I started. It's long
past time."

Bianka's gaze scanned her from head to toe, and she
gave a curt nod. "Yah. I understand. But you need us, you
call. Any time. Yes?"

Polina flung her arms around Bianka for one last hug.
"Yes."

"Good girl. Now, let's work."

Hours later, the extended oblong table in the dining
room held eleven gleaming place settings, one extra for the
possibility of an unexpected visitor. Beneath the pristine
white tablecloth lay a bed of scattered hay, meant to
represent the Christmas stable.

In the living room, the air was redolent with the
delicious aromas from the surrounding areas of the house:

yeasty bread, candles, fruit, and gingerbread from the kitchen; pine from the tree; the crisp bite of snow from outside.

Polina stood in front of the beautifully decorated Christmas tree, unlit until the first star appeared in tonight's sky. At the very back, against the wall, behind the mounds of gaily-wrapped packages, her gifts waited to surprise their recipients. Pleased to see them so well disguised among the holiday glitter and geegaws, she gave herself a secret thumbs-up. Mission accomplished.

She'd had to wrangle Henryk's help in her gift for Rhys, but since Rhys already knew about what she'd created for the Nowaks, she supposed turnabout was fair play. Her nerves jumped and danced inside her. Tonight, all her hard work would be on display. She would be on display, too, with Bianka's relatives in attendance. For tonight's festivities she wore her nicest outfit, but even so, a pale blue cable-knit sweater and faded jeans didn't do the occasion justice. She wished she had something nicer to wear. The last thing she wanted was to shame her hosts. Or Rhys.

For the first time since she was a child, she longed for something pretty, something feminine, to wear. She stole a glance at Bianka, at her shining hair, curvaceous figure, and the forest green dress that enhanced all her best features. Polina wasn't vain—not really, anyway.

"Stop brooding," Bianka scolded. "All is good. You'll see."

Maybe. But something gnawed at her, some dark feeling that she'd encased herself in a soap bubble and a child loitered too close with a hatpin.

Before she could pursue that line of thought any farther, a husky voice whispered in her ear, "Have you been a good girl?"

"Rhys!" Polina didn't wait for him to remove his jacket before launching herself at him.

"Wow." He enfolded her in his arms and kissed her soundly. "That's quite a greeting, sweetheart. I've got everything I want for Christmas right here."

Panic sped up her speech. "You're here for the night now, right? You won't leave again?"

"Of course. Why?"

She stood on tiptoe to whisper to his cheek—as close to his ear as she could get. "What if they don't like me?"

"They're going to love you. Even if you weren't charming and smart and Bianka's ideal 'good girl,' they'd still love you. It's tradition. You're the visitor. They have to love you."

"They do? Why?"

"You're a stranger to these people. You bring luck and good fortune with you. An extra place is always set at the table. If a stranger should appear in their midst on *Wigilia*, Polish families welcome the visitor as a harbinger of good fortune for the coming year, and that place setting secures the visitor's seat at the table. Tonight, you're the visitor."

She shook her head. "No. That's not right. I set an extra place earlier today. Ten guests, *including* me. Eleven settings."

He chuckled. "That's just Bianka hedging her bets. She made me show up early to ensure that the first guest to enter the house tonight was a male. Male visitors bring good luck."

Already knowing the answer, Polina arched a brow and asked, "And if the first guest who arrives is female?"

"Locusts, famine, thirty days of darkness. The usual."

"Ha-ha."

"Relax. Bianka has it all under control. She'd hate to have another stranger appear on her doorstep when she doesn't have an extra place setting available. So, she added one anyway. Trust me. You're already the visitor that represents good fortune and happiness to the hosts in the coming year. But if you don't believe me, go on. Take a walk to any of the Nowaks' neighbors' homes and knock at their doors. No matter where you go tonight, you'll be greeted and fed and cared for like a princess."

No wonder her mother hadn't worried she'd have trouble finding somewhere to celebrate a traditional Polish holiday in a strange city. "You mean, I could knock on any stranger's door tonight and instantly be made welcome?"

"Yes," he replied, "but I'm very glad you wound up here tonight."

Her heart warmed.

"If you weren't here," he continued, "Henryk would have

invited Katia from the company's compliance department to be my date." He gave an exaggerated shudder. "She's a cold one. Cold *and* ugly."

Fighting back a giggle, she punched his shoulder. "You stink."

"I'm serious. It's a bad omen to have an uneven number of guests at the *Wigilia* table. Superstition says a table with an uneven number will see one of the guests die before next Christmas. So if Kacper hadn't run into you last week, I would have been forced to sit next to Attila the Hun's great-great-great-great-great granddaughter, Katia the actuary."

Hands planted on her hips, she pleated her forehead and narrowed her eyes. "That's the only reason you're glad I'm here?"

In one swift move, he pulled her into his embrace and nuzzled her neck. The lime and sea breeze scent of his cologne wreaked havoc with her brain matter, and she relaxed into him.

"I have a thousand reasons," he murmured. "Chief among them that you are the best thing to come into my life ever, and if I had my way..." He let the statement trail off by placing soft, moist kisses from behind her ear to the notch where her neck met her shoulder.

♥

When all the guests were seated at the table, Henryk rose and held out the *oplatek,* a large wafer, similar to a communion host, blessed by the local priest. Seated beside Polina, Rhys leaned closer and translated the man's speech.

"Tonight, I wish my wife, Bianka, good health in the coming year and thank her for her love and for all that we share. I beg her forgiveness for any wrongs I may have committed toward her and our family. May all her dreams come true for she is a good and loving woman." He broke off a corner of the wafer, ate it, and then passed the larger piece to Bianka before regaining his seat.

Now, Bianka rose. "Thank you, Henryk. May the coming year bring you much health and happiness. I am grateful to have such a warm and loving husband. I ask his forgiveness for any wrongs I may have committed toward him over the year and wish him a bountiful year ahead."

After breaking off a piece of the wafer and eating it, she passed it to her sister.

"Each guest," Rhys explained to Polina, "from oldest to youngest will now do the same. They will wish their hosts good fortune in the coming year, beg forgiveness for past transgressions, break a piece of the *oplatek* to eat, and pass it on to the next person younger in age." He paused, cocked his head. "How old are you?"

"Twenty-eight. How old are you?"

"I'll be thirty-two in the middle of September. When's your birthday?"

Her eyes narrowed. "Why do you want to know that?"

"Because it's customary for a man to know those details regarding the woman he cares about."

"Why?"

"Usually so they can celebrate those special occasions together, for one thing." Grinning, he poked her with his elbow. "What's the big secret? I told you when my birthday was. The fourteenth of September if you want to be precise. When's yours?"

She shrugged.

"Polina," he persisted. "When's your birthday?"

"I don't know," she mumbled.

"What do you mean you don't...?" He didn't finish the sentence, didn't need to. Her embarrassment was obvious in her pink cheeks and the way she turned her gaze away from him. "Isn't it on your passport?"

"All my legal paperwork says I was born on June 15th. CPS gave me that date when I couldn't tell them my real birthday." Another shrug. "It was never important."

Because no one had ever made the date important for her. No one had ever cared enough about her to make her birthday special.

"My caseworker said they chose that date because it was smack-dab in the middle of the calendar year."

Christmas Eve was not the time to discuss the shortcomings of her upbringing. Giving her hand a quick squeeze, he let go of his concerns. At least, temporarily. "Twenty-eight makes you the second youngest tonight. I'll pass to you, and you'll be passing the *oplatek* to Feliks when you finish."

"Me?" Her voice strained to stay soft despite her growing panic. "I can't. I don't speak Polish. I mean, I learned a little, but that's for later. During presents."

"Say it in English. I'll do the same." He gestured at the rest of the guests, watching Bianka's brother-in-law speak his wishes from his place at the table. "They won't mind. Many of them speak English, and if they don't, someone else will translate for them."

"Okay. I guess I could do that."

"Atta girl."

When Bianka pointed at Rhys, her brother passed the *oplatek* to him. After taking the bread, he stood. "First, I want to thank Henryk and Bianka for their generosity. I wish them both a year ahead filled with health and all the good things they deserve. And for Polina..." He turned to look down on her, seated beside him. "I wish you a safe journey home. May you find what you're searching for and return to me soon." He broke his piece off the bread and handed the remaining piece to Polina. "Your turn."

With trembling hands, she took the bread and rose while he sat. "Umm..." She cleared her throat.

After eating the *oplatek*, Rhys brushed his hand near her waist. "Go on. You can do this."

She took a deep breath. "I'd like to thank Henryk and Bianka for welcoming me into their home. I am so grateful to know these wonderful people and I wish them health and happiness today and all the days of their lives." She turned to Rhys. "I wish I'd found you later. But I'm glad you found me on the sidewalk that night." She broke off her piece, passed the bread to Feliks, and sat.

That was it? That was all she intended to stay? Nothing about the future? Not even a wish for his continued good health? Or a thank you?

Feliks stood and uttered his wishes, but Rhys paid no attention to the boy. She wished she'd found him later. What exactly did that mean? She'd made her speech in English, as he'd advised, so a language barrier didn't explain her bizarre statement.

Once Feliks finished, he broke off his piece and waved the larger piece still remaining. "The rest is for Kacper now.

Right, Mama?"

"Yes, *ukochana*. After dinner. Now, we eat."

While everyone else around the table dove into the splendid feast set before them, Rhys decided to seize the opportunity to say *something* to Polina. But before he could form a cohesive argument, she leaned toward him, the back of her hand covering her mouth.

"I screwed that up, didn't I?"

He looked at her, noted the sorrow in her eyes. Pity stabbed him. She was nervous. Unsure. Afraid. Why, he couldn't fathom. But he wouldn't allow her to feel those emotions tonight. Feigning confusion, he furrowed his brow at her. "Did you?"

Her eyes widened. "Didn't I?"

"No, sweetheart." Taking her hand from near her face, he brushed a kiss across her palm. "You were utterly charming, as always."

14

When the last course was finished, the family retired to the living room to exchange gifts. As he rose to join them, Polina took his hand to hold him back.

"Can we wait 'til everyone goes to mass before we do presents?" she whispered. Pink spotted her cheeks. "I'd prefer it was just us with Henryk and Bianka."

The *szopka*. She must have been embarrassed about how her arts and crafts project turned out. Poor Polina. He'd tried to warn her. Luckily, he'd signed her name to the gift he'd brought for the Nowaks. He had something special for her, as well, and yes, now that she mentioned it, he'd also rather be alone with her when he gave her the first of what he hoped would be a lifetime of gifts.

"Fair enough," he told her, "but let's watch the others open their gifts in the meantime, all right?"

For the next hour, they sat together on the couch and watched the melee of ripped paper, appreciative kisses, and exuberant thank yous. Through it all, Rhys kept his hand clutched around Polina's fingers. How would he possibly find the strength to let her leave when he couldn't sit here without remaining tethered to her?

"You okay?" she asked.

He nodded and leaned down to brush his lips across her temple. The clock kept ticking, and while his heart still beat, the rhythm slowed. He wanted to breathe her in, memorize every aspect of her face, find a way to make her stay, dammit!

"Polina," Bianka announced, drawing his attention. In her hands, she held a small, perfectly square, wrapped gift, with a pretty silver bow on top. Feliks and Henryk stood behind her, beaming. "This one is for you—from us."

"Oh." Clearly flustered, she exchanged a panicked glance with Rhys. When he nodded, she accepted the box with shaky hands. "You didn't have to...I mean...you've done so much for me already. I really wasn't expecting anything..."

"Open." Bianka folded her arms over her chest and waited.

Polina swerved her gaze to him again. "Rhys? Help me?"

Help her? With what? The box was small and certainly not heavy. "Just rip into it, sweetheart. This gift is for you."

Doubt clouded her eyes, but she dug a fingernail into the wrapping paper, poking a wide hole into the package. At that point, he realized he'd better help before she damaged whatever contents lay inside.

"Easy," he murmured. "It's just paper. Like you're opening an envelope."

On a surreptitious nod, she continued destroying the paper, this time with a little less force. She revealed the box inside, and was about to thank them. Somehow, he knew she was about to thank them for a cardboard box.

"Let me help you with that," he offered. "The corners are taped."

He took the box from her and pried open the lid to reveal the gift, layered in tissue paper underneath. After pushing the tissue out of the way, he passed the gift back to her so she might see what lay inside. A sterling silver frame enclosed a photo of the Nowaks in front of the living room fireplace, Kacper lying at their feet.

For the first time since dinner started, Polina smiled.

"To remind you," Bianka announced. "You have a family here who loves you."

Her smile grew brighter, and her face glowed. "Thank you. It's wonderful."

"Also useful," Bianka added. "Back of photo has our telephone number, postal address, our email. No excuse for you. You talk to us all the time. Let us know you're all right."

"I will. I promise."

"Good girl. Now, all the presents are done—"

Polina shot to her feet. "Wait. I have a gift for you. It's in the back of the tree." Dropping to her knees, she wriggled under the lower boughs.

So much for waiting 'til they were alone. Oh, well. In hindsight, it wasn't easy to receive a gift, watch everyone else exchanging gifts, and not become caught up in the excitement, he supposed. He should probably grab her gift from its hiding place to make things even.

But when he started to rise, Polina, from under the tree branches while she reached for the package, halted him with a quick hand gesture. "Stay there, Rhys. I want you to see this. After all, I couldn't have done it without you."

Great. That was just what he'd feared. Equal responsibility in a wreck.

She re-emerged slowly, backing her way out from under the decorated tree on her knees. When she finally turned toward the crowd, a beaming smile lit up her face. The sad package she held had been wrapped in plastic shopping bags with a quaint red bow tacked on top. Rhys's heart sank to his feet.

"Henryk, Bianka, you brought me into your home and handled me like family," she said in awkward Polish. "I want to say thank you." So that's what she meant at the table. She'd practiced a speech to go with her gift. Charming. Awkward, but charming, nonetheless, which pretty much described her to a tee. Switching to English, thank God, she added, "I'd like to ask Feliks to unwrap this since it was his special request."

When she signaled with a crook of her finger, the boy scampered forward, clapping his hands and chattering too rapidly for Rhys to catch any of what he said. His excitement, however, couldn't be misinterpreted. She knelt in front of the child, still holding the dismal package. "Be careful," she admonished, "what's inside is fragile."

As the boy painstakingly removed the plastic, Rhys looked away with a wince and stared hard at the other guests. If one of them so much as snickered, he'd—

A hush fell over the room. All eyes stared agog, all but Rhys's. Poor Polina. God, it must be worse than he thought. The way a driver couldn't look away from an accident scene, he felt himself drawn to see the hideous spectacle. When he finally focused on the gift, his jaw dropped.

What had she told him? This wasn't meant for competition. This was made from love.

And magic. She'd created magic. The *szopka*, approximately the depth of the family's mantel clock, was exquisite in detail. Three spired towers of hammered copper, complete with delicate filigreed balconies and triple-arched doorways housed the infant and his adoring parents. Painted foil in vivid red and royal blue caught the lights off the Christmas tree and twinkled in a prism of colors. She'd even created tiny manger animals from clay. And in a golden crown above the center doorway, she'd added a large N. N for Nowak. A monogram.

"It's also a music box," she said proudly. Turning the *szopka* around, she showed Feliks the key in the flat, unadorned back.

That's where she'd cut corners to complete the project on time. Competition *szopki* were three-dimensional. Hers was all front so that it would seat with no issue on the family's fireplace mantel. And she'd added a music box that played *Silent Night*.

Pride filled his chest as he looked from her to the *szopka* to the expressions on the Nowaks' faces. She'd actually created something beautiful and touching out of some silly supplies from a local craft store.

Bianka threw her arms around Polina. "Oh, my, it is so *byooti-full!*"

Henryk hugged her next. "Truly magnificent, Polina. Thank you."

"No," she replied. "Thank *you*. I hope you'll enjoy this for many years to come."

The other guests clustered nearer to pat her shoulder and nod their approval. Over their heads, Rhys caught her gaze and gave her silent applause. She beamed brighter than the sun glistening on Christmas snow. His focus strayed to the ever-present, ever-running clock.

♥

When the rest of the family left on their walk to church for *Pasterka*, the midnight mass, Polina and Rhys lingered behind in the living room before the now-lit *choinka* with the Nowaks.

Bianka, with her perfect timing, poked her husband in the shoulder. "I clean up. You put Feliks to bed. Leave these two alone." With a curt nod in their direction, she returned to the dining room. Henryk took Feliks's hand and after goodnight kisses were exchanged, the boy, with a lusty yawn, followed his father out of the room. Alone. She and Rhys were finally alone. The time had come to give him the present she'd created just for him.

She'd watched the surprise register on Rhys's face when Feliks unwrapped the *szopka*. If he'd gone so quickly from dread to awe to appreciation for the music box, *his* gift should stun him speechless. *Should.* But would he react the way she expected? Or would he reject it outright? Would he prefer something bought from a store?

She still knew so little about him. And, as evidenced by her lousy speech with the *oplatek*, he turned her upside-down and sideways. He was her Zipper ride, come to life. Her nerves jumped and bounced every time he asked her about her past. She might have made peace with her mother, but that didn't mean she'd made peace with the life they'd led. Gift-giving was a new experience for her. To be sure she didn't screw it up, she'd confided her plan to Bianka and Henryk, and they both agreed it was a wonderful idea. But...what if they were wrong?

Don't be stupid. Give him his present.

On a deep breath to calm her jitters, she unwound herself from his embrace on the couch. When he tried to follow her, she stayed him with a quick hand bounce. "Sit. I want to get your present."

"Shouldn't I get yours, too?"

"No. One at a time. Ladies first."

He quirked a brow. "I would think that means ladies get to open their gifts first."

Yeah, he *would* think that. But she didn't want any distractions when he saw what she'd done. "Ladies' choice," she amended and, before he could argue, dove under the tree to retrieve the last sad, lonely gift left beneath the boughs.

The intricacies of gift wrapping eluded her, and she'd

resorted to plastic shopping bags tied around the package. Sure, it looked pathetic. But what was inside...well, this was her masterpiece. Decades of working with steel machinery gave her an edge at creating mechanical structures. She wiggled out from under the branches on her knees and elbows, the heavy gift cradled in her hands.

Rising to her feet, she thrust the awkward package at him. "Merry Christmas, Rhys."

"Thank you." He took the gift and almost dropped it, clearly not prepared for its weight. "What the—? What's in here? Cement?"

"You'll see." She stood before him, toes curling and uncurling inside her thick socks while she waited. When he continued to stare at her, motionless, she jerked her head at him. "Go on. Open it."

With the gray bag balanced on his lap, he loosed the knot on top. "Anything special I should know about opening this?"

Ooh, good point. She should have realized. "Don't pull it out from the top. Keep it supported on the bottom."

"All right, then." He slid the bag down at a snail's pace, increasing the anticipation. She held her breath and waited for the big reveal. As the piece came into view inch by inch, her heartbeat kicked up tempo, and her mouth dried. What if he didn't like it? What if he laughed at her? No. He would never do that.

Would he?

While doubts flew in her skull, she pinned her gaze on Rhys. She needed to see his first reaction—before a polite mask could descend and hide his true feelings. Just in case.

As she studied him, his eyes, muddied with confusion, turned to widened delight. His entire face lit up as he freed the sculpture from its plastic surroundings.

"It's *Smok Wawelski*." He ran a fingertip down the snout. "It's a perfect replica. How did you do this?"

She sparkled. His approval meant so much to her. More than it should, her conscience chided, but she reveled in the moment, unguarded and unafraid. "Henryk helped. He took me back to the cathedral so I could sketch the details of the dragon, and then he picked up the materials I needed to recreate it. Turn it around. Look at the front."

He hefted the bronze dragon higher and slowly spun the face toward him. In the center of the statue's base sat a very small clock face. "It's a desk clock."

"Uh-huh. Henryk said to tell you that most of the bronze came from a specific site in the Nowa Huta district. He said you'd consider that important." She cocked her head at him. "Care to tell me why?"

"Nowa Huta is one of the oldest districts in Kraków," he murmured, fingers still stroking the dragon's lines. His gaze remained focused on the statue, tracing the hooved limbs, the jaw open and ready to emit flames.

"So that means there's a chance some of the bronze I used might have come from some broken ancient artifact." Well, that made her feel a whole lot better. She'd have to remember to thank Henryk for going that extra distance for her.

At last, Rhys's fingers touched the black face of the timepiece embedded in the base, and he looked up, a puzzled frown on his lips. Self-consciously, she rubbed the bare spot on her wrist. "Polina? Sweetheart? Where's your watch?"

She shrugged.

"You used your mother's watch to make this for me. Why?"

Another shrug. "Just the face. The works inside are new so you don't have to hand-wind the clock like you would with the watch. No big deal."

"Yes, it is. You didn't have to make it a clock. It would have been gift enough as a sculpture. And you know that. Come here." Placing the piece on the table, he grabbed her hand and pulled her back on the couch beside him. "Sometimes I'm a bit thick-headed. What am I missing? What's the significance?"

She stared at the dragon, embarrassed to look him in the eyes when she explained her thought process. He'd probably think it stupid. Or childish. "Tradition. You love traditions. I don't have anything of value that my mother left me—certainly nothing like your grandfather's treasures. I have the watch and a beat-up mobile home that we rented from my Uncle Leo. Not much of a legacy, I'm afraid."

And yet, she'd given him that one treasure, unconditionally. Not only that, she'd created this unique gift from bronze from the site at Nowa Huta. She didn't know the significance, but Henryk did. Whether or not the bronze came from a broken artifact didn't matter. It came from a site where his grandfather had worked and studied. A place where he'd acquired one of his artifacts. That meant more than she could possibly imagine.

"My turn." Polina sat up straight and folded her hands in her lap, drawing him out of his morose thoughts. "Where's my present? Gimme, gimme."

His gift to her would pale in comparison, but he retrieved the package from its hiding place behind the living room sofa.

"Wait a minute." She arched a brow. "How long has that been there?"

"Since the day I took you to the Father Bernatek Bridge. While you were at the bridge with me, Bianka stowed your gift here."

Clucking her tongue, she rubbed one index finger over the other. "Sneaky."

"Yes, I am." He passed the large wrapped box to her with an apologetic shrug. "I'm afraid it isn't the most sentimental gift in the world. I screwed up. I opted to get you something practical."

"I like practical," she said.

Yes, she did. Because it was all she'd ever known. He should've realized that sooner.

While he ruminated, she tore the wrapping paper and revealed the box—labeled in Polish. "What is it?"

"Open it and see."

With a fingernail, she pried open the tape and finally lifted the lid off the box. The down-filled coat with its rich fake fur collar lay beneath the layer of green and red tissue paper. "It's beautiful." Getting to her feet, she pulled the coat from the box and slipped her arms into the sleeves. She twirled, her face wreathed in smiles. "How do I look?"

"Perfect."

"Thank you. I love it." She kissed him on the mouth, light and sweet, then flitted away to remove the coat and nestle it back in its box.

As happy as she was with his gift, he couldn't stop castigating himself for his choice. He should have gone for broke. Should have heeded Henryk's advice to buy jewelry. Should have shown the same courage she had and found a gift that came from the heart. When the hell had he become like his father—losing the magic of sentimentality?

For a while they sat in silence, the only sounds coming from Bianka humming while she worked in the kitchen. Polina tried to rise. "I should help. She's been working so hard all week."

But he stopped her by holding her tightly. "If she needs you, she'll call you. She and Henryk are giving us time alone. They know what's happening."

She looked at him, her expression a complete blank. "What's happening?"

This time, he couldn't hold back his laughter. "You, me, how little time we have left before you leave."

"Oh. Right." She frowned. "I forgot about that."

He wished he could. That clock ticked in the back of his mind on a continuous loop. He hated how quickly she'd burrowed under his skin and into his heart. He'd never been a needy man. He stared off at the white lights twinkling among the lush branches of the fir tree.

"Rhys? What's Christmas like where you come from? Is it the same as here?"

"It's the same everywhere, for the most part. The meaning, the joy, the solemnity. Only the traditions change. The holiday is all about family, love, togetherness, feasts and presents."

She'd never before celebrated a Christmas. Or a birthday. Never received a gift.

Time and again, he wondered about her mother. Why she insisted on this trip at Christmastime, why she'd written such explicit directions regarding what her daughter should accomplish while here for the holiday. He remembered what Polina told him the night he met her. Her mother had sent her to Kraków to discover the magic. His brain landed on a new thought, and he seized it with greedy claws. What if he'd misunderstood the meaning behind "magic?" What if they both had?

Part of him wanted to demand to see the letter her

mother had written. To find out if she'd misunderstood. But he didn't. He didn't have to. All he needed was to talk to someone who'd read the letter and could decipher it. Someone who had Polina's best interests at heart.

Bianka. He'd have to talk to Bianka. Maybe, between them, they could decipher the letter's true meaning.

15

On Christmas morning, Rhys returned to the Nowak household early enough to guarantee Polina would still be asleep. He sat with Henryk and Bianka in the immaculate kitchen, imbibing on coffee and one or two last sugar cookies, while they held an impromptu whispered conversation. After all the fuss and revelry for *Wigilia*, Christmas Day would be a quiet affair of leftovers and visits to neighbors.

As he reached for his second *chruschiki*, Bianka slapped his hand. "No more sweets. Bad choice for breakfast. Bad for teeth. What you want? Why you come so early today?"

"I want to know about Polina. About her mother. And her childhood."

"Ask her."

"No. I want to know things I don't think she understands, and I don't want to embarrass her." Or anger her. Since he refused to share his own secrets, he sensed asking her for more details about *her* past would be met with a solid wall of resistance.

"So?" Bianka sipped her coffee. "What you want to know?"

"Polina's never celebrated anything in her life, has she? Not Christmas, not New Year's, not even a birthday."

"True." Shaking her head, she clucked her tongue. "Mama not good woman. Hard life for little girl. No fun, no presents, no love. Work. Work and scraps."

"Scraps?"

"Scraps. Grew up very poor. Not enough food. Not

enough money. Not enough love. Always getting by on the scraps of life. That's why we do everything grand this year. We had all the traditions for *Wigilia*. Now, we do all the traditions for *Sylwester*. Do old traditions and new ones, too. You'll take her to ball. We bake doughnuts, hang pans on fence. Make everything *extra special*. Maybe she'll like so much, she'll stay."

Well, well. He had an ally. A strong one. "Have you talked to her about that possibility?"

Bianka folded her arms over her chest. "I can't make her stay. Nor can you. Polina is a troubled girl. She needs time. Needs space. Needs love. Needs food. She's much too skinny."

His happiness dimmed. "Troubled? How?" Bianka shook her head again, saying nothing. "Do you know something about her you're not telling me?"

She shrugged.

"You read the letter from her mother."

"Yes, I did. I had to. I had to know she's a good girl."

He held up a hand. "I'm not judging. I'm actually glad that you did. What exactly did the letter say?"

"Not your business." She clamped her lips into a tight line.

"I'm not being nosy, Bianka. I'm concerned about her. Originally, I wondered if I was missing something important that her mother wanted her to experience here. But now that you say she's troubled—"

"If you want to know about my mother's letter," Polina announced from the doorway, "you should ask me."

He jerked toward the sound of her voice and found her standing beneath the carved lintel. Nearly swallowed up whole by a white terrycloth robe, hair mussed from sleep, eyes narrowed, Polina-the-not-quite-alert-angel-of-recrimination frowned at him. She'd caught him in the act. He couldn't deny the accusation in her expression that clearly said, *Spying on me?*

"I would have asked you directly, but I didn't think you'd talk to me about it."

"Oh, right. Much better to go behind my back and try to wheedle the information out of Bianka?" The words pelted him like ice chips.

Hoping to break the tension, he arched a brow and pitched his tone toward teasing. "Wheedle? I, madam, do not wheedle. I might charm. Or perhaps, even, cajole. When all else fails, I'll sweet-talk. But wheedle? Never."

She rolled her eyes toward the ceiling and sighed. "Do you want to see the letter or not, Mr. Roget?"

"Yes, I do—if you'll allow me."

"Fine. I'll go get it." She turned and headed down the hall, the stamp of her bare feet on the wooden floor a clear indication of her impatience.

In the wake of her exit, Rhys sat stiffly in his chair, trying not to squirm. Bianka glared daggers, and Henryk lifted his coffee cup to his lips to hide his smile—unsuccessfully.

She returned a minute or two later with a couple of pages, crumpled, stained, and reeking of cigarette smoke. Shoving them near his nose, she said, "Here."

He took the letter and stared at the childish scrawl on the paper, the mixture of block and lower case letters, the misspelled words. *This* was written by her mother? An adult woman?

Polina,

No "Dear Polina." Just straight to the woman's name. As if she was an employee. Or a virtual stranger.

UnklE lEo will only givE you this lEttEr whEn I'm gonE. BEttEr that way. No more fighting.

You nEEd to do onE morE thing for mE. You must go to Poland, rEturn my ashEs to my homE so I can rEst with my parEnts in thEir krypt at Salwator's SEmEtEry.

I want you to go at ChristmastimE. UnklE lEo has thE dEtails of your trip. WhilE you are thErE, follow my instruktions on thE nExt pagE. MakE surE you do thEm all beforE you go homE. Find thE magic. You nEvEr bEliEvEd in magic.

I did the bEst I could with you. I know you hatEd mE. You thought I was wEak. MaybE I was. EddiE was thE first but hE wouldn't bE thE last. ThErE are monstErs hErE.

Rhys glanced up. "Eddie?"

Polina's complexion blanched, but she waved him off. "Not important."

Lie. Clearly, this Eddie character was one of the monsters. He returned his attention to the letter.

You wErE nEvEr an Easy girl to undErstand. So difficult. Always judging EvEryonE, ExpEcially me. You wErE nEvEr likE mE. I hatEd you for that. Now I know it was for the bEst. NEvEr trust anyonE. You arE strong. StrongEr than I EvEr was. You will survivE. But do what I ask first. ThEn you can bE frEE of mE for good.

Why did parents fight so hard to control their children's futures? His father, her mother. Peas in a pod, he supposed.

There was no signature on the letter. No "Love, Mom."

No love anywhere within the chicken-scratch writing, truth be told. Nothing that commented on how proud she might have been of her daughter, how clever and resourceful Polina was. No mention of her beauty, her generous heart, or the memories they'd shared over the years. She didn't even bother to say goodbye. What kind of mother wrote a letter like this?

A pang of loneliness overwhelmed him, borne of the life Polina must have led before coming to Kraków, before he found her. And yet, somehow, she'd managed to light up the dark corners of his life, simply by being herself. By being the person her mother clearly resented. How had she managed to live on scraps, as Bianka said, without becoming bitter and hard?

On the second page was a bullet point list that began with:

1. *Go to Kraków.*
2. *Go to Old Town.*
3. *Visit Planty GardEns.*

Again, nothing personal found its way onto the paper. Although, he did smile at *5.Follow thE dog* and *8.Kiss a strangEr.*

The rest of the page detailed most of the activities

they'd already completed, except for the New Year's celebration still to come, which included writing out her problems on a piece of red paper then burning the paper, and drinking *tokaj* to see the bubbles.

Finished, Rhys sat back in his chair, digesting all he'd read. And all he hadn't read. Nothing conclusive leaped out at him, no sudden awareness flashed in his brain. Her mother hadn't included explanations why these particular traditions were so vital. The red paper thing was symbolic—a way to make sure the problems of the past didn't carry forward into the future. And the bubbles in the *tokaj*—they told of what she could expect in the coming year. But was that her mother's last stab at getting Polina to believe in the mystical? Or did these tasks hold some hidden meaning he'd yet to decipher?

"Well?" Polina prompted. "Did you find your answers?"

Yes. And no. If anything, the letter had only confused him more. But he wouldn't admit that to her. To do so would minimize the enormity of her trust in allowing him to read something so personal. Or, in this case, so impersonal. "Feel like going for a walk?"

She looked down at her fluffy bathrobe and bare feet. "Give me ten minutes." Whisking the letter off the table, she turned and walked down the hall for the second time that morning.

Bianka rose from her chair. "Need breakfast. No cookies. I make *kanapki* for you to take with you. Eat while you talk."

With both women gone, Henryk placed his cup on its saucer and glared at Rhys. "What are you looking for?"

"I'm not sure."

He frowned. "Do I have to remind you that Polina is not like one of your grandfather's artifacts?"

This argument again? Had Polina discussed her theory with Henryk and Bianka? "Don't be ridiculous. I know that. What on earth are you jabbering about?"

"I mean, my friend, you can't pick her up off the street, scrutinize her for flaws and merits, polish her up, and then keep her on a shelf once you decide she meets your criteria."

Discomfort rippled through him, and this time, he did

squirm in his chair. "That's not what this is about."

"No?" Henryk cocked his head, forehead pleated with worry lines. "You listen to me and listen well. You brought that lovely lady into my home. Bianka thinks the world of her, treats her like a little sister. Break Polina's heart, and my wife will break you."

"I have no intention of breaking her heart."

"Then what is your intention?"

"To get to know her. And to help her. But I want to be sure I understand why her mother sent her here and that I haven't missed anything."

"Is that all it is? Or are you studying her pedigree?"

Rhys's ire rose, burning his cheeks and throat. "You're not her father, Henryk. Let it go."

"In honor of Christmas and because we're friends, I'll say nothing more. Just remember what I told you. Tread carefully." He rose, picked up his cup and saucer. "If you want my opinion, I'd say her mother sent her here to find peace. Bianka's intention is to make sure she leaves here with a very large dose of tranquility." He winked. "And more meat on her bones."

"Oh? And what's your intention?"

"To keep my wife happy. Don't do anything that will put you at cross-purposes with us."

Outside the Nowak house, the neighborhood lay still and quiet. Peaceful.

Polina drew in a deep breath, tasting the clean, crisp air. "Bianka's wrong, you know."

Rhys, standing beside her on the sidewalk with an insulated food carrier Bianka packed in his hand, cocked his head. "About what?"

"About my mother. She wasn't a bad woman. I think she was lonely."

"I think that's a very generous way to look at things. And yet, in her letter, your mother accused you of judging her harshly."

"I did." She scraped arcs in the freshly fallen snow with her booted toes. "I never really thought about what she might have gone through, being dragged from Poland, probably still in shock at the loss of her parents, to America to work herself to the bone every day for the rest of her life."

"Did you two butt heads often?"

"Every day. And as I got older, the fights got uglier."

"You were a child. A child with adult responsibilities long before anyone should have to shoulder those burdens." He grinned and ran a gloved finger down the slope of her nose. "And that gives me an idea about what we have to do for the next week."

"It does? What?"

"I'm going to give you a real childhood. Come on." Taking her hand, he walked at a rapid pace away from the house.

She hurried to keep up, but her cursed boots hindered both speed and agility. "Rhys, slow down. Please. Where are we going?"

He stopped, giving her a minute to catch her breath. "Sorry. Can't help it. I'm excited. I'm taking you to the local park, for starters."

At a slower pace, but with a determined bounce in his step, he escorted her around the corner and pointed at a chain link fence enclosing a field of snow-covered steel structures. "We're going in there."

She stared at the area then gave him a dubious look. "Why?"

His smile never dimmed. "Come on. I introduced you to magic. Now, I'm going to show you how to have fun."

She stopped short at the edge of the open gate. "I've had fun before."

"No, you haven't."

"Of course I have. I told you. I used to test all the rides at the carnival. I've had lots of fun."

He took her gloved hand in his and curled his fingers outside hers. "You tested the rides as part of your job. Maybe you liked doing it, but it was still a job. If you've never done anything just because it felt good—and not because someone ordered you to—you've never had fun. Come on." He led her to a snow-covered lump on the outside radius of the rest of the lumps. Using his jacket sleeve, he brushed off the snow to reveal a wooden table underneath. "Let's have breakfast first. Ever gone on a picnic?"

"No."

"Well, you're about to." He placed the soft cooler on the table, then proceeded to brush snow off the connected bench. "Sit." He patted the clear spot. "It's a little damp, but you're going to get your bum wetter before we're done here."

This was sounding less and less like fun to her. "I'll stand, I think."

"Relax. Sit," he said again and plopped on the bench himself, not the least concerned about his...what had he called it?...*bum* getting wet. "It's just frozen water, Polina. It won't hurt you."

Well, of course not. She knew that. Did he think she was afraid? She sat, though images of frostbite nibbling on her backside danced in her brain.

He removed the foil wrapping and handed her a sandwich, flavorful steam rising in the chilly morning air. "Here. Let's eat the *kanapki* while they're still warm."

While she bit into the layered bread, meat, and vegetables, he pulled out a Thermos and poured coffee into two insulated cups. She inhaled the nutty aroma and smiled. "God, I love Bianka! She thinks of everything." After grabbing the closest cup, she sipped and allowed the beverage to do its magic. Her first picnic. Though, if eating breakfast on a bench in the cold outdoors was all there was to picnicking, this was more like her millionth. She'd eaten outside lots of times. Breakfast, lunch, dinner. Lather, rinse, repeat.

They sat together on the bench, saying nothing, while the day woke up around them. Church bells sang on the frosty air, sunlight glinted on snow. A squirrel skittered down a tree, its claws clicking over the frozen bark. The quiet and easy, no-rush, no-pressure atmosphere relaxed her. She thought for sure Rhys had devised this outing to get her to spill more secrets—to talk about Eddie—which was why she'd immediately headed him off with her thoughts regarding her mother. But, he hadn't said a word since he'd handed her the sandwich. About anything.

And she liked it. She liked that she could sit here beside him, absorb the stillness, feel no urge to fill the air with useless talk. It was nice. Not fun, exactly, but nice. Peaceful.

Snow slid off the bough of a pine tree, landed with a muffled thud.

"It's pretty, isn't it?" she said.

"Mmm-hmm." He leaned closer to her, his shoulder pressed to hers. "Are you cold?"

"No. I'm good. Really good." Finished with her sandwich, she balled the foil and slipped off the bench, aimed for the trash can at the edge of the treeline. "Be right back. Can I take yours, too?"

"Sure." He rolled his foil into a tight ball and handed it to her. "Thanks."

"You're welcome."

She trudged through the ankle-deep snow, but a pair of golden eyes glowing from beneath the stark branches and tangled vines behind the trash can halted her in her tracks. Barely breathing, she locked her gaze on those shiny eyes. On a sharp rustle, the animal streaked out of its hiding place and raced across the field, red coat a sharp contrast to the pristine white landscape.

"A fox," she said to herself as the creature disappeared over the ridge. "How lovely."

She had to hand it to Rhys. While she'd eaten many meals outside in her lifetime and seen her share of wild animals, none of those other moments filled her with as much joy as today. He'd actually shown her how to have fun. Real fun. By simply relaxing and enjoying a moment's peace. In a snow-covered field, and with the twitch of a fox's tail.

"Hey." His hand rested on her shoulder, and she turned to see him, expression dark with concern. "Is everything all right?"

"Did you see that fox?"

"Mmm-hmm. There are a lot of them in the woods here. Come on. We're not done yet."

"We're not?"

"Nope. We're going to use those." He pointed a finger at the steel structure of an old-fashioned swing set.

16

Over the next several days, Rhys showed Polina what children did to have fun. On Christmas morning, she learned to pump her legs to propel her swing higher and faster and laughed with delight at the breeze kissing her cheeks and ruffling her hair. Incredible. No motor or engine. No centrifugal force like the swings she was used to. This time, the only force came from her legs and feet reaching higher and farther with each upward swing.

He took her to the city's zoo, where she loved watching the sea lions play with beach balls in their icy pool, giggled at the monkeys' antics, and gawked at the size of the elephants. The nearly extinct Przewalski wild horses were beautiful and graceful, but then again, oddly enough, so were the penguins.

On December 30th, he finally took her ice skating—not for long, since Polina discovered she didn't care much for the sport. Riding a single blade atop the slippery surface definitely didn't make her feel safe. Back at the Nowaks' with hot chocolate and marshmallows, snuggled with Rhys in front of a roaring fire, she told him about her observations.

He arched a brow at her. "This coming from a woman who spent her life testing amusement park rides?"

"Oh, but," she argued, "they're much safer."

"Flying around at top speeds dozens of feet off the ground is safer than ice skating?"

She shrugged. "If you're talking about on a thrill ride, yes. They're created based on solid physics and kinetic energy, whereas snow sports like skating and skiing and sledding are designed to defy gravity. There's a greater chance for human error."

"How so?"

"Well, take roller coasters, for example. Roller coasters work on the physics of potential energy. Riders crest that first hill, and gravity pulls the cars down. The higher the hill the coaster ascends, the greater the speed on the downslope." Using her hands, she demonstrated the up and down motion. "Simple."

"And you consider that safe?"

She nodded. "It's controlled chaos. All roller coasters work on the same principle. There are three basic types: wooden, inverted steel, or suspended steel. Wooden's all about the construction—a lattice-type platform of cross-beams and cross-ties, tracks like train tracks, and cars with wheels that fit into those train tracks. Not much you can do with a wooden coaster to make it daring. No loops, no curves. It's just a lot of highs and lows. Riders get their thrills from the rickety nature that seems like the entire ride could collapse at any minute."

"Yeah, I see your point," he remarked dryly. "Defying death with every curve."

She nudged his upper arm. "It's not really going to collapse. It's the noise, that clickety-click of the wheels over the railroad ties, and the herky-jerky motion that makes the rider believe there's a danger. Now, steel coasters are very different. Because tubular steel can be shaped into curves and arcs, steel coasters can do almost anything: upside-down, loops, sharp curves, whatever the designer can imagine. The cars on suspended steel coasters hang from an overhead rail with a flexible joint that allows them to swing back and forth. That adds to the feeling of helplessness, of nothing supporting the rider. It's like being strapped in a chair on a really high clothesline, anticipating a huge windstorm that you know is gonna blow you around and might actually make you fall from the great height. With suspended coasters, a rider can be placed in almost any position. He or she can seem like they're flying or practically somersault in their seats. Upside-down, heartwrenching drops, a combination...the possibilities are limitless.

"Inverted coasters are rigidly fixed to the track, but the thrill comes from the speed and the intricacy of the loops and curves. In both cases, the rides are fast, smooth as satin, and constructed to produce an exhilarating, but safe, experience."

"As opposed to ice skating and skiing—"

"Where there are few safeguards in place. If the ice is too thin, you could fall through. If you slip, you could break a bone. You could collide into someone or something else, like a tree or an outbuilding. Coaster designers spend years creating new thrill rides, always pushing the envelope, but always keeping safety in mind. Physics and computer technology minimize the risks."

She sipped her hot chocolate, reveling in the sweet, rich taste. She might not have cared much for ice skating, but she loved the after-party of hot chocolate and warm cookies. And snuggling. She cuddled closer to Rhys, allowing his arm to enfold her into his embrace.

"You seem to know quite a lot about roller coasters as well as physics."

He sounded so shocked at the idea, she couldn't suppress her smirk. "Of course. Physics and all kinds of engineering: mechanical, electrical, drafting. It's what I do. I'm a roller coaster designer." At his dropped jaw, she added, "It makes sense, doesn't it? I spent my life working on them, assembling them, disassembling them, fixing them."

With wide eyes, he shook his head. "Sure. It makes perfect sense, but..."

She smirked. "But you just assumed I was some poor, ignorant rube with a sot for a mother who had no formal education, no way to make a living." There was no malice in what she said. Why would there be? She didn't blame him for his assumptions. Most people couldn't look past her carnival past, the abnormal part of her upbringing, to figure out how she became who she was today.

"I thought you came here straight from the carnival world."

"I did. But not the way you think. I was taken from my mother's care when I was sixteen." After Eddie did his damage. She stifled a shiver and raced past that sorry episode of her youth. "Spent a few years in foster care, earned a full scholarship to college where I did all the things other college students did, got my degree, and apprenticed with an engineering firm before plunging out on my own. I only returned to the carnival when my uncle contacted me to say my mom was sick."

"You've been to the zoo before."

She laughed at his crestfallen expression and the disappointment in his tone. "Yes, but it was sweet of you to take me anyway. And I've never been to a planetarium or spent time on a child's swing set. So you did show me a lot I've never seen before. Not just the fun we've had this week, but the dragons, this warm and loving family, a traditional *Wigilia*. I could never have done it all and gained the knowledge and insight I have without you. I'm grateful. In fact, what you've done for me in the last few weeks has inspired my best ride yet. Wanna see?"

At his nod, she unwound herself from his warm circle and headed to her pretty, sunny guest room. After rooting around in her backpack, she pulled out the tablet, turned it on, and accessed her latest project.

She returned to the living room where Rhys waited and vaulted back beside him on the loveseat. "Here. Look. It's an inverted steel coaster, capable of speeds of about ninety-five miles per hour."

"Ninety-five...?"

"Mmm-hmm. See?" She pointed at the drawn images. "Riders will begin in this darkened cave, which only ratchets up the tension while they're waiting for the coaster to move. I'm thinking about adding some creepy music piped in from hidden speakers, too—or animal growls. That could be cool. Really get them anxious. At launch, the cars will hit top speed within three seconds as they climb to the top of the first peak, about a hundred-fifty feet off the ground. Then they'll descend through two hairpin curves before the final straight plunge back to the base."

He studied the drawing, the formula and measurements all carefully laid out on the sketch. "I'm impressed."

"Don't be. It still needs a lot of work." She turned off the tablet and placed it on the table beside her. "But to thank you for what you've done for me, I plan to name this ride after you."

"You do?"

"Yup. I'm going to call it 'The Dragon's Tail.'"

♥

Leaving Polina in Bianka's very capable hands, Rhys headed straight to the local shopping center before the stores closed tonight. He wandered past the first row of storefronts and stopped at the entrance to a unique shop. His heart pounded against his ribs, and the hair on his nape danced. *Keep it cool, Rhys.* He rubbed a palm over the back of his neck. *Don't give away how much this means to you.*

After taking several deep breaths to calms his racing nerves, he strode inside, and the bell on the door jangled.

A lone man, short and stocky with a round sunny face, stood behind the row of gleaming glass cases. As Rhys stepped inside, he looked up and greeted him in Polish.

Rhys stumbled his way through a reply in the same language before switching to English. "Mr. Kozlow, please?"

"Ah!" The man held up one index finger and disappeared behind a black curtain that, no doubt, led to the storeroom.

While he waited, Rhys strolled through the shop, glancing at the various pieces of jewelry, collectibles, and electronics people had sold for quick cash. On the opposite side of the room, something caught his eye, and he stopped in front of the middle case.

"Yes, sir?" A new clerk, this one tall and cadaverous with sunken eyes in his gaunt face, entered the sales area from behind the curtain. When Rhys looked up from the case, recognition flared in the other man's expression. "Ah, Mr. Linsey. Good to see you again. You got my message then?"

"Yes. You have the piece?"

Mr. Kozlow nodded. "Of course. It's a rare find, you know."

"Not that rare," Rhys remarked blandly. "Samarind coins can be found all over Europe, thanks to the Viking trade routes."

The clerk blinked, as Rhys knew he would. Now that they'd established neither one of them was an idiot, they could bypass the bartering nonsense and conduct business.

"One moment," Kozlow said and disappeared behind the curtain.

Rhys returned his attention to the item in the center case. Fate. Again. He'd come here in search of something for his collection and might have discovered an ideal gift for Polina at the same time. Still, he needed to be careful, to tamp his impulsive nature. He was determined to not repeat his poor judgment at Christmastime. A coat. Why the hell did he buy her a damn coat?

He thought back to yesterday's conversation about her rollercoaster. He had done exactly what she'd accused him of. He'd heard she'd grown up in a carnival, did an hour or two of internet research, and drew some ugly conclusions. Yet, she not only didn't hold his assumptions against him, she planned to name her latest project for the time they'd spent together. The Dragon's Tail. How perfect. And yet another gift that came from the heart. Which was why he wanted something special to present to her tomorrow night.

First, though, he planned to purchase that coin. Then he could focus on a possible gift for Polina. If he did the tasks in the opposite order, he'd be too distracted by the lure of the artifact to choose wisely for her.

The clerk returned with a black velvet drawstring bag dangling from his hand. "Mr. Linsey? Do you see something else you like?"

"As a matter of fact, I do." Pointing to the gold band with the dragon's head perched on a black velvet finger mold, he added, "Is that a gimmel ring?"

The man's smile widened. "Indeed, sir. You have a sharp eye. Early Georgian period. Would you like a closer look?"

He nodded. "But first, I'd like to see the coin."

"Of course." He withdrew the Persian collectible from the bag and laid it on another block of velvet beneath the stark lights.

The harsh spotlight above the piece notwithstanding, the etchings on both sides of the copper were phenomenally clear. Based on the markings, the coin came from the

Samanid dynasty, ninth or tenth century. He shook his head in disbelief. Imagine. He'd found this piece—his Holy Grail—here. In this teeny pawn shop in a small village outside Kraków. In Poland. An almost perfect replica of his grandfather's Persian coin.

"It's an extremely fine piece," Mr. Kozlow said. "You can see the markings of the overlord, Nuh I, in the margin. Very little discoloration and no weakness."

He quoted a price slightly below the coin's worth, and Rhys nodded. "I'll take it." Transaction complete. No need to argue or bargain. Thanks to their earlier conversation, each of them was satisfied. "Now, let's talk about the gimmel ring."

17

Poland sure seemed to love their dragons. Sylwester's Eve, celebrated on the last day of the year, honored Pope Sylwester I who, according to legend and legend-maven Rhys, had conquered a fire-breathing, man-eating dragon.

"Another one?" Polina asked as they sat together in the dining room after a late lunch of kielbasa and pickled herring. She was crossing off the final items on Mama's to-do list. They'd already hung wet pots on the fence outside to drive away the old year, gone sledding in a nearby park, and baked bread in the shape of animals.

"Of course," he said. "*Smok Wawelski* was long dead by this time. Sylwester's dragon was named Leviathan, and he boasted he would end the world on the first day of the year 1000."

"This particular beast could talk?" She quirked a brow at him. "That's a new trick."

"That's what the legend says. I wouldn't know for certain. I wasn't there. But, do you know what happened next?"

"Since the world is still here, I'm guessing Leviathan failed to destroy the earth."

"Yes, he did. Thanks to Pope Sylwester, who climbed down a hundred and fifty steps into the dragon's lair, ensorcelled the beast, and then sewed its mouth shut."

"Clever."

"Thank you, but I had nothing to do with it."

"No more chit-chat," Bianka announced. "Much to do. In your room, Polina. Something on bed for you."

"Something?" She exchanged a puzzled glance with

Rhys. "Quick. Get me a needle and thread in case it's a new dragon."

"No dragon," Bianka replied with a throaty chuckle. "Better. Come. I help you."

Help her? Why? What was on her bed? Amusement transformed to concern. "Rhys...?"

"Go." He shooed her with his hands. "It's a surprise. I think you'll like it."

A surprise? She usually hated surprises. They never turned out good. "O...kay." She followed Bianka down the hall. In her room, draped on the bed lay a shimmering river of shiny blue fabric.

"Dress," Bianka said. "Tonight, you Cinderella. Go to ball."

"I don't understand."

"Saint Sylwester Eve. We all go to ball in city. Pulaski Hotel. You, too. Can't wear jeans. Wear dress. Shoes, too. No silly plastic boots or running sneakers."

"Where did they come from?"

"We buy." She thumped her chest with a fist. "Henryk and me."

"Oh, I couldn't...I have to pay you back. This is much too—"

"Stop. Not loan. Not charity. Gift."

A gift. Never in her life had she seen such an abundance of gifts.

"Go wash up," Bianka commanded. "Then we get you dressed and do your hair."

"But...I've never been to a ball." Panic set in, speeding up her words. "I wouldn't know what to do. Or how to act."

"What's to know? You no act. Just be you. Eat, dance, laugh. Fun. You'll see."

"I don't know how to dance. And I can't wear this." She brushed her fingers across the whisper-soft material, and fresh doubts assailed her. "Maybe I could just stay here tonight. You all go on without me. I can babysit Feliks. If I don't put on the dress, you can return it to the store and get your money back, right?"

"Wrong. You wear tonight. Feliks going to friend's house. No need babysitter. Mama insisted on all traditions. That means ball. Dancing. Fireworks. Now, go wash up.

Much to do before we leave."

Dropping the fabric from her hands, she shook her head. "I can't, Bianka. I just can't."

"Yes, you can. You will like. I promise. Big fun. All the people from the bank will be there. You come, too."

"Bank? What bank?"

"Rhys and Henryk's bank. Where they work. Bosses make big party every year. Invite all the workers, their spouses, and boy-or-girlfriends. Rhys wants to take you. Show you off. Sweep you off your feet. They have fireworks, too. Best party in city tonight. You'll see."

Well, this just kept getting worse and worse. A party with Rhys's coworkers? And his bosses? She couldn't possibly stand up to the scrutiny of people who dealt with that much money on a daily basis! She was still her mother's daughter, cheap material wrapped in a shiny dress. "You don't understand. I'm not—"

The woman yanked her into a fierce hug and ran her hand down Polina's hair. "I know, *ukochana*. But we love you. Just as you are. That's why you must come to the ball tonight. Make night perfect. No worry."

The woman's words and actions were meant to soothe, and they did, to some extent. Gifts and comfort. Two things she'd never known before coming to Kraków and being carried into the Nowak household.

She swallowed hard. She wouldn't repay all that kindness by giving into childish fears. They wanted her to attend.

Rhys wanted her to attend. Why? To sweep her off her feet? Hadn't he already done that? Ever since the moment Kacper collided with her on that sidewalk outside Hubert's Bakery, he'd picked her up—physically and emotionally. When she became despondent, he lifted her spirits.

Or did he want to show her off like she was his latest trinket? But that made no sense. She wasn't fancy enough for him to show off to his friends, no matter how hard he tried to polish her up. Even while wearing a ball gown and a pair of real shoes, she was still Polina from the carnival world. Back home, she never worried about how she looked. Then again, back home, no one ever wanted to sweep her off her feet or show her off, either.

"We will all be with you all the time," Bianka said, and for a moment, Polina wondered if she was talking about tonight or after she returned to the States. "We have fun. Drink *tokaj*, see the bubbles. Bubbles rise slow in glass, calm year ahead. Bubbles move fast, new year bring many changes. This is what Mama wanted."

Funny. She didn't remember her mother's letter mentioning anything about attending a ball. Oh, sure. Number twenty-two on the list detailed drinking *tokaj* and finding out if the bubbles rose quickly or slowly inside the glass. But Mom didn't specify where Polina had to be while drinking the stuff.

Bianka pulled away and used two fingers to tilt Polina's face toward the light. "Go on now. Wash up. Face and hair. Use shower. And smile. Not a bad thing. You like. I promise."

"Yes, ma'am." With leaden feet, Polina shuffled into the bathroom. She didn't want to be Cinderella, didn't want to go to any ball. What if she said something stupid? Or tripped over her own feet and collided with a waiter who carried a tray of expensive wine glasses? The imagined crash echoed in her head, and she groaned. What if Rhys's boss found out he'd brought her and fired him for his lack of judgment?

She had no business going to a ball. At the Pulaski Hotel, no less. That sacred altar of snobbery. The whole idea made her itchy. But if that's what they all wanted...

After stripping to her underwear, she turned on the shower. The glorious spray hit the tiled wall, and she stuck a hand under the water to feel the heat. Now, more than ever, she was convinced her mother sent her here so she might gain some insight. To understand how a little girl who'd begun life with these conveniences, with parents who'd loved her completely, couldn't cope when she found herself suddenly thrust into a much harsher world. And how that new reality destroyed all the good in her heart.

God knew, Polina struggled with the idea of going back to her real world. Not when she could remain in this lovely fantasy. She couldn't bear to leave all she'd discovered here. But if she stayed, she could easily become complacent, needy, and then, if some tragedy occurred like what befell her mother so many years ago, the demons might take hold of her, too. Yes, her mother had said she was stronger. But she was stronger out of necessity. Because she'd grown up without luxuries like hot water and love. And because she was stubborn enough to want them, yet strong enough to work for them. Bull-headed, her mother used to call her. Bull-headed, stubborn, and selfish.

Which brought her full-circle to tonight's ball. Her selfish side flared to the forefront. She only had two days left here. She didn't want to spend these last forty-eight hours amid a crowd of strangers. She wanted Rhys and the Nowaks all to herself. But apparently, her wants conflicted with theirs. So, o...kay. She'd go along with their wants and do her best not to shame them in the process.

♥

Rhys would have preferred to spend the night someplace a lot quieter. More intimate. Just the two of them or, worst case scenario, the five of them. But here he stood in the Pulaski Hotel ballroom, surrounded by at least a hundred people, awkward and tongue-tied whenever he glanced at Polina. She glowed in the blue silk dress the Nowaks had chosen, the hue an almost perfect match for her sparkling eyes. Bianka had arranged Polina's hair swept up, leaving her neck and shoulders deliciously bare in the strapless gown.

Gone was the urchin he'd picked up off the pavement a few weeks ago, replaced by a goddess of enchantment. When he escorted her into this private party, he'd sensed the eyes of his coworkers watching—many widened with admiration or narrowed in grudging respect. A pride of ownership washed over him. He always sensed the quality under the grit. In business, in his artifacts, even in Polina.

She kept his streak alive.

Wrapping an arm around her waist, he pulled her up against him. Let them all see the beauty he'd captured.

Murmured conversations hummed over the soft, orchestral music while couples swirled to the tunes. Tuxedoed wait staff carried silver trays laden with crystal flutes full of the sparkling wine known as *tokaj*. Many of the guests sat at the tables that circled the dance floor, eating, laughing, and indulging in chitchat. Henryk had whisked Bianka away for some romantic waltzing the minute they checked their coats, and they'd yet to return from the dance floor. That was a couple completely in love with each other.

For the moment, Rhys stood with Polina on the outside of the party atmosphere, giving her time to adjust to the crowds, to drink in the experience, and to make certain everyone had a chance to see them together. Several coworkers approached to greet him, their gaze locked on the beauty at his side. Each time, he made the obligatory introduction, but added some small gesture of possession to ward off any possible poachers. He'd brush the hair off her bare shoulder, place his hand at her waist, or, in particular when his boss sauntered over, place a soft kiss near her eyebrow.

Mine, he thought to himself. She's all mine. Leaning closer, he whispered in her ear, "Dance with me?"

She stared at him, eyes rounded in panic. "I don't know how."

"I'll teach you." He took her hand, noted how icy her fingers felt against his, sensed the tension stiffening her posture. "Relax. Why so nervous?"

"I'm not used to being around so many people."

"Of course you are. You worked at a carnival. Surely you were around much bigger crowds than this."

"Well, yeah, but I didn't have to talk to them. Or sit and eat with them. Or *dance* in front of them."

She gave the word, "dance" the same hushed gravity as she would "commit murder," and he bit back a smile.

"Come on." He drew her out to the dance floor where dozens of other couples slowly spun to the orchestra music. Once in the center of the action, he stopped and took her in his arms. He might as well have held a mannequin. "Loosen up, sweetheart. Just follow my lead. Don't worry about stepping on my toes or anything. I won't go too fast. And no one can see your feet beneath your gown."

He started slowly, a basic box step, but judging by her furrowed forehead, for her, the simple movements were more complicated than Euclidean geometry. "Just count the steps with me. One. Two. Three. Four. Make a simple square. You can do it."

She followed, but the second time she stepped on his toes, she stopped and dropped her hands to her sides. "I'm sorry. I told you I couldn't dance."

Taking her hand again, he waited for her to tiptoe back into his embrace. "Come on. You can do this. You're not going to let a simple dance defeat you, are you?"

She stiffened, but placed her other hand on his shoulder again. "No."

Although she continued the steps with him, her frown indicated she didn't enjoy the dancing at all. He couldn't have her frowning on New Year's Eve. Not when he had a special surprise in store for her. "Have I told you how beautiful you look tonight?"

"Rhys, please," she said through gritted teeth. "I'm trying to concentrate."

Laughter bubbled up inside him. Any other woman would have preened at his compliment. But not Polina. The box in his pocket practically burned through the wool of his suit jacket. Maybe now was the time to spring his question on her. "Let's take a walk."

Before she could argue, he led her off the dance floor and out of the ballroom. The lobby, however, was packed with people in various states of party attire from formal to casual to costumes. The last thing he wanted for this moment was a circus atmosphere. No help for it. He'd have to take her outside and hope the temperature hadn't dipped into the single digits yet. He headed for the revolving door leading outside.

She pulled back. "Wait. Where are we going?"

"For a walk. It's too warm in the ballroom."

"But...my coat." She craned her neck toward the alcove where partygoers had checked their coats. "I should—"

"Leave it. We won't be long. I promise. There's something I want to show you."

"And you couldn't show me before we came in? You know, when I still had my coat on?"

"No. I have to show you now."

"O...kay."

Outside the hotel, the night air was chilly, but not frigid. There was no breeze. He found a spot near the valet parking area where a portable heater blew warm air, a nearby streetlight encircled them in its halo, and they had a modicum of privacy. Even so, he didn't speak right away. He needed to figure out where to start.

"So...umm..." She glanced around at their surroundings. "What'd you want to show me?" Her right foot traced invisible semi-circles in the sidewalk. Her tell. She was obviously confused and probably cold. All the more reason to get on with this.

He removed his suit jacket and slipped it over her bare shoulders. "What if I told you that you didn't have to leave in two days? You could stay here. Well, at least for a little while longer."

Her surprised gaze leveled on his expression. "What do you mean?"

Releasing her, he reached for the box in his pocket, flipped open the top, and showed her the gimmel ring. "Look. Do you know what this is?"

"Some kind of dragon jewelry?" She took the box, studied the piece inside, traced an index finger over the delicate creation, now polished to a brilliant hue.

"It's called a gimmel ring. Like a...promise ring. Do you know what that is?"

She shook her head.

He removed the bit of gold from the box and showed her how the two circlets came apart into two separate rings, one with a dragon head, the second revealing two entwined hearts. "Centuries ago, a man would give a gimmel ring to his lady, and she would wear the dragon part alone until the day she and her man married. Then, she'd put the hearts in their place, and the completed set became her wedding ring."

Her complexion paled. "Rhys, I like you, but—"

His laughter cut off her gentle, polite rejection. "I'm not asking you to marry me, if that's what you're thinking. We barely know each other. There's no pressure here. I just saw this in a shop and thought..." He paused, trying to figure out the best way to say what he really wanted to tell her—without sounding needy or possessive. "I thought about the circles that are so important to St. Sylwester, about how each year is supposed to bring us full circle, and how...no. Wait." He sighed. "No, that's not really what I was thinking at all."

"Then, what *were* you thinking?"

"About you. And your childhood. How little you've seen and done in your life. And about how much I'd want to teach you and show you if we had more time. About how much of the real world you've yet to see. And how I want to be the one to share those experiences with you."

She folded her arms over her chest, and the sleeves of his jacket, much larger than her slender frame, flopped to cover her hands. She blew air through her lips, releasing a cloud in the chilly night. "Anything else?"

"I don't understand..."

"Is there any other reason you wanted to give this 'promise' ring to me?"

"Well, it's a symbol. When I spotted it in a little shop in town, I thought it was...I don't know...appropriate, I suppose."

Another puff of air escaped her lips. "Appropriate."

"Yes. Gimmel rings have long been a symbol of two people becoming a couple. And the dragon head made it seem like...fate. We always seem to come back to dragons, you and I." Her expression remained guarded and, sighing, he shook his head. "I'm making a muck of this." He took a deep breath, tried again. "What I really wanted to say is, don't go back to the States. Not now. There's so much more for you to discover in the world. Stay. Please. You could move in with me. Or if you're not comfortable with that, you could continue to live with the Nowaks. They love having you. I'm only in Kraków for another few months. Then I can transfer anywhere that has a financial district. And I've got a list of places that I planned to visit—to retrace my grandfather's journeys. I'd love to have you come with me. We'll travel the world together—"

"No."

An icy claw gripped his chest. "No? You don't even want to think about it?"

"No. If I think too much, I might give in."

"Oh, well, sure, we wouldn't want that, would we?" Acid filled his tone, but he couldn't hold back his shock. Or his disappointment. This was not what he'd anticipated. He'd made no backup plan for her denial.

"I'm sorry, Rhys." She dipped her head. "I like you. A lot." Her head stayed down, her fingers opening and closing the jewelry box again and again. *Snap. Click. Snap. Click. Snap. Click.* "But I can't stay here with you."

"Can't or won't?"

She didn't reply, but her teeth captured her lower lip as if she held back an argument. Or another puff of breath.

"Why? What's so important that you won't consider staying?" He hammered the questions at her, needing answers that made sense. "It's not like you have a family to return to. Your relatives are all here in the cemetery crypt. And as far as I know, no one in the States cares about you. Certainly not the way I do. Not the way the Nowaks do."

"I have to go back," she murmured over the rapid open/close/snap/click of the jewelry box. "I have my own journey to continue."

"So what? Who says you have to continue it in Texas? What's waiting for you there?"

"Nothing. I told you. I don't intend to stay in Texas. I'm only going there to tie up a few loose ends."

"So then, what's the rush? You told me yourself you didn't get the last bid you submitted. It's not like you have a project waiting for you. Or a family. Or anyone who means something to you. Think of all the fun we could have."

She took a step back, removed his jacket, and handed it to him. "No. I think I want to go back inside now. Get my coat. I'll ask Bianka and Henryk to take me home."

"No. Stay."

"I've told you before. I'm not a dog, Rhys."

"Of course you're not. What I'm saying is, there's no reason for you to go back there when everything you need is right here. Stay with me, here in Kraków. At least, as long as I'm here. Then we'll move on to a new adventure. See where life takes us."

She shook her head. "I have responsibilities at home. People waiting for me."

"Who?" Impatience sharpened his tone. "The carnival workers? The ones who never celebrated your birthday or gave you a Christmas gift? You really think you owe them anything? Wake up, sweetheart. You owe those people nothing. They never cared about you."

"I owe them *every*thing." She slapped the velvet box into his open palm. "You really think it's some great crime that I never got a Christmas gift? I didn't need a Christmas gift. I needed food on a daily basis, which they gave to me. I needed clothing, which they made sure I got. I needed an education, which I received from one of 'those people.' We didn't have a lot of money. So what we had, we shared. We were—*are*—a community. A family that you could never understand or appreciate." She plucked at the skirt of the beautiful dress as if having it touch her skin irritated her. "With them, I never needed fancy clothes or a fancy man on my arm for people to see my true character. Most people in my world judged me on my actions, and they never found me lacking or in need of improvement. They just accepted me as I am, without trying to change me or polish me for safe-keeping on a shelf. You should try that some time."

Turning on her heel, she headed back inside, leaving him with the gimmel ring and a slack jaw.

What the hell just happened? How could he have misjudged the situation so badly?

18

"Polina, wait!"

She didn't. She couldn't. Not with her heart breaking and the panic attack slipping precariously close to the surface.

How could she have not seen it? How did she miss the monster lurking behind Rhys's mask?

Once back inside the hotel lobby, she aimed straight for the one place he couldn't follow. The ladies room. Safe within the pink-papered walls and line of stalls, she leaned over the bank of marble sinks, grabbed a tissue from the wall-mounted dispenser, and dabbed at her eyes in front of the mirror.

Breathe. Find the good. Breathe. In, one. Out, one. In, two. Out, two...

Find the good.

She couldn't come up with a single thing.

Why, why, why, why? Why did she have to meet and fall for a wanderer? Worse. A wanderer who saw her as a pet. Someone he could train. He wanted to show her things. Teach her things. Rearrange her dreams and mold her into his possession. He tried to shackle her with a ring—a ring that meant nothing. A useless piece of shiny metal. What on earth would make him think she'd be awed into submission by something shiny?

How could she have been so blind to his faults?

A snide voice echoed in her skull. *Not so smart after all, are ya? You're as stupid as your mother, taken in by some man's charms. Worse. Because her example should've made you smarter.*

Stupid, stupid, stupid. She clapped her hands over her ears, but the voice still lingered, loud and clear.

The door to her left opened and closed several times as other women came and went, but Polina remained inside the rest room, mentally flogging herself for being taken in by Rhys's good looks, smooth talk, and appealing cologne. After what seemed like hours, Bianka appeared at her side.

"Enough, *ukochana*. No more pouting. Time to rejoin the party."

Polina shook her head. "No. I can't do this anymore. I want to go home."

"Not yet. Wait 'til midnight. See the fireworks. Then, we'll go."

She shook her head even harder. "No, I want to go home-home. To the States. It's time."

"What happened?" Bianka gripped Polina's fingers in a tight clasp. "Between you and that scoundrel?"

"He asked me to stay with him."

Her forehead puckered in lines of confusion. "Is that all?"

"It's the way he asked. Like I was some lot lizard like my mother that he could just buy for a while. Like, since I didn't have anything better going on and neither did he, I might as well hang around with him until he got bored with me. Because I haven't done enough bouncing around in my life already, I should cling to him so we could 'See where life takes us.'" She curled her fingers around the last sentence. "So he can show me off when he wants. As if I'm not a person, I'm just another possession for him. Then he tried to give me some kind of promise ring—a promise ring with no promise attached." She sniffed. "Like I'm dumb enough or shallow enough to accept a piece of circus candy to keep me from realizing I'd become another ratchet in his gear shaft."

"I don't understand. He gave you candy? What is this gear shaft?"

She shook her head yet again. At this rate, she'd become one of those bobble dolls. "Circus candy. It's an expression back home. It means something shoddy in a pretty box. And the gear shaft..." How could she even attempt to explain that? "I just meant he thinks I'm going to become another girl he could..." Embarrassed, she looked away.

"Ah." She nodded. "The latest mare in his stable, yes?"

Close enough. Though, she had to admit, she didn't much care to think of herself as a mare.

"Did he say that?" Bianka patted her shoulder in her maternal way.

Say what? Somewhere, she'd lost track of their conversation. Oh, right. The circus candy—his promise ring. "That it was a promise ring without a promise attached? Yes. As to the rest, I figured out his intentions on my own."

"*Idiotka.*"

Well, that word needed no translation. But she did need some clarification. "Him or me?"

"Both of you, most likely. But, at the moment, I'm referring to him. He knows better than to make you unhappy on New Year's Eve. No quarrels tonight. No quarrels tonight means harmony all year long. He knows. I had big plans for you. For tonight. Do all the things your mama wanted and things she maybe didn't know. Make your last two nights with us special. So you would remember. Always remember and smile. Now he ruined everything. *Idiotka.*"

The regret Bianka voiced burrowed past Polina's shield of self-pity, and she straightened with a hard sniff. "No. He didn't ruin anything." She refused to allow Rhys to destroy whatever plans the Nowaks had made for her. Studying her reflection in the mirror, she pasted on a smile. When she thought she could face Bianka and not look like a total fake, she did so.

"Ach. You'll have to do better than that," Bianka grumbled. "You're not a very good actress."

"I'll work on it." She linked her arm around the older woman's waist. "Come on. Let's go make some memories."

♥

Seated at their table in the ballroom, Henryk glowered at Rhys. "You better hope my wife can undo whatever you did or said to upset Polina."

"I have no idea what I did or said," Rhys admitted with a grimace. "She took everything the wrong way for some reason."

"Mmm...I wonder why." He turned his head toward the wall, muttering insults in Polish.

Regardless of the language barrier, Rhys got the gist. "Why are you blaming me?"

Henryk veered his attention back to Rhys, pounding a fist on the table with enough force to make the china clink. "Because I warned you. I told you to be careful not to hurt her. But you obviously bulldozed through her in spite of my advice. What exactly happened between you two? Where'd you go?"

"Just outside. I wanted a little privacy."

"Privacy for what?"

Rhys bounced his hands. "Simmer down, Henryk. Nothing nefarious happened. I told her I wanted her to stay here in Kraków. What's so bad about that?"

"I don't know. Yet." His glower increased to feral. "What did she say?"

"She kept saying no. That she had to go home. She had responsibilities." He sipped from his water glass to ease his throat, which suddenly felt hotter than the Gobi Desert on a summer afternoon. "I pressed her on that. I mean, what's she in a rush to get home to? A cadre of losers who don't give a damn about her? She'd be so much happier here."

"For the love of..." Henryk scrubbed a hand over his face. "Please tell me you didn't say that to her."

"Not in those exact words, but—"

"Good grief, man! What else did you say?"

The heat inside the ballroom overwhelmed him, and he loosened his tie. When that didn't help, he unbuttoned the first two buttons on his dress shirt. "I gave her a promise ring." Seeing Henryk's eyes widen, he added, "Not for anything serious. It was just a bauble I picked up at the exchange shop. Of course I had to explain to her what a promise ring was, but I told her not to panic. I wasn't making her promise to marry me. After all, we barely know each other."

"Very romantic and chivalrous of you."

"I wasn't aiming for romantic. Or chivalrous," he

retorted. "I was being sensible. We just met a few weeks ago. No one falls in love that fast."

"I did. So did Bianka."

"Fine. I stand corrected. But I didn't. And neither did Polina. We just happen to have a good rapport with each other. When I showed her the ring, I thought she'd immediately understand the connection and we'd share a laugh."

"What connection?"

"Well, the ring had a dragon's head. She and I have this running joke about dragons, and I figured, based on the traditions about circles on St. Salwator's Eve..." Henryk didn't speak, but his complexion remained mottled. "It sounds silly now, but trust me. It should have been amusing. I was hoping to show her how happy she could be if she stayed here with me."

"Until you leave Kraków. Then what? You tell her it was fun while it lasted and ship her home with her dragon ring and a kiss farewell?"

Rhys shook his head. "Wrong. You've got it all wrong. I asked her to accompany me wherever I went next."

"Mmm-hmm. What else did you do?"

"Now you sound like her. Like I've done something unforgivable. What am I missing?"

"Well, let's see, shall we?" Henryk counted on his fingers. "You insulted her, insulted her background, minimized your relationship with her, minimized her life goals, gave her a joke gift two days before she leaves us— possibly forever..."

He gripped the table, white-knuckled, and thrust his head forward, closer to Henryk. "That's not what I did! You're twisting it all around."

"Really? I'd wager Polina saw the entire exchange more my way than yours."

"Then you're both wrong. I just wanted to make her stay with me. With us."

"By belittling her and everything that matters to her. Very clever."

"No! I asked her to stay, showed her the ring, explained it wasn't meant to pressure her, and things seemed to go downhill from there. I don't know why. I don't understand what makes this a hard choice for her. You love her. Bianka adores her. Why wouldn't she want to stay with people who genuinely care about her?"

Henryk appeared thoughtful, and Rhys leaned back in his chair, waiting for some indication his friend would finally see his side of the argument.

"So, it's true then," Henryk replied.

"What's true?"

"That I'm sitting next to the stupidest man on the planet."

His body sagged in the chair. "Oh, now, that's unfair. You weren't there. It really wasn't as bad as you think."

"Obviously it was worse. What happened next?"

"Nothing. She said no and that she wanted to grab her coat and go home, then locked herself in the rest room."

Henryk released a heavy sigh. "Thank God."

"What? What'd I miss now?" He looked up, swerved in his seat to face the front of the room, and tracked Henryk's gaze to the ballroom entrance where Bianca stood with a beaming Polina at her side. "Oh." He stood, caught Polina's eye, and strode across the room to meet them. "Everything all right now?"

"Always was," she replied and sailed past him.

Oh, no. Not again. With so few hours left before she was gone—possibly for good—he wouldn't allow some silly misunderstanding to ruin their final two days together. He caught up to her in a couple of long strides and took her arm. "Dance with me." Not a question this time.

"I'd rather not." Her eyes blazed.

"Then we can argue right here in front of everyone," he threatened. "Your choice."

Her face blanched, and she glanced around the room at the crowd of strangers. He was bluffing. The last thing he wanted was a scene in front of his coworkers, but he knew Polina well enough to risk she'd be even more terrified about drawing attention to herself.

"Fine," she said under an expelled breath.

He led her out to the dance floor and took her in his arms again. She was stiff, unyielding. Not nervous this time around. Angry.

Get on with it, Linsey.

"I'm sorry. I said some things I shouldn't have."

"Darn right you did."

He couldn't stop the grin that quirked his lips. Her resilience was one of the things he liked most about her. "It's your fault, you know."

"*My* fault?" She stumbled over his feet, nearly upending them both.

"You make me nervous."

"*I...*" She stopped dancing. "...make *you...*" Her palm pushed into his shoulder. "...nervous?"

"Crazy, isn't it?"

"Crazy, impossible, ridiculous. Take your pick."

"But it's true. Every time I get close to you, all I can think about is you. The way you smile, the way your hair smells like sunshine. The way your nose crinkles when I say something you don't believe." He brushed an index finger across her brow. "Like right now."

She blinked and stepped back, out of reach. "Don't."

"Why not?"

"Because you'll take away my mad. And I'm not ready yet to give that up."

"But you have to." He swept her into his arms again and continued their simple box step around the floor. "Didn't Bianka explain how you're not supposed to hold grudges on New Year's?"

"Is that why we're dancing right now?"

"We're dancing now because I can't get enough of holding you in my arms. We're *talking* right now because I don't want you carrying any ill will toward me into the new year. Bad luck for both of us."

She smirked. "I knew it. You're afraid of Bianka."

"I'm more afraid of never seeing your smile again. And not that twist of your lips like you're wearing now, but an honest-to-God, make-the-sun-come-out-and-the-clouds-disappear smile. So, what can I do to help you get over your 'mad'?"

She didn't reply right away. In fact, she seemed to look past him, over his shoulder. The music swelled around them as it neared its crescendo, much like the beating of his heart. Still, she said nothing. At last, she tilted her head toward his neck and murmured, "I want you to tell me about you."

This time, *he* stumbled in the dance. "I'm sorry? What?"

"You know all there is to know about me, but I still know almost nothing about you. Tell me. Tell me about your grandfather. Tell me why you didn't get along with your father. Tell me about your mother and the rest of your siblings. I want to know all about you."

He frowned. "You already know everything that matters."

"No. I know everything you want me to know. There's a very big difference."

The song ended, and he stopped dancing, but didn't release her from his arms. "There's not that much to tell."

Her gaze leveled on his. "Tell me anyway."

Good God, she was deadly serious. He sighed. "Not here. And not now."

"Why not?"

"Too many people. I'd rather we were alone, if you don't mind."

Her face clouded, and she stepped out of his embrace for the second time. "Uh-huh. Got it. You'd rather not."

"Honestly, I promise I'll tell you what you want to know. But not here."

"Rhys!" Henryk appeared beside them. "Stop hogging this lovely lady to yourself. It's my turn to dance with her."

"Not right now, Henryk."

"Actually," Polina said, "I think his timing is perfect." She turned away from him and lifted her arms toward Henryk.

And there it was. The best part of his day. Of any day. Her brilliant smile. Aimed at someone besides him.

19

She managed to avoid Rhys for quite a while after their one dance, probably thanks to Bianka and Henryk's continual interference. After her dance with Henryk—a clumsy affair for both of them—he escorted her to the table where Bianka waited. Rhys took several steps in their direction, but Henryk waved him away. They pinned her in at their small circular table, a human wall of upset and umbrage.

During the buffet dinner, after she placed small amounts of sausage, smoked salmon, *pierogis*, and something called farmer's bread on her plate, Bianka steered her to a table full of women she "had to meet." Meanwhile, Henryk monopolized Rhys in a far corner of the ballroom. Of course, the subterfuge would have been less obvious if any of the women Bianka introduced her to spoke English.

After ten minutes of awkward smiling and polite nods while she picked at her food, Polina excused herself. When Bianka rose to follow, she shook her head. "Stay. Spend time with your friends. I'll be fine."

Bianka pointed to Polina's plate. "You no eat much."

"I'm not very hungry."

"Too skinny." She clucked her tongue and translated her comment for her companions. At least, that's what Polina surmised based on the sudden body scans, nods, and chorus of tongue-clucking that ensued from the other ladies at the table.

One last smile and nod, and Polina managed to escape the crush of people, climb the stairs, and exit the ballroom.

The lobby was even more packed with people than earlier when she'd followed Rhys out. When he tried to give her that...what had he called it?...that *gimmel* ring. A promise ring without a promise. Because she was...what? Disposable? An object to hold onto for a while and then discard when she outlived her usefulness? Certainly, he didn't deem her worthy enough to share his secrets with. His travels, yes. His truths, no.

Finding an empty chair away from the crowd in an alcove off the lobby, she sat and rested her chin in her hand.

"Still fighting your future?"

She looked up to see the gypsy girl standing over her, in her vibrant scarves and gold medallions. "You again? Are you following me?"

"I could ask you the same thing. But I'm more curious about what you've experienced since I last saw you."

"Sorry." She plucked at the skirt of the deep blue gown pooled around her lap. "You'll have to tell someone else's fortune tonight. I don't have any money on me."

"I'm not asking for payment."

"Well, then, you're a lousy gypsy."

"Maybe. But at least, I'm a true Rom. Not like you or your mother, pretending to be gypsy to fool strangers into giving money for false fortunes. I have a gift, and I use it the way I want to."

God, she was so tired of arguing with people tonight. Wasn't this supposed to be a festive occasion? She could've stayed at the house alone and had a better time. "What do you want?"

"To help you. You sought me out when you first arrived here. Whether you believe me or not, my running into you here is a coincidence. But, I'm guessing it's also fortuitous. Don't you know it's bad luck to be sad on St. Sylwester's Eve? Unhappy tonight, unhappy all year..."

Her head jerked up, and she glared at the gypsy. "Oh, for God's sake! Isn't there anybody in this entire city that doesn't fall for all that magic and superstition you spout?"

The gypsy shrugged, and her medallions clinked. "Kraków is the Magic City."

"But it's not real. Don't you see? Good luck, bad luck,

magic, dragons. It's all nonsense. It means nothing in the real world."

"Ah, but that's where you're wrong," she replied with a wagging finger. "Magic and luck and yes, even dragons mean hope in the real world. When life gets ugly—and you don't have to travel very far in this part of the world to see the ugliest moments in human history—sometimes, only hope for a better day can ease the pain. We all have dragons we need to slay. You should know better than most. Didn't you ever wish for anything when you were a child? In those nights alone in your trailer, when you were bone-cold, bone-tired, and bone-hungry?"

"Sure. I wished for a lot of things."

"Like...?"

She sighed, forced her mind back to those bitter days. "Like...I wished my mom didn't drink so much. I wished my father would come to take me away from everything. I wished Eddie hadn't—"

She skipped that wish. The details of what happened that night would never leave her lips again. She'd told the police, endured the humiliating exam in the hospital, pressed charges, and watched him skip away when she couldn't prove to the judge's satisfaction that she hadn't "wanted it." Never again.

"I wished I had good shoes and a decent coat and a real bed and food to eat and a thousand other things. Big whoop. *None* of them came true. You know why? Because wishes aren't real. Magic isn't real. Anything you want in life, you have to work for."

"And what do you plan to work for, now that your mother is gone?"

"The same things everyone works for. A house of my own, a little money in the bank, security, maybe a family someday."

"All the things you wished for when you were a child."

Polina opened her mouth, closed it again. Thought about what the gypsy said. She couldn't deny it.

"Magic doesn't happen with wands or abracadabras or sleight-of-hand," the gypsy said. "Magic occurs when we live to our fullest potential. As children, we wish for things we hope to gain. Children *wish* because they have no other means of achieving what they desire. As adults, we work to achieve many of those same dreams from our childhood. Why? Because with adulthood comes independence. We have the means to realize our dreams. All we need to do is seize the opportunities that come to us."

"And I plan to. As soon as I'm finished here."

"When I first met you, I told you to follow the dog to find your future. So, why, now that you've found him, are you running away?"

"You mean Rhys? What makes you think he's my future?" The gypsy opened her mouth to answer, but Polina cut her off with an upraised hand. "Don't say it. Whatever you may believe, I sincerely doubt Rhys and I have any future. And for the record, I'm not running away. I was never meant to stay here."

"Neither is he."

"Yes, but he and I are traveling in opposite directions."

"Sometimes our opportunities aren't found in a straight line. All your life, you've been looking for someone to love you, someone who'll make the ache inside you go away, someone to keep you warm. And now that you may have found that someone, you're throwing stumbling blocks in the way to prevent you from connecting with him."

"He's not interested in a real future with me." Polina shook her head. "I'm just a diversion for a month. A date for the holidays so he doesn't have to be stuck with the actuary from his office at all these parties. A pretty bauble. He's looking for temporary. And I've had enough temporary in my life."

"If he asked you to marry him tonight, would you accept?"

She laughed bitterly. "Of course not. We barely know each other. And I've got a lot I want to accomplish before I start thinking about marriage and family."

"Then why would you expect him to offer you more than a temporary arrangement? What he offered you is what you would have offered him. What you both want for now. You're two people who agree it's too soon for a permanent relationship, but you like each other enough to hope there might be something more somewhere down the road. Sounds like a perfect match to me. So, I ask again. Why are you running away from your future?"

"I already told you. I'm *not* running away."

"You're out here by yourself. All dressed up and pouting. Why?"

"I'm not pouting. I'm just...disappointed." She didn't like admitting that some of what the girl said made sense. "Rhys is not an innocent party, you know. He refuses to tell me anything about his past."

"And if he told you, would it change how you feel about him?"

"Of course not. I'm not that shallow."

"Then what does it matter?"

"I don't know. It just...does. I told him all about my upbringing. He should be willing to share with me equally. I won't accept halfway from anyone. I've had enough temporary and enough halfway."

"And when you asked about his past, what did he tell you?"

"Not now. Not here."

"You mean here?" She gestured to the floor around them. "At a great big party, in front of a bunch of strangers? You, who've always been so ashamed of your mother and your upbringing? Would you be willing to tell everyone here about your past? Risk having them overhear you and judge you?"

She considered that. He *had* seemed panicked when she'd asked him on the dance floor. But was that because he was afraid to share his secrets with her? Or because he feared others might become privy to what should be between the two of them alone? She didn't know. "I suppose I'd want to wait until we were alone—especially for something devastating."

The gypsy nodded. "And so you have your answer. Go. Seize your future. *Do siego roku!*" The traditional Polish greeting on New Year's Eve meant, "I wish you well." With that simple statement, she turned and headed into the crush of people, leaving Polina to consider all they'd discussed and decide what next step she should take.

♥

Rhys stood in a corner of the ballroom, his ears listening to his boss drone on about the continued regulatory issues with the Brazilian bank while his gaze kept searching for Polina. He'd watched her leave the table where Bianka sat with a cluster of women, noted the slump in her shoulders as she climbed the stairs toward the exit. Guilt stabbed his conscience. He'd put that slump there. The sooner he got her out of here where they could talk alone, the better. But Bianka insisted they stay for the fireworks.

To hell with the fireworks.

Besides, if he planned to talk about the old man when they were alone, there could be plenty of pyrotechnics scorching the air.

"So, Rhys, what do you think?" Jon Adamiak's question broke his focus on Polina and their coming discussion.

What did he think? About...what, exactly? He'd have to make up lost ground. Or divert the conversation.

"Why don't we table this until after the new year? After all, tonight's a holiday party, not a business function. We can discuss your concerns in more detail on the second of January."

Adamiak stroked his chin. "Doesn't give you much time to prepare. But, you're probably right." He clapped Rhys on the shoulder. "*Do siego roku!*"

"*Do siego roku,*" he replied. Now, to get out of this place and find Polina before someone else stopped him or Henryk blocked him from reaching her again.

And suddenly, there she was. At the top of the stairs near the entrance, scanning the crowd, shoulders back, a hope-filled expression lighting up her face. For a full minute, he couldn't move. He simply drank her in, wondering how she could have come to mean so much to him so quickly.

A month ago, nothing would have distracted him from a conversation with Jon Adamiak. Gaining an audience with the CFO of Volker-Kellogg Bank was like getting the opportunity to talk to God. To have God seek him out and ask his advice on a forex issue? Unheard of! But instead of treating the auspicious moment with the deference it deserved, he'd chucked the entire conversation into the back of his brain. Meanwhile, all he could think about was a strawberry blond waif and her hurt feelings.

Her *gaze* connected with his, and *bam!* Fireworks. Who cared how or why? All that mattered was her, and the magic she brought to his life. With determined strides, he weaved through the clusters of partygoers, his vision fixed on where she stood, waiting. He scaled the carpeted steps, and she held out her hand. He clasped her as if she pulled him from some abyss.

When he stood beside her, he whispered, "Would you like to get out of here?"

She beamed. "I thought you'd never ask."

20

Throughout the ride back to the Nowaks' house, neither spoke. Polina pinned her gaze on the buildings they passed, the multitudes of people celebrating in the streets, and the perfect crescent moon that hung above them like a pirate's earring. Now that she'd left the ball, she wondered if she'd made the right choice. Too late to change her mind. She'd have to deal with whatever burst out of the Pandora's box she'd opened. What on earth could he reveal that would be so awful? A sense of dread crept into her bloodstream, and she shivered.

Rhys flipped up the heat, and the warm air whooshed through the vents. "Cold?"

"A little," she lied. "Thanks."

What if he told her he was already married? With kids, back home in jolly old England? Did that explain why he offered her a promise ring with no promise attached? Did he think to himself, *like mother, like daughter*? Like Eddie had? The thought chilled her down into her bones, and she hugged herself to stay strong. Better to learn the truth now, rather than later, she supposed.

Once he escorted her inside the house, he removed her Christmas coat and offered her another glass of *tokaj*.

She shook her head and blew air out her pursed lips. "You really think you need to get me drunk to tell me the truth?"

He flushed. "No. Of course not."

Liar. "Uh-huh." She sat on the sofa in the room where she'd spent so much time in the last few weeks and glanced at the clock on the mantel, perched beside the *szopka* she'd given the family a mere week ago. A lifetime ago.

Eleven-fifteen. Midnight would be here sooner than she'd like.

How ironic Bianka had pronounced her Cinderella tonight, and now she sat in a beautiful ballgown, watching the clock inch closer to twelve. What exactly would happen at that witching hour? Would all the magic of the last four-and-a-half weeks vanish? Was she going to wake up from some dream state and find herself lying on the slushy sidewalk, where Rhys had first found her, to discover a wolf about to rip out her throat? Or would Rhys become the wolf—offering her half a life because his real, *quality* family waited for him back home?

Rhys paced ruts in the carpet—back and forth, back and forth—making her dizzy. "Where do you want me to start?"

She quirked a brow. "Seriously? I gave you all this time to think and get your speech together, and you squandered it? What'd you do on the ride over here? Plan a mental grocery list?"

"You threw a lot at me."

His pacing grew frenetic and, grabbing his hand, she pulled him down beside her. "Stop this. Just tell me. Somehow, I doubt it could be as horrible as you're making it out to be." At least, she hoped so.

He raked a hand through his hair. "You have no idea."

"Yes, I do. You're a good man, Rhys. A decent, honest guy. I know that much." The words were said as much for herself as for him. He'd been so good to her, good *for* her, since the moment they met. How could he be a monster? She had to believe in him—until he gave her a reason not to.

"You don't know about my father."

Huh? His father? His secret was about his father? In all the wild scenarios her imagination had concocted, something about his father had never entered her mind. She expelled a relieved breath. "Is that all?"

"Is that all? You don't even know what I'm about to say. What did you think I would tell you?"

"I dunno. I was...scared you'd say you were married or something."

His eyes rounded, and he scrubbed a hand against his chin. "I already told you I wasn't. Why on earth would you leap to that conclusion?"

"The gimmel ring." He shook his head rapidly, as if trying to wake up his brain cells, and she added, "The promise ring without a promise attached. I thought maybe you couldn't make me a promise because..." She could barely look into his eyes, much less finish her accusation.

Enlightenment sparked, and he nodded. "Because you thought I might already be promised to someone else."

She sat up straighter, hands folded in her lap, chewed on her lower lip. "I didn't know what else to think."

He knelt beside her, took one hand in his. "No. Polina, no. The gimmel ring was meant to be a gift, a memento. Something to remind you of our time together here. When I spotted it in a little shop in Nowa Huta, it made me laugh. I thought you'd also find it amusing. The dragon and all. I knew the meaning behind it might frighten you off. But I never expected you'd doubt my sincerity because of it. I simply didn't want you to feel pressured into a future you're not ready for by accepting it. You and I have a lot we both want to accomplish before we can commit to each other."

"I know." She squeezed his fingers. "A friend explained it to me."

"What friend? Bianka?"

She didn't identify the gypsy. After all their disagreements regarding the existence of magic, the last thing she wanted to admit was a belief in a fortune-teller. She still wasn't a hundred percent sure how the girl knew everything she did, but had no desire to pursue that train of thought. "I overreacted. And I'm sorry."

"I'm sorry, too. I bumbled the whole event. In fact..." He dug into his pocket for the box, opened the lid and presented the ring to her. "I could try again, if you like."

She folded his fingers around the box, closing the lid, and hiding the gift in his palm. "No. Hold onto it. When we're both ready to live up to the promise behind the ring, then I'll wear it proudly. Until then, tell me what we came back here for. I want all the details—don't hold back. What's with you and your father?"

"Nothing. Not anymore, anyway."

When he didn't elaborate further, she rose on a sigh laced with false defeat. "Apparently, I've misjudged you. Again. Twice in one night. I'm off my game." She strode toward the hallway leading to the bedrooms, her legs trembling beneath the swish of her silken skirt. What if he called her bluff and let her go? Only one way to find out. "Happy New Year, Rhys. Don't bother seeing me off the day after tomorrow. I'm exhausted now and going to bed. You can let yourself out."

"No. Wait. Please."

She turned slightly, looking at him over her shoulder, her annoyance a hum in the air between them. "For what?"

"Do me a favor and get your tablet. It's easier to show you."

She didn't move. Was this a trick? Did he hope to distract her, get her talking about the Dragon's Tail so he wouldn't have to tell her his secrets? Well, he wouldn't succeed. Returning to the sofa, she folded her arms over her chest then sank into the cushions again. She jerked her head to the far corner of the room. "It's on Henryk's desk there. You've got five minutes."

He found the tablet on the writing desk, powered on, and typed. Whatever website he wanted, he found it fairly easily. Straightening, he held the device out toward where she sat and said, "Meet my father."

The expression on his face chilled her. With trepidation, she crept closer, her gaze pinned on the photo in the left-hand corner of the online article. The resemblance was there—slight, but there. Something in the eyes. And maybe the slope of the nose. But the man in the photo wore arrogance in his crooked grin and very expensive-looking, tailored suit. She didn't like him on sight, but was that her own intuition or Rhys's obvious animosity muddying her opinion?

Go on, coward. You wanted this. Read the headline.

She had to drag her attention to the bold font at the top of the screen. "The Man Who Broke the Bank: 'Black' Jack Quinn and the Downfall of the Empire of Greed." Frowning, she looked up at Rhys. "I don't understand."

"Read it," he said. "And if you still don't understand, pick another article out of the list. There are thousands, many of them more inflammatory than that one."

So she kept reading. And learned that "Black" Jack Quinn earned his nickname when his multitudes of failed derivatives trading resulted in massive losses—losses he hid in secret accounts. Derivatives trading? She looked up from the screen. "What exactly are derivatives? And how do you trade them for money?"

"It's a very risky form of financial investment. People place their money in certain securities that are dependent on returns from other assets. Thus, the profit is 'derived' from those other stocks or options. You could be a net winner or loser, depending upon where the price of that stock sits when the call comes due. My father poured lots of money—lots of other people's money—into those trades, all the while claiming wild profits when they were actually devastating losses."

According to the article, Jack Quinn's subterfuge was only discovered due to a simple clerical error by a low-level employee in their Singapore branch. By the time his employer, Rochford World Bank, caught up to him, the firm had lost what translated into billions of dollars and was forced to file for bankruptcy.

She looked up again. "Billions?"

Rhys's lips were set in a grim line, and his eyes...oh, the pain in his eyes! She wanted to hold him, to heal the hurt that beat him down. Who knew better than she how the sins of the parent often revisited themselves on the child? But she held back. There was more to this story, and she needed to hear it all. Her eyes flicked to the clock again. Time was not on their side.

"Billions." He picked up a pen from the desk, flipped it in slow increments between his fingers. "He never told us anything. Not even my mother. He just left one night, claiming he'd been called to Singapore on business. We found out the next morning when the press showed up on our doorstep. My father had disappeared, and no one knew where."

"How old were you?"

"Thirteen. Overnight, everything we believed—his entire curtain of lies—was shredded. Our house was over-mortgaged, our bank accounts empty. He'd been selling off our family assets for years, including all my grandfather's artifacts. Anything of value had disappeared long ago—and we never knew."

"Wait! You mean the artifacts your grandfather left you when he died? He *sold* them?"

"Every single one of them. But not just *my* inheritance. Everything my sisters and mother received, as well. We were not only broke; we were in debt. Lots of it. After he maxed his own credit limits early in the game, he borrowed against all of ours. We were ruined before any of us were old enough to hold a job."

Billions. "Where did all that money go?"

"Some went to the investors he'd defrauded, some went into new investment plans that were supposed to recoup everything he'd already lost. My father was the worst sort of gambler. Every time he pulled ahead, even slightly, he thought his bad luck streak had ended and reinvested those profits in the same doomed cycle. He risked everybody's money. And lost it all. A staggering amount."

"Billions," she repeated, awestruck. How much was a billion? And how many times over would she have to count to reach an amount capable of bringing down a bank that had been in business for over a hundred and forty years?

"Billions."

"What happened to him?"

"He got off easy. A very public trial, a five-year stint in prison, and he walked out with a clean slate. He can't ever get a job in finance again, but..." He shrugged. "For the most part, he returned to a normal life. The rest of us weren't so lucky. We had to change our names, start over."

"So your real name isn't Rhys Linsey?"

"It's been my real name since 1996. My birth name was Rhys Quinn. Rhys John William Quinn. Linsey was my maternal grandmother's maiden name. After my father's arrest, my sisters and I all started life over with her surname to protect ourselves from the negative publicity and poor credit ratings. All scrubbed clean. Like most kids our age. Except we weren't like most kids our age. We'd been betrayed by the one man who should've always had our backs."

She rose, placed a placating hand on his shoulder, felt

the hard tension in his muscles beneath his suit jacket. "I'm sorry. It must have been hard on you."

"It got better when I didn't have to see him. I was at university when he was released from prison, and I found myself recruited right after graduation for an ex-pat job. The timing was perfect. I didn't have to go home at all. I took the bank's offer, and I never looked back."

He resumed his pacing, but his strides now had a lethal determination to them. She was reminded of a caged tiger she'd once watched at a county fair. Penned in and only allowed out at showtime, the beast loped the short distance over and over, snarling at anyone who came near. For days on end, she'd watched him until she got up enough courage to approach the cage and slip him bits of sausage whenever his trainer wasn't looking. Over time, she came to commiserate with the big cat over their shared trapped existence. She understood the tiger's desperation, and now recognized the same emotion roiling in Rhys. Too bad she didn't have any sausage handy to win *him* over. Instead, she'd have to dig at the root of what troubled him.

"You're still holding a grudge against your father? That's why you haven't gone home in years?"

"Yes." He showed no shame at the admission.

"On New Year's Eve? Isn't that a bit hypocritical? Especially after the lecture you and Bianka both gave me about not beginning the new year with any ill will in my heart? If you keep holding this grudge toward your father, doesn't that go against everything you believe in?"

"It goes against everything the *Polish people* believe in. But I'm not Polish." He poked her shoulder. "You, however, are."

She pulled back, cocked her head, stared at him, seeking some kind of playfulness in his expression. She found none. "Did you just use the I-know-you-are-but-what-am-I defense on me?"

At last, he had the grace to flush and look away from her intense scrutiny. "Maybe. Try to understand. It's not only about what happened in the past—it's also how those actions can still impact my future. I'm in the same business world where my father once reigned as the financial wizard. Until the day his wizardry was revealed to be a farce. If anyone were to find out I'm the son of the notorious 'Black' Jack Quinn, I'd be destroyed. No financial institution would ever trust me with their funds."

"Can I ask...?" She wrapped an arm around the chair back. "Surely, you knew the risk. You were barely a teenager when the scandal with your father broke. Why go into the same line of work if you were afraid of discovery?"

"Because I was a naïve kid and because I really do love what I do. Originally, I hoped to make up for my father's mistakes. I thought, if I could succeed honestly, I could reclaim my name for all of us. And I'd show the whole world that just because my father was a screw-up didn't mean the rest of us were."

"Why can't you do that now? You're successful in your own right."

"Do you think I'd hold onto any of that success if my coworkers knew who my father was?"

"Sure. Why not? You're not your father. Surely, they know that."

He shook his head. "The higher up I climb in the financial world, the more I have to lose by revealing the truth."

"You really believe the financial world would hold you liable for your father's mistakes? Haven't you proven to them that you're honest, reliable, and trustworthy by now?"

"That depends. Will you ask them before or after they discover I've been living under an assumed name?"

"It's not an assumed name. You've been living under that name since you were thirteen, right? All your school records, financial standing, and employment have been under that name. That makes it yours. You didn't steal it from someone else for immoral purposes." She leaned forward, hands on her lap. "Tell me something. If you could go back to being Rhys Quinn tomorrow, would you?"

"No. At this stage of the game, I've been Rhys Linsey longer than I was ever Rhys Quinn. Everything and everyone attached to Rhys Quinn is in my past."

"Including your family? You're willing to leave them behind forever? Like they don't exist? Do you think that's fair to them?"

"You want to talk about fair? My father served five years

in a Singapore prison. When he was released, my mother took him back, no questions asked. All was forgiven. And my sisters fell in line to keep the peace. I can't do that. I have no choice but to cut off most ties with my family. I don't visit on holiday, don't correspond. I occasionally chat with my sister online, but even that contact is limited to special occasions and sporadic conversations. I don't dare go home and risk anyone linking me to my ex-con father. Which makes me the one serving a life sentence in prison. Meanwhile, he's with them, free as a bird, celebrating New Year's Eve in my grandparents' home while he works on his memoirs. His *memoirs*, for God's sake!" He tossed the pen back on the desk with a clatter. "God help us if he ever publishes them. That will only renew the scandal all over again. Muckrakers will go back to research the original event, and it won't be long before someone wonders, 'What ever happened to the son?' And his crimes will destroy everything I've built for the second time."

"Why? Even if someone should discover the truth, he served his time. Society forgave him. The rest of your family forgave him. Why can't you?"

"Because he ruined our lives."

"Really? Take a look at yourself, Rhys." She raised a hand to frame him between her fingers, slowly moving from his head to his feet. "You hardly look ruined to me. You've got everything you could possibly need: a career you love, enough money to eat and keep a roof over your head, a family that loves you."

"I don't have my legacy."

She shook her head. "I don't get it. What legacy? You already said you've been Rhys Linsey longer than you were Rhys Quinn. And you've made a new name, complete with a shining future for yourself. I would think that alone would show your boss—and anyone else—that you've distanced yourself from your father's influence." A sudden thought exploded in her brain and she blurted, "Unless you're talking about the artifacts." The grim set of his mouth confirmed she'd nailed it. "Really? You really consider your life ruined over the loss of a few old knick-knacks?"

"Knick-knacks? They were my inheritance! My father stole them, and I want them back. I won't rest until I get what should be mine."

"You plan to travel the world, city by city, until you visit all those sites and find every artifact to replace the ones you lost? All while still working this job you love so much? How is that even possible?"

"If my grandfather could do it, so can I. I've been lucky so far. My first job was in Athens, and I discovered my office was just a few miles away from one of the archaeological sites where my grandfather had worked. I visited the area around the site and found a little shop that had a similar artifact to the one my father sold out from under me. At that point, I realized I had a unique opportunity. From Athens, I transferred to Ankara, to Brussels, and a host of other cities before I found myself here in Kraków. In each city, I managed to find an artifact to replace the one I lost. Now, I won't rest until I regain an exact replica of every single piece. All seventy-five of them."

"What if there is no Volker-Kellogg Bank nearby one of your grandfather's sites?"

"I'll travel to those locations on holiday."

"Uh-huh." He certainly seemed to have figured it all out, but she didn't like what it meant. "How many years did your grandfather spend traveling to acquire that kind of collection?"

"I'm not sure exactly. At least fifty, I suppose."

Fifty years. More than half his life. "What if..." Her throat clogged, and she swallowed hard. "What if you can't find a particular object? I imagine some of those pieces were pretty rare."

"I'll keep searching until I do." He shrugged. "I'm not in any rush. I can take as long as I need. And go where I have to."

Her heart dropped. "Do you ever intend to settle down somewhere?"

"Absolutely. Once I've regained everything I lost."

Fifty years. In fifty years, she'd be seventy-eight. If she lived that long. Cancer killed her mother before the age of forty-five. What if *she* only had seventeen years or so left? Could she risk wasting them on a man who valued the past more than the present or future?

"You know, in the grand scheme of things, they're just

things. They can't bring you happiness the way people can. And even if you replace every piece you lost with an exact replica—an impossible task, if you ask me—it won't make you feel better. The artifacts you acquire will never be the same pieces your grandfather discovered, painstakingly dug up, cleaned, and preserved for you. So they'll always seem like shoddy imitations to you. Because they're not the real thing."

"And you're an expert on what's real."

"No, I'm an expert on what's fake." She rose from the desk chair, placed a hand on his shoulder. "Don't you see, Rhys? You're chasing a false dream. And you've turned your back on what really matters in your life to pursue it. You'll never find peace that way."

"I haven't turned my back on anyone."

"No?" She cocked her head. "What about your family?"

"I told you, they made a choice. They accepted a criminal back in their midst. A thief and a liar."

"You won't ever forgive him, will you?"

"Why should I?"

"Why shouldn't you? He made a mistake. He paid for it." Plopping back in the desk chair, she rifled through the various papers and folders on top of the desk.

"What are you looking for?"

"I know Bianka put red paper here for tonight. Where is it?"

He shook his head. "Sweetheart, I appreciate what you're trying to do, but writing out my troubles and burning them isn't going to change my situation."

"Have you ever tried?"

"No."

She finally found the two sheets of red paper in a manila folder, and she waved them at him, victorious. "You and I are both going to do this now. Me, for my mother and our unresolved issues. You, for your father. *And* your mother and sisters."

He frowned. "I'm not holding a grudge against my mother and sisters."

"Yes, you are. You blame them for forgiving your father. You've distanced yourself from them for years. Don't you think it's time you put an end to this impasse? Before it's too late?" Her voice shook with emotion. Tears glistened in her eyes, and she swiped them away with her fists, leaving smeared make-up on her knuckles. She'd told Bianka she shouldn't wear the stuff. "Don't make the same mistake I did, Rhys. Time is so precious, and there's never enough of it."

"Trust me. Our situations are *not* the same."

"Our situations aren't very different. We both have parents who weren't perfect. And we both wish they were— like kids sometimes do. The only difference is, your father is still alive. That gives you an opportunity to put your animosity aside and start over. Please don't squander it. New Year's Eve is for starting over, whether or not you're Polish. Time's not on our side, Rhys. Not for you and me, not for you and your parents, not for you and your sisters. Don't squander whatever time you might have left. Do this with me. It might make you feel better. Who knows? You might even make peace with your father." She sensed his hesitation and pushed her advantage. With a meaningful glance at the clock, she wheedled, "Eleven fifty-five is no time for dithering."

Pausing in his to-and-fro across the floor, he followed her gaze toward the clock and sighed. "Hand me the paper. I'll write out my grudges and burn them if you want, but don't ask me to make peace with the old man. That ship sailed long ago."

Hiding her disappointment, she passed him a sheet of red paper and a pen.

21

The next morning, as instructed, Polina woke early and touched the floor with her right foot first to ensure an abundance of energy and good luck all year. When she left her room a short time later, she found Bianka and Henryk snuggling near the stove in the kitchen, giggling and whispering like lovebirds. A wave of longing overwhelmed her. The child she'd once been and the adult she was now craved a special someone who lit up whenever she was in the same room, someone who'd plant kisses on her neck in the kitchen, in the living room, or anywhere else the idea grabbed him. She'd thought that someone might be Rhys, but not if it meant waiting while he chased objects instead of staying with her. Smile, she chastised herself. *Don't let anyone see your pain.*

Bianka tilted her head and caught Polina staring.

Heat rushed into her cheeks. "Oops. Sorry." She began to back away from the intimate scene, but Bianka's lighthearted voice stopped her.

"Come in, *ukochana.*" She broke out of her husband's embrace and pulled a frying pan from a low cabinet. "I make breakfast now. You have good time last night?"

"Yes."

Henryk poured coffee into the three porcelain cups lined up on the counter. "You and Rhys left the ball before the fireworks. Everything all right between you two?"

"Mmm-hmm." Polina took the cream from the refrigerator and placed it beside the coffees. "We needed some privacy to talk so we came back here."

"You solve all your problems?"

Not quite. But she had made some decisions. In

addition to her unresolved issues with her mother, she'd written her troubles regarding Rhys on her red paper—troubles she hadn't shared with him—before they burned their lists in the fireplace, according to tradition.

Although she'd pushed the doubts out of her mind for the rest of their time together last evening, when she went to bed, the questions returned with a vengeance to ruin her sleep. His long-held animosity toward his father and his obsession with his trinkets nagged at her. Sure, she had goals to accomplish that required a lot of her attention. But *her* goals—a permanent home, a family—directly conflicted with *his* main objective, to travel the world for up to fifty years in the acquisition of a bunch of dusty old stuff before finally settling down to have a true life. A life that would probably come too late for her. No probablys about it, actually. She'd already waited almost thirty years. She couldn't see herself waiting any longer.

The effects of her sleepless night must have shown on her face because Bianka wrapped an arm around her shoulders and crooned to her, "Come, *ukochana*. We make breakfast. Then we'll bake doughnuts and bread. You remember why, yes?"

"To make sure we're never hungry in the coming year," she replied by rote. The idea held no joy for her. The entire holiday had been sucked dry of celebration after last night.

Bianka nodded. "Know why else? To keep our hands busy so we don't smack sense into stupid, stubborn men."

Polina snorted a bitter laugh, but didn't reply.

"That's not true!" Henryk raised an objection. "Not all of us are stupid and stubborn."

"Come." Bianka tugged her into the heart of the kitchen and turned to Henryk. "All men are stupid and stubborn, just in varying degrees. You, not so much. Rhys? To be decided at a later time. For now, go get our son. We'll have big breakfast when you come back." She swept her hands at him, shooing him out of the room.

"But I haven't had my coffee yet," he argued.

"You have all your life to drink coffee," she replied. "Today's my last day with Polina. Go get our son. We need...what they say?...time for lady talk."

"Girl talk," Polina corrected.

"Yah. Girl talk."

She didn't say another word until Henryk, muttering to himself about stubborn women, grabbed his coat and closed the front door behind him.

"Good," she announced after her husband departed. "We're alone now. We don't have to talk if you don't want to. I want today to be good day. Best day. Don't talk if talk upsets you. Don't do anything to upset you. Rhys is supposed to show up in about an hour. You tell me you no want him here, I tell him, 'Stay home.'" She folded her arms over her chest, becoming an impenetrable wall of disapproval.

"No. It's okay. He should be here. No one's supposed to be alone on New Year's Day, right?"

"Is that the only reason you want him to come here?" Bianka planted her hands on her hips.

"No. I know you've set him up to be your good luck visitor this morning, too." Another Polish tradition. The first visitor of the year, if male, brought good luck with him. Once again, women got the short end of the luck stick.

Bianka shook her head. "You two have another disagreement after you left last night. Yes?"

"Not really. I just wish..." She didn't finish the statement. How could she explain she wished he cared more about her than about a bunch of dusty old artifacts?

Luckily, Bianka buried herself in another cupboard in search of a mixing bowl and missed the expression on Polina's face. When she turned around again, she asked, "Are you sad because you leave tomorrow? You want to stay? We fix. You stay. No leave. Stay as long as you want. See? No trouble."

"No. I mean, I wish I could stay. I've really loved being here with you."

"Then it's Rhys who put the sadness in your eyes again. May God save me from stupid, stubborn men. I will let him come, if that's what you want, but I don't have to be cordial to him until he apologizes."

"No, don't do that. Please. It's fine. He really didn't do anything wrong."

After measuring flour into a cup, Bianka dumped it into the mixing bowl. "Hmmph. He made you unhappy. That's wrong enough for me."

"But not for me," Polina insisted. "I'm unhappy because I expect more from him than he's willing to give me right now. That's on *me*, not on him."

She cracked two eggs into the bowl and pointed an empty shell at Polina. "It's on both of you. You good girl. I don't think you ask him to steal from bank or kill someone."

"No, of course not."

"Then he's too stupid or stubborn to do something or be something that's good for him, and you're wasting your last few hours together too stubborn to let him learn from his mistakes on his own. Men are stupid and stubborn. Women, we're just stubborn and more stubborn. But don't tell Henryk I say so."

Polina bit back a smile. "Right. Better to keep some mystery."

"Smart girl. Good girl. Mystery, not secrets, yes? Mystery, fun. Secrets, dangerous. Once you know all the secrets, you can understand problems and solve them together."

"What if you know the secret, but he doesn't see it as a problem?"

She shrugged and whisked the batter in the bowl. "Most men don't. That's why they're stupid. And it's up to us women to fix their problems for them. Only when you've solved the issue will he realize you were right the whole time."

Great. She had less than twenty-four hours to get Rhys to change his mind about his life priorities.

Piece of cake.

♥

This time around, Rhys opted for the phone over the computer.

She picked up on the third ring. "Happy New Year, brother mine."

"Happy New Year to you, too, Eliza. You sound chipper. Not too hung over this morning?"

"Quiet night. Just me and the parentals. I watched the

fireworks on the telly in my pajamas, snuggled up with a bag of crisps."

"Hard to believe you're the same person who was tossed from St. Rose's Girls Academy for slipping out of her room after midnight."

"Ah, but that was in my wicked youth. Now, I'm a staid old unattached lady with no prospects. So I spend all my time with Mummy and Daddy and an obscenely overweight cat. It's a glamorous life, you know."

"Alex didn't deserve you. You need to get out and socialize again."

"I will. Eventually. Right now, I need to let my heart heal first."

He had no idea how to respond to that. Advice for the lovelorn wasn't exactly his forte. "So, umm... How's everything else?"

"Since last week's conversation? The same. Be careful, Rhys. Someone might start to think you're homesick."

"Ha-ha. Are you going to be home today?"

"That depends. Do you need someone to pick you up at Heathrow?"

"No. I'm still in Kraków."

"Then, in that case, I'll be around."

He chuckled. "You're a cheeky sort."

"Thankyouverymuch. Seriously, what's up? Why the phone call? Are you all right? You sound...odd."

"I'm fine. I just called to tell you to keep your computer on. I'll have a surprise for you later."

"What kind of surprise?"

"A secret, for-your-eyes-only surprise."

"Oh, goody! When?"

"An hour or so. Maybe later. And that's all the information I plan to give you right now so don't pester me."

"Come on, Rhys. That's not fair! Give me a hint. Something to make the wait go by faster."

"If you're not around when I ding you, you'll lose out." With that last riposte, he hung up.

That should keep Eliza on edge all morning. Maybe now, with this crazy plan of his, he could take the edge *off* Polina at the same time.

♥

Polina was still distant with him when he arrived at the Nowaks'. Oh, she put on a good face. Just not good enough to fool him. After all their time together, simple things gave away her aloofness: how stiff she felt in his embrace, the quick brush of her lips against his, her murmured "Happy New Year" greeting without a scintilla of emotion behind it.

Bianka didn't make the situation easier. She glared icicles at him over the breakfast table, ignored him when he asked her to pass the salt, and (he believed) purposely burnt his toast. Naturally, Henryk wouldn't overtly go against his wife, and Rhys caught the man shaking his head several times. The only ally he found in the household was Feliks, who chattered about the fun he had at his friend's house the night before, the new trick he wanted to teach Kacper, and the possibility of sledding later in the day.

After the awkward breakfast, he pulled Bianka aside, asking her to allow him a few private moments with Polina before the family rejoined them for the day's festivities.

She slapped his cheek—lightly, but he still felt the sting. "You do what she says, eh? She has what's good for you in her heart."

"So do I," he replied.

While the Nowaks cleaned the kitchen, he led Polina into the den and turned on the tablet. "I want to show you something."

She maintained her distance, hovering a few feet from where he stood at the desk. "Mmm-hmm."

"Come here."

She inched closer, her gaze on the blue square glowing on the screen. "It says, 'Eliza says, *Ahoy, Rhys!*' What does that mean?"

"It's the greeting I use when I chat with my sister."

"Your sister?"

"Yes. My sister, Eliza, is on the other side of that chat box. I thought you might like to meet her."

Some of the stiffness left Polina's posture, and joy lit up her face. "Yes." She nodded emphatically, and her light laughter tinkled in the air. "I'd love that, in fact."

He pulled out the chair. After she took the seat he offered, she pulled the screen closer and typed, *Ahoy, Eliza. This is Polina. I'm a friend of your brother's.*

The window popped open, and his sister's familiar face filled the screen. "Are you Rhys's somebody?"

"Knock it off, Eliza," Rhys growled. "Her name is Polina."

"Your somebody?" Polina asked, her brow furrowed with confusion.

"Pay no attention to my sister. She's a fool."

"Ooh, you sure are a lot grumpier now than you were earlier this morning. What happened, Rhys? Did someone burn your kippers?"

"You're burning my patience."

"I can't help it. I'm excited. You promised me a surprise." Eliza raised her voice, managing to sound both triumphant and enticing. "But I had no idea you intended to introduce me to your somebody—"

From off-screen, a familiar voice squealed, "She's there? The mystery girl?"

Rhys groaned. "I thought I told you this was a for-your-eyes-only secret."

"Are you joking?" Eliza retorted. "You think I could keep this kind of secret from *her*?"

And *bam!* There was his mother, knocking Eliza out of the way to get closer to the computer lens. Too close. Good God, he could examine her nostrils at this angle.

"Back up, Mother. We can't see you."

She did as he instructed, settling into the chair with Eliza now bent over her left shoulder to see as well. "Is that better?"

"Yes, thank you."

With her hands folded on the wrist rest in front of her keyboard, she smiled—all teeth. "Introduce me, Rhys."

"Is this really necessary?"

All three females echoed, "Yes!"

After a heavy sigh of defeat, he obliged. "Mother, I'd like you to meet Polina Kominski. Polina, this is my mother, Vanessa Linsey."

"Quinn, dear," she corrected. "Vanessa Quinn."

He ignored that. "And the pest on her left is my baby

sister, Eliza."

True to baby sister form, Eliza stuck out her tongue at him. "Rotter."

Meanwhile, Polina mirrored his mother's pose, right down to the hands clasped atop the desk, and she sat arrow-straight in the chair. He held back a smile. Yes, his mother had that kind of effect on people. "Hello, Mrs. Quinn. Eliza. It's nice to meet you both. Happy New Year."

"Call me Vanessa, darling girl. Oh, she speaks English so well!" his mother cooed. "Almost like a native."

Now he was stuck mirroring Eliza, draping himself over Polina's shoulder to be seen by the women on the other side of cyberspace. "She's American, Mother."

His mother's eyes rounded, and she batted her lashes. "Are you really? How delightful! And yet you met my Rhys in Poland? What are the odds? Do you two work together?"

"Umm...no," Polina replied, gazing up at him, her confusion only deepening.

"I hope you don't mind, Polina," Eliza interjected, "but I have a thousand questions for you. My brother's been keeping you a secret from us, and we're all dying to know about you."

Polina's gaze hardened, her eyes flashing like flint. "I could say the same. In fact, I only learned about you all last night."

"That's our Rhys," his mother chimed in. "Always so tight-lipped."

"Where are you from in America?" Eliza asked.

"All over. My family traveled a lot."

"I should say so, if you wound up in Kraków with my brother. What brought you there?"

"Umm...a plane?"

Both women on the other end of the screen laughed. "I mean, why are you in the city? On holiday?"

"My mother passed away recently, and I was bringing her ashes home to be placed in the family crypt."

"Oh, you poor dear! I'm so sorry," his mother gushed. "My sincerest condolences to you."

"That's kind of you, Vanessa. Thank you."

"Enough sad stuff," Eliza said. "How'd you meet Rhys?"

"We ran into each other my first night in Kraków.

Literally. He was kind enough to volunteer to chaperone me around the city during my stay here. We've been together ever since."

"How chivalrous of you," Eliza said with a sly grin.

He didn't rise to her teasing. Instead, he sat back and let the ladies become acquainted. Throughout their conversation, Polina's frozen exterior cracked and thawed. She laughed and chatted, her usual warm personality returning to the forefront, thanks to the gentle coaxing of his female relatives. Excellent. This could be worth his discomfort after all.

After several minutes of back-and-forth, his mother said, "It was lovely to meet you at last, Polina. You've been such a positive influence on my son. I hope I'll get the opportunity to one day thank you in person. For now, I'll say goodbye and let you young people talk. Cheers, Polina."

She disappeared from the screen, leaving only Eliza in front of the camera, that goofy smile still splitting her cheeks.

"If you ladies have had enough..." He rose, ready to disconnect the chat, but Eliza stopped him.

"No, wait!" She bent closer to the camera lens on her side, her features becoming enormous, and whispered, "Now that Mum's gone, I can ask. Are you bringing Polina to the party?"

Once again, Polina's questioning expression landed on him. "Party?"

Rhys frowned. "I haven't said I would definitely come. What makes you think I'd drag Polina into our family squabbles?"

"It's our parents' anniversary party," Eliza told Polina, intentionally ignoring him. "I don't know if Rhys told you, but he's not a big fan of our father."

Polina nodded. "I know."

"You do? What'd he tell you?"

"The truth," he interjected.

Her lips curled in a moue. "Hmm. I bet. What do you say, Polina? Is my brother reacting rationally to the situation, or is he behaving like a stubborn ass?"

"Don't answer that!"

"She doesn't have to," Eliza crowed. "Your reaction tells

me she'd agree with me. It's time to stop holding a grudge and come home. Talk to Dad. Tell him to go to hell, if you want. But do it in person. And hear him out first."

"Even if I decide to take you up on the invitation, Polina isn't coming. She goes home tomorrow."

"That's what planes are for, brother mine. Pull the crowbar out of your bum, pry open your wallet, and buy her a round-trip ticket from her home to ours. You can afford it. Besides, you heard what Mum said. She brings out the better man in you. That could come in handy for this event."

Polina turned to him, her eyes alight, but narrowed in doubt. "I don't have to be there, if you don't want me. But you should go. This is your chance to set things right between you two."

"I have nothing to say to him."

The words barely left his mouth before her walls rebuilt and shut him out again. "O...kay."

"Give me your email, Polina," Eliza said from the other side of the computer. "Maybe you and I can talk him into it."

Her icy gaze never left his face. "I doubt it. Your brother seems to think some sins are unforgiveable, no matter how much atonement the accused performs. But I'd love to keep in touch with you anyway." She rattled off her email address and jotted down Eliza's on a pad atop the desk. "It was very nice to meet you, Eliza. Good luck with your parents' party. Happy New Year."

"Same to you. Bye, Polina. Safe travels!"

The two women disconnected, and Polina rose from the chair behind the desk. "Thank you. That was kind of you."

She'd say the same thing—with the same lack of inflection—to a stranger who held a door open for her. This time, he knew what brought back the ice princess, but he refused to be emotionally blackmailed into ruining his life. Even for her.

With a deep sigh, he turned off the tablet. "My family is a complicated issue."

"It's your life, Rhys. I can't make you do anything you don't want to. Even if I think you're making a mistake."

"You only think that because you don't understand

what's at stake."

"Oh, I understand. *You* don't."

"I'm not just talking about my relationship with my parents. I'm talking about my career. My entire life. It's not as easy as you think."

Nodding, she rose and, with a sigh, smoothed a hand over her jeans. "So it seems."

She turned to leave the room, but he stopped her cold with his next comment. "What gives you the right to tell me how to handle my life?"

"Excuse me?"

"Forgive me for saying this, but you haven't exactly had a perfect existence with stellar parents as role models."

"Don't you see?" She took a few steps closer to him. "That's why I can help. I know how it feels to be on the fringes of society."

"You're going to compare your life to mine?" He gave a bitter laugh. "Ridiculous. My situation is vastly different. I come from a family line that has always been honorable. Dignified. Until my father ruined that by being a total screw-up. And dragging down an entire international bank in the process. Lucky you, your mother's dead. Her low-life activities can't harm you anymore. I don't have the benefit of that luxury just yet."

Her posture stiffened to marble statue status. "I'm going to forget you said that. You're upset, confused, and lashing out at me. You don't mean what you're saying."

"I don't need you to justify my words, Polina. What would you know about the shadows I live under? You've spent most of your life in dirty, gritty carnival world. For you, this is all an adventure. After all, when you're living on the lowest of society's rungs, the only place left to go is up. You've never had to worry about your reputation because you never had a good reputation to begin with." Another laugh came from him, this one full of disdain. "But, by God, look at you now. Warm, comfortable, well-fed. If not for me, you'd still be in that miserable hostel in town, barricading your door every night."

Unshed tears glistened in her eyes, but she didn't deny his accusation. How could she? He spoke the truth, harsh as it was.

"Enough, Rhys." Henryk stood in the doorway between the living room and kitchen, his face florid. Behind him, Bianka hovered, clearly even more enraged. Even Feliks looked on, eyes round and jaw slack. "You've said enough. I think it's time you found another place to spend the holiday."

When Kacper started growling, Rhys got the message. He'd just crashed and burned.

22

After their disagreement on New Year's Day, Polina made the decision to avoid seeing Rhys again. It hurt too much. She asked Henryk and Bianka to take her to the airport five hours before her scheduled flight—plenty of time to get through security and into the safety of the lounge before Rhys would even notice he'd missed her. A perfect plan. Perfect, provided she didn't consider how deeply his words had cut her and how much she'd wished for a different outcome between them.

Back in the States, when she spotted Uncle Leo—tall, rail-thin, and hawk-faced—outside the baggage claim area, she burst into tears.

"Quitcher caterwaulin'," he grumbled. "We got work waitin' for us."

Anxiety burst from her like a supernova, spreading into her limbs and freezing her to the floor. Ignoring her, he turned and headed for the exit, leaving her to stumble after him. Before she wound up in full-blown-panic-attack-mode, she counseled herself to breathe. *In, out. In, out.*

Find the good.

She thought about Bianka and Henryk and Feliks, her newfound Polish family, who had accepted her and loved her unconditionally. Too bad with memories of the Nowaks came memories of Rhys. His loss stung a lot. She was honest enough to admit she'd come to care for him—maybe even loved him—until he'd disappointed her in the end.

Oh, well. Some people were meant to be alone through life, she supposed. Not her. The Polina who'd returned from Krakòw wasn't the same cold, unfeeling mannequin who went there. She was now in full possession of *all* her emotions, ready to give and accept love for her own. So what if Rhys turned out to be an inappropriate target for her newfound romantic side? He'd helped her discover she *had* a romantic side and for that, she would always be grateful. The pain of his departure would ease. Eventually. Probably. Next time around, she'd be more receptive when the right man came along. Smarter, too.

Goodbye, Rhys. May you be as happy as knowing you made me.

The tightness in her chest eased, and she lifted her head as she passed through the automatic doors where brutal Texas heat nearly wilted her resolve. One more deep breath, shoulders back, she followed Uncle Leo into the parking lot. She was only here temporarily, a day or two at most, before she started the next leg of her journey in life.

Once on the highway, he didn't turn on the radio. White lines whizzed by, along with row after row of steel electrical towers, fields of dirt, strip malls. And cows. Brown cows, black and white cows, cows with calves, cows in groups, cows that stood alone. Texas seemed to have more cows than people.

"Why are there so many damn cows in this state?" she exploded.

Uncle Leo glanced sideways at her and clucked his tongue. "I told your mother not to send you on that trip. Fool waste of good money, if you ask me."

Waste of money? No. Her memory lingered over Bianka's warm hugs, Henryk's steadfast affection, and Feliks's boyish exuberance. So much love, all hers for the taking.

Coming back to Texas was a waste of money. She should've cashed in her ticket for a different destination— started her new life immediately. She really only came back to Texas to say goodbye to ones she loved: Tiny, Ralph, Sasha, Lena. Not Leo. She had nothing to say to Leo. She probably should have stayed in Poland, where she was happy. But, no. Her life was here, somewhere. Not in Poland where she'd constantly face memories of Rhys, not in Georgia where she'd gone to school and settled down until her mother got sick. She'd had hopes that Wild Rides would give her the opportunity to settle in Arizona for a while, but that rejection was probably for the best. She hated the heat. Wherever she went, she'd have to go on without Rhys, since he was still determined to collect his artifacts. She'd waited twenty-eight years to start her life; she couldn't wait another fifty for him. As painful as all those decisions had been, she'd made the right choice to say goodbye to Rhys and to Poland.

"I bet you're glad to be back in the good old U.S. of A., huh?" Uncle Leo remarked.

She offered him a wan smile. "Maybe I will be, after I've slept for a day or two."

Shrugging, he refocused his attention on the traffic. "Yeah, well, sleep's gonna hafta wait. The Zipper's down. I need you to take a look at it when we get to the yard."

A sigh escaped before she could stifle her reaction. In his mind, nothing had changed. She was still the Fix-it Queen for all the carnival rides. Inside her, however, *everything* was different, and the sooner he realized that, the better for everyone. "I told you before I left, Uncle Leo. I'm not coming back to the carnival circuit."

He glared out of the corner of his beady black eye. "What you gonna do, Pollyanna? You ain't equipped for nothin' else in life *but* the carnival circuit, regardless of your fancy degree."

Pollyanna. She bristled. He always called her Pollyanna as an insult, a dig at her tendency to remain positive, no matter how rough times got. She wouldn't rise to his baiting now.

"Your mama shouldn't have put them grandiose ideas in your head. I've been good to you and your ma, took you in, fed you, gave you a decent life. You owe me."

Although his words pelted like red-hot pellets, she steeled herself to remain calm. A million images cluttered her memory. She recalled Uncle Leo kicking some skin-and-bones mutt caught eating the moldy hot dogs in a nameless dirt town in Missouri. Sasha, the Russian immigrant, forced by Uncle Leo to work through the flu during a heat wave in New Mexico, had nearly died of dehydration. Tiny, a former mathematics professor whose real name was Morgan Rosenfeld, joined the circuit after too many years of alcoholism caught up with him at a state college in Rhode Island. Uncle Leo had coined the nickname, Tiny, because the professor only stood four-foot-eleven-inches tall. It was mean-spirited and small-minded, which kind of described Uncle Leo to a tee, now that she thought about it.

She remembered Tiny teaching her to read and write in the back of the bunkhouse, and how Uncle Leo had chastised them both. "Why're you wasting time on her?" he'd sneered. "She's as dumb as her mother. Might as well teach a goat to speak Latin."

At the time, his insults had infuriated her. She was *not* like her mother. And if only to prove him wrong, she'd worked harder to learn, soaking up knowledge like a thirsty sponge. She read every book she could find, whether it involved history or science or literature. Now, as she looked across the truck at him, clarity burst into her brain with the fury of fireworks on the fourth of July.

Mom was seven years old when Uncle Leo brought her to America from Poland. Had she been able to speak any other language besides her native Polish? As an adult, Mom's language skills weren't exactly stellar, but Polina had always chalked that up to the booze and pot. But what if she'd never really learned English? Even Feliks, well-educated by his parents, had struggled to wrap his tongue around the unfamiliar language. What had it been like for her mother, alone and terrified in a foreign country—a country not always as welcoming and open to strangers as her native Poland?

If Polina had never believed Uncle Leo when he told Tiny she was too stupid to learn, why on earth had she ever believed the same derision about her mother?

"You belong with us, Pollyanna." His gruff statement jolted her out of her thoughts. "We understand and accept you in a way the real world never could."

Polina glanced up at the hazy sky. *You never had a chance, did you?*

No wonder Mom had lost herself in an endless round of drugs, alcohol, and men. She was homesick and alone. And even her own daughter had never understood her pain.

Along with this new awareness came an epiphany. Her trip to Poland had never been about finding magic. Mom had sent her to Poland to find herself, to find the courage to be who she was meant to be. The courage Mom had never been able to muster.

I won't let you down, Mom. Thank you.

♥

She received a queen's welcome when she and Uncle Leo arrived at the winter quarters of Jablonski Enterprises. The minute the truck's horn pierced the air with a quick toot-toot, dozens of workers raced to the center of the yard, waving their hands in the air. As she stepped out of the beat-up old truck and onto the dusty ground, cheering erupted.

Sasha reached her first and scooped her up to spin her in his broad arms. "Velcome home, Polina," he shouted. "Ve missed you."

"I missed you, too," she told the Russian bear.

"You should not have come back," he whispered. "I miss you when you leave, but I was happy, too, knowing you got away."

She understood. "Don't worry. I'm not staying." She placed a kiss on top of his head before he set her back on her feet.

"Welcome home, Polina," Tiny said and hugged her. "I hope you brought back those books I asked for." Books were code for anything to be discussed in private. Like her future plans. He leaned close to murmur in her ear, "I want to talk to you later tonight."

"Every one of them." She hitched up the straps of her backpack, feigning excessive weight in the contents. "Stop by my trailer after dinner, and we'll go through them."

"Good girl."

Ralph came up to her next. "Fridge is stocked," he said, pulling her into his embrace. Since he ran the sausage and peppers stand, she had a pretty good idea what was stocked in her refrigerator. "Don't stick around here too long."

After weeks of Bianka's fabulous meals, her stomach would not be happy to go back to her normal fare, but beggars weren't choosy.

Behind Ralph stood Lena, her mother's replacement, who no doubt would have another message for her about getting out of here fast.

The entire scene would have been comical, reminiscent of a jail break in an action movie, if it weren't so pathetic. Everyone here knew she planned to leave the circuit and had agreed to help. Everyone except Uncle Leo, who wanted to keep her here, slaving away for below minimum wage, expecting her to show him gratitude for her indentured servitude.

"Pollyanna!" Speak of the devil. Uncle Leo stood on the outskirts of the group, a cigarette dangling from between his thin lips, fists planted on his non-existent hips. "Get to work on that Zipper. We need it up and running by tomorrow night. Your tools are already there." His baleful gaze encompassed the other carnival workers clustered around her. "The rest of you get back to work, too. This ain't no holiday."

He stalked off, and the others took a moment to kiss her and whisper a hasty message or two before scurrying to their various tasks.

"Last time, Uncle Leo," she muttered as she headed for the popular attraction of flipping cages on a rotary track.

♥

By mid-afternoon, Polina's back ached from spending too many hours bent over, or crouched beneath, or stretched into various nooks to repair and maintain the mechanics on the Zipper and a half-dozen other rides. Sweat plastered her t-shirt to her back, and she craved a shower in Bianka's luxurious bathroom. Unfortunately, she'd have to settle for the tepid trickle of her childhood shower stall. As she approached the old trailer she'd shared with her mother, her stomach growled. Recalling Ralph's whispered message, she grimaced. *Oh, tummy, you are going to be sooooo disappointed.* As disappointed as the rest of her.

She opened the padlock on the door and stepped into the dim interior. Years of misery greeted her. The air smelled of stale booze and pot smoke. The same battered furniture, coated with a thin layer of dust, waited for her attention. Housekeeping had never been high on Mom's priority list. And in the last few months of her mother's life, Polina couldn't find the energy to care for the dying woman, the carnival rides, and the trailer. Something had to give. She'd opted to let the cleaning fall off her to-do list. Now, she'd pay the price.

First things first. She opened all the windows and blinds, hoping for a refreshing breeze and some sunlight to ease the dismal atmosphere. She began in the cramped kitchen, scrubbing countertops and appliances, moved on to the living room, and wended her way down the hall to the bathroom where she got a good look at her reflection. Good God! One day back, and she looked like she'd crawled out of a swamp. Rhys wouldn't even recog—

Cripes. Rhys. She didn't want to think about Rhys now. Not now. Not ever.

After her pathetic shower, she pulled out her tablet, accessed her email, and scrolled through the list of replies. When she spotted the new mail from Riverside Amusements, her normal ritual began. *Oh, please, oh, please. Let this be the one.* Fingers crossed, she clicked on the email to read their reply:

> *Dear Ms. Kominski,*
> *Thank you for your interest in designing our new ride for Riverside Over San Diego. We received many unique proposals and several competitive bids, which made our decision difficult...*

She sighed. Here we go again.

> *...While your design was not chosen for this particular project, we are interested in speaking to you regarding a long-term assignment for our newest property, Riverside Over New England—*

A banging on her door made her jerk. Tiny. She'd forgotten she'd told Tiny to stop by after dinner—a dinner she hadn't yet eaten. Who could eat now? She had a job! Her feet shimmied across the cracked linoleum floor before her brain cautioned her. *You might have a job. Maybe. Don't celebrate yet.*

Bam! Bam! Bam!

"Just a sec," she called toward the door before Tiny's knocks became loud enough to be heard all the way in Poland.

Turning off the tablet, she raced into the bedroom to stow the device inside her backpack, which she shoved under the bed, out of sight.

She trusted Tiny. And Sasha. And even Ralph. But there were too many townie families here, the employees who didn't travel with the Jablonskis, people who would love to get their hands on anything they could sell for as little as a pint of whiskey. For something as valuable as her tablet? Some townies weren't above breaking and entering to get what they wanted.

Tiny pounded on her door once more, and she hurried to let him in before his assault left permanent dents. Not that the old trailer didn't have its share of scars and depressions from the years of use and neglect. "Hi. Sorry. I was trying to get a handle on the mess in here. I'd forgotten the sorry condition I'd left this place in 'til I walked inside an hour ago."

"You didn't have to clean up for me, Polina. I know what you've been through." He stepped inside, brushed a kiss across her cheek, and cocked his head to study her in the waning sunlight that streamed inside from the open door. "You look better than when you left. Healthier. Happier."

She shrugged and strode into the kitchen area. "It was an interesting trip."

"Wanna tell me about it?"

Nodding, she gestured to the kitchen table. "Come, pull up a chair. Want a glass of water? I'd offer you something else, but it's all I've got right now. Unless you'd like some sausage and peppers?"

He waved her off as he took a seat across from her. "Tell me. How did everything go? What'd you do? Did you have any problems? Were you able to finish the whole list your mom left?"

She gave him a brief rundown of what she'd seen and learned in Kraków, never mentioning Rhys and relegating the Nowaks to the status of "host family."

When she finished, he stared at her, unblinking. "Sounds like a nice trip. All very pedestrian, which means you're leaving stuff out. What aren't you telling me?"

She looked out the window where the setting sun framed the kitchen cabinets in an aura of burnt orange. "Nothing. It *was* all pedestrian."

"Uh-huh." He clasped her hand across the table, refocusing her attention. "Talk to me, Polina. I'm not some stranger you can slough off. I changed your very first diaper the day you were born and a thousand others after that. I sat up with you all the nights when your mother's drunken tirades frightened you. I bought you shoes and clothes when I could. Taught you everything you know, which coincidentally, is everything *I* know. You've never lied to me before now. Don't break in new bad habits when you've got a chance to make a fresh start. Tell me what really happened to you. Maybe I can help."

Her lips twisted, and a sardonic laugh escaped. "I doubt it." But she told him anyway. How could she not? She started with her very first night in Kraków, the gypsy girl, the barking dog, how Kacper knocked her to the ground and how Rhys swooped her up. She shared her love for the Nowaks, and celebrating holidays. Throughout the tale, Tiny never interrupted, encouraging her continuation of the day-to-day details with occasional nods and smiles. By the time she reached the argument on New Year's Day and the overwrought goodbyes at the airport, a new block of tears clogged her throat.

Still holding her hand, Tiny squeezed her fingers. "Sounds like these people became pretty special to you."

Emotionally drained from the retelling, she could only nod.

"So, what happens now?" he asked.

She eked out a squeaky sigh, but nothing more.

"You still planning to leave the carnival behind for good?"

Her nod was emphatic. Burning determination renewed itself inside her. She sat up straight and felt strength return to her spine, her bones, her blood. Beneath the shadow of all the dismal, soul-crushing events of the last several hours—of the last several days—she'd never forgotten her goals. At last, she found her voice again. "Yes. Now, more than ever."

"Good. Because now it's my turn to tell you a few things."

She smiled. "Oh? Like what?" Here came one of his endless lectures regarding hard work, striving for success, and waiting for someone worthy of her. She'd heard the same speech since before she could talk and could probably recite the advice in her sleep.

His face took on an earnest expression. "I want to start by saying I'm sober. Haven't touched a drop of booze since your ma died."

"You haven't?" Her smile broadened. This was big news. Huge. Although never the stumbling drunk her mother was, Tiny was rarely seen without his trusty flask. To give that up? He must have had some kind of major league awakening.

"Nope."

"That's terrific." She squeezed his hand. "I'm so proud of you!"

"There's more."

"More?" What else? Excitement waged a battle with fear. What if his newfound sobriety came from some kind of medical condition? Could he be sick? Was that why he'd suddenly quit drinking? Oh, God. Would she have to stay here longer now? Not that she wouldn't take care of him if he was sick. Tiny was the closest thing to a real parent she'd ever had. She'd never turn her back on him.

"You know I've always treated you like my own little girl."

Her reply was wary. "Uh-huh."

"Well, part of the reason for that is 'cuz I love you."

"I love you—"

"Lemme finish. You were the only baby we ever had here. That alone made you special. We all felt like you were ours. But..." He let go of her hand, allowing his index finger to trace the ancient knife scars in the aged Formica tabletop. "But, there's also a pretty good chance you really *are* my daughter."

What?! Polina couldn't so much as blink. A million thoughts buzzed inside her head. All the years she'd followed him around, the thousands of days and nights in the bunkhouse with books and scraps of paper while he taught her mathematics, reading, history, science.

Her father? She'd always thought her father was some carnival customer, a guy with an unsuspecting family who'd stuck around after the show closed for one night's extra-curricular fun, then disappeared into the ether. It had never occurred to her that the man she sought was beside her all along. Why would it? "Why didn't you ever tell me?"

"Your mom wouldn't let me. I think she believed it better for you to be 'everybody's kid.' This way, you never got singled out by any of us, for good *or* bad."

She understood what he didn't say. Uncle Leo's animosity toward Tiny and most of the workers here was legendary. If he suspected anyone of them had been her father...

Still, a spark of resentment flared. "How old do I have to be before everyone stops protecting me? You and my mother wanted to protect me from big, bad old Uncle Leo. Uncle Leo claimed he was protecting me from the real world and people who wouldn't understand the way I was raised. Rhys wanted to protect me from the dangers of Kraków. Bianka and Henryk wanted to protect me from Rhys. You wanna know what happens to people who are 'protected' their whole lives? They either grow up to become like my mother—addicts too fragile to handle the world around them when they face the slightest adversity—or they expect everyone to cater to their every whim for the rest of their spoiled, pampered lives. I don't want to be either of those. I want to be a real person with real problems I figure out on my own, real accomplishments, and a real life. A life I've put on hold for..." She ran out of steam for a second or two, but finished with a flourish that included a whirling hand wave. "...forever!"

She shivered and wrapped her arms in a self-hug.

Tiny's lips quirked in a half-smile. "Are you finished now?"

"I think so."

"Feel better?"

She took a moment to analyze herself. The anger had flooded out, hollowing her. "Not really," she confessed, her tone whisper-soft. "And now my head hurts."

"You were never good at tantrums." He squeezed her hand. "I can't tell you what your friends in Poland thought or why they sought to protect you. But when it came to my reasons, I did what I thought was best for you because you were always my baby girl."

"What makes you think you're my father?"

He turned his hands palm-up on the table. "Mind you, I'm not a hundred percent sure. No one is. Not even your mom ever really knew. But you're built like me—like my sister. Tiny." Crimson stained his cheeks. "*Petite,*" he corrected and lifted one hand in mid-air to reflect the similarities in their heights. "You know what I mean."

"You have a sister?"

"Anna. Your hair's the same color as hers, too. And you've got her quick mind. She was a civil engineer. If I had a picture of her, I'd show you."

"Where does she live?"

Eyes downcast, he shook his head. "She's gone now. Before I came here. That's when my drinking took off— when I lost her. Until you came along, I thought I'd lost everything when Anna died. You gave me a reason to keep living."

"So why tell me all of this now?"

He offered her a sad smile that did little to ease the worry butterflies in her stomach. "Because I couldn't let you leave for good without you knowing the truth. I love you, Polly. You're my daughter, whether it's 'cuz I made you one night in the heat of passion or just 'cuz I raised you every single day. I love you and I'm damn proud of you. And I quit drinking because I want you to be proud of me."

She placed her hand over his. "I'm leaving here. Tonight. Do you want to come with me?"

23

On a squeal of brakes, the bus lurched to a stop, and Polina jerked awake. Blinking, she struggled to regain her senses. No wonder she fell asleep. She thought the cows in Texas were excessive? Those cows had nothing on the rows and rows of dead corn stalks lining the Midwest. The never-ending scenery and the continuous rocking of the bus on the road were more effective than sleeping pills. Toss in her natural exhaustion from hours of hard work, world travel, and jet lag, and she did a swan dive into oblivion before they hit the main highway. She'd covered an awful lot of mileage in the last twenty-four hours: from Poland to Texas and now enroute to her new life with Tiny.

Their escape from the carnival was even more ludicrous than her homecoming. Sasha planned to take Uncle Leo's truck into town for some supplies. Lena promised to keep Leo occupied while she and Tiny made their getaway in the truck's cab, huddled beneath a tarp. After Sasha dropped them off at the bus station, she bought two tickets to Massachusetts.

The email she'd received from Riverside had been a job offer, designing not one but *all* the rides at a new theme park the company had acquired in the Boston area. She'd be working with a full dynamics team and a number of top-notch mechatronics engineers, planning where each ride would go, how much they'd cost to construct, and coming up with a series of concepts that would revolve around one specific theme.

Now, as the bus doors opened in front of another non-descript building, she turned to Tiny in the seat beside her.

"Where are we?"

"Somewhere in Kentucky. How are you feeling?"

Kentucky. So they were heading...north...east? She paused to take stock of her current pitching emotions. "Dizzy." How could she not be? Shuffled between countries, learning Tiny was quite possibly her father, racing away from the carnival in the dark of night, and on her way to a future she'd only dreamed of. What if she screwed up? What if she got there and they hated her ideas? Bad enough she'd left everything she'd ever known, burned her last bridge, but she'd allowed Tiny to strike the match. Her chest tightened.

Tiny patted her hand. "I know you're anxious. You've waited a long time for this. Worked hard for it. You can do this. Okay?"

"O...kay."

God-knew-how-many-hours and how-many-cheese-crackers-with-peanut-butter-snacks later, he poked her arm as she dozed. "Wake up, Polina. This is us."

She glanced out the bus window at the piles of dirty snow showcased by the waning afternoon sun and the florescent lights of the windowless bus station. *This is us?* What a depressing thought. "Please tell me that's not a metaphor."

Laughing, he rose from his seat. "Come on. Grab your gear. And be careful stepping off the bus in those boots." He pointed to the familiar plastic footwear that had been the bane of her existence in Kraków. "It doesn't look like you've got any traction on those soles. You're likely to slip on the ice and hurt yourself."

No kidding. "Where were you when I was in Poland?"

"First half of the month, I was in Alabama. Second half, Texas. But you already knew that."

He slid into the aisle, and she followed. As soon as her feet hit the pavement outside, the blustery wind sliced into her exposed skin. "Brrr!" Zipping her jacket up to her throat, she burrowed her chin into the emerald fleece beneath. Immediately, her thoughts turned to Rhys. Where was he now? What was he doing? Did he think about her at all? Stop, she chided herself. Stop obsessing about Rhys.

"New England in January." Tiny took her arm. "Come

on. The motel's this way."

They strolled through a pretty village with hand-painted signs advertising an old-fashioned ice cream shoppe, antique store, a café, coffee house, and at least two seafood restaurants. As they walked, other people rushed past them, zigging and zagging like pinballs, no doubt heading to warm homes with families and hot dinners waiting.

The concrete sidewalks became cobblestones, and the stores gave way to houses with gingerbread scrollwork and wraparound porches. Lovely. Welcoming. Familiar. If she blinked, she'd swear she was back in Kraków.

A sense of peace enveloped her, leaving her lighthearted and optimistic. This was it; this was the place she'd dreamed of all those desperate years.

At last, she was home.

♥

For a week after Polina left, Rhys buried himself in work. Although nothing disastrous occurred, nothing positive happened, either. No tingles on his nape, no spurt of adrenaline. He'd become dead inside.

Polina had stolen his magic. An enormous black cloud seemed to loom over him, shading his outlook, his mood, his daily life.

Worst of all, she'd shut him out since her departure.

He checked online at different times of the day and night, hoping to see her icon that would tell him she was accessing the internet. Once, her icon lit up while he surfed, but a second later, she went dark again. Total radio silence. No replies came from the flurry of emails he sent. He finally broke down, swallowed his pride, and stopped by Henryk's desk.

"Have you heard from her?"

Henryk looked up from his monitor, brow furrowed. "Who?"

"Polina. Who else?"

"You mean you haven't?"

He didn't reply. Instead, he repeated his question—this time more slowly so it sank in.

"Have...you...heard...from...her?"

Henryk shrugged and clicked on his keyboard. "Bianka spoke to her the other day on that chat thing they do."

"She was online? When? How is she? Where is she? Why hasn't she contacted me at all?"

"I don't know. Ask her."

"I've sent her a half-dozen messages. She doesn't answer. I haven't heard from her since New Year's Day."

Henryk stopped typing and gave him a skeptical look. "Hmm...I wonder why that is. You don't suppose anything happened on New Year's Day that soured her on you, do you?"

A trickle of guilt splashed his conscience, but he tamped it down. "I don't regret what I said that day. I'm sorry we ruined your holiday, but she had no business getting involved in matters that didn't concern her."

"Yes, I remember you saying so that afternoon. Quite emphatically, in fact."

"You think I'm wrong, don't you?"

"It doesn't matter what I think. It only matters how Polina feels about it. And, judging by her silence, I'd say she's made her opinion known. Leave her alone. Let her be. You're happy with your life; now, she can seek out the life that will make her happy."

"Who made you her father?"

"*You* did, when you brought her to my house that first night. What do you want from her, Rhys? You want a pretty girl on your arm?" He waved a hand around the office. "Pick one. Polina deserves better than someone who doesn't really care about her as more than another acquisition."

"Of course I care about her."

"Not enough. You know, you're more like your father than you care to admit."

"What do you know about my father?" Only one person could have revealed that secret, and his anger heated at the apparent betrayal. "What did Polina tell you?"

Henryk shook his head. "She didn't have to tell us anything. We all heard you shouting at her. And for what it's worth, when Bianka insisted you were no longer welcome in our home, Polina defended you. A lot more admirably than you deserve, in my opinion."

"Why? What did she say?"

"About your relationship with your father? Nothing specific. Just that he'd hurt you deeply and she hoped that, eventually, you'd find some kind of peace between you." Henryk cocked his head. "Pretty generous, don't you think? Especially after the way you denigrated her *and* her mother?"

Very. And he wasn't worthy. Hadn't been from the start, never really seeing her true value. "Do me a favor? The next time Bianka talks to Polina, would she be kind enough to send a message? Tell her I'm sorry?"

The older man's eyes narrowed. "Why? It's better this way. You didn't love her. You went out of your way to show her your time together was temporary. What's the problem now? You wanted to be the one to end it? On your terms? Too bad. Let her go."

"I just want—"

"Let...her...go."

Hoisted upon his own petard. With a nod of surrender, he returned to his own desk. Let her go? Hell, no. Not when he just realized how much he wanted to win her back. This time, for good. Of course, considering she wouldn't talk to him and no one would help him, he'd have a terrific fight to tell her that.

Then again...no one *in Poland* would help him. But he knew someone in another country who would. The idea was crazy. And desperate. But he had to admit, he was both of those things right now. Crazy in love with Polina Kominski and desperate to let her know. To find out if she might feel the same way about him.

Mind made up, he sent a quick message to Eliza:

I'm coming home.

24

This was the stupidest thing he'd ever done. But Eliza had promised she'd make sure Polina saw him, saw this moment. He didn't ask how, didn't want to know if she planned to live-stream his humiliation to a bunch of carnival workers somewhere deep in the heart of Texas. Well, so what if she did? He swallowed his pride, felt the burn from gullet to belly. Whatever he had to do to win back Polina. She was worth any cost.

He'd embarrassed her, shamed her, when he should have cherished her and listened to her counsel. He'd do his penance willingly. And hope it was enough.

Now, here he stood, on the outskirts of his parents' surprise anniversary party in the hotel ballroom, sweat beading his nape and his nerves skittering in anticipation. From his hiding place in the empty room next door, he watched his sisters laugh and mingle with family and friends he hadn't seen in decades. Because of the party room's setup, he could only see the backs of his parents' heads. Probably best, since he needed time to come to grips with what might happen when he and his father were face-to-face at last.

There were about forty or fifty people in the room— some he recognized, others he didn't. The lady talking to Eliza was a mystery, perhaps a coworker or friend he'd never met. And on the subject of friends, was that really his old mate, Martin Barnard snuggling up to the shrimp platter? Marty had put on a few pounds since their days at boarding school. Lost some hair along the way, as well. The adorable imp in the blue dress who continually flared her skirt and spun in the middle of the dance floor until she fell from dizziness? Could only be Rhiannon. His namesake. A child he'd never seen or held. Well, he'd remedy that lapse as soon as he got through his speech.

Fourteen years. How could he have let fourteen years pass by without once coming home? Why did he believe the occasional phone call or internet chat could take the place of seeing his sister's smile, getting a kiss from his mum, swooping in and swinging his beautiful niece in his arms to hear her laughter? What had he gained in return? An ancient trinket or two? Meanwhile, he'd lost touch with so many people he loved. By choosing *things*. And pride.

I am an idiot.

He'd always thought his absence would punish his father and maybe, it had. But he'd also punished himself. Now, more than ever, he needed to talk to Polina. He had to apologize, tell her she'd been right. *One task at a time. Speech, reunion, and then, when the uproar my surprise appearance creates dies down, I can retreat to my hotel room and try, again, to contact Polina. Maybe this time, with Eliza's help, she'll talk to me.*

As if on cue, Eliza popped up behind him. "You ready, brother mine?"

"Not yet. First…" Turning, he wrapped his arms around her waist then kissed her forehead. "I'm sorry. I should've come home a long time ago."

She beamed up at him. "I'm just glad you're here now." She pulled away and straightened her dress. "Now, you know what you're going to say?"

"No," he admitted. "I wrote a bunch of things down, but, I have no idea what will fly out of my mouth when I see him."

Rather than berate him, she nodded sympathetically. "Just think of Polina watching you. That should help you keep your boorish behavior in check."

He could've said something about her sass, but his worries took precedence at the moment. "Are you sure she's going to see this?"

She patted his upper arm. "Trust me. I planned every detail. I may not be a genius at controlling my own love life, but when it comes to fixing everyone else's troubles, I'm the goddess of perfection. I guarantee she'll see it."

He took a deep breath, exhaled, rolled his shoulders.

"You look wonderful. You know that? A little tired around the eyes, but I doubt Mum will notice." She winked. "Or Polina."

Mumbling thanks, he ran a hand down his suit jacket, smoothing invisible creases.

Meanwhile, Eliza traipsed out the door and back into the other room, took the microphone from the stand near the band's dais, and blew into it. When she walked too near the speaker system, a squeal of feedback pierced the air. The partygoers halted in mid-sentence, mid-sip, and in Marty Barnard's case, mid-shrimp.

"Sorry about that," she said into the mic. "But now that I have everyone's attention, I'd like to ask you all to find your seats." She faced the small table where their parents sat, their backs still to Rhys. "Mum, Dad. Happy thirty-fifth! My siblings and I have worked really hard to put this surprise party together for you. And we all want a chance to tell you how much we love you."

That was Rhys's cue. He left his post and crept toward the ballroom, waiting at the edge of the doorway, still out of sight to most guests, including his parents.

"In the spirit of fairness you instilled in us," Eliza continued, "we'll go in age order."

Their sister, Sara, two years his junior, rose from her seat, prepared to take "eldest sibling in attendance" status.

"Not so fast, Sara," Eliza said. "There's someone else here who gets to go first." She faced the doorway. "Come on in."

Rhys strode into the room, and a hushed gasp rippled through the crowd. Unease itched his skin, and he yanked on the cuffs of his crisp white dress shirt to release some of the tension. For a full minute, no one moved. No one spoke.

Until he locked eyes with his mother, who shot up from her chair and raced toward him. "Rhys!"

He caught her in his arms and bent slightly to kiss her, but Vanessa Quinn cradled his face between her hands, staring at him as if she hadn't seen him in years—which, technically, she hadn't. Contact via computer screen didn't count. He should've realized that long before now.

"Oh, my sweet, sweet boy. Welcome home!"

While the rest of the guests applauded madly, Rhys found himself surrounded by women as his sisters rushed to enfold him in a circle of fancy dresses and happy tears. With each kiss and each greeting, he reveled in reconnecting with his family.

A loud, "Ahem!" pierced the joyous bubble, and the ladies stepped back, leaving Rhys facing a stooped old man who looked decades older than his fifty-eight years. "Welcome home, son."

Black Jack Quinn was a broken shadow of the man Rhys had feared, respected, and eventually despised.

"Thank you, sir." He stood stiff and straight, hands fisted at his sides, unsure what to do or say next.

His father stumbled forward, and Rhys shot out a hand to steady him. To his surprise, the old man lurched toward Rhys and collapsed against him, weeping openly. "I'm sorry, Rhys. You have no idea how sorry I am."

This was *not* the man he'd thought about all these years, the man he'd recalled with animosity. This was a man full of regrets, a man to be pitied. Or forgiven. Or perhaps, both. He was so small, so frail-looking. What happened to the arrogant, unrepentant bully Rhys remembered?

His head swimming at this turn of events, Rhys could only hold his father and murmur polite acceptance. That sent his mother careening into him again, and he wound up holding both of them as they clung to him and sobbed. Over the old man's penitent head, Rhys's gaze found Eliza's smiling face. When she connected with him, she jerked her head to the closest corner of the room near the table where his parents had been seated earlier. He tracked his sister's visual nudge and discovered...

Polina, aglow in an aura of sentimental happiness, as she looked on.

"H-how?"

Because Rhys had his hands full with his parents, Eliza signaled Polina to join them. "She got here about two hours ago. When I told her you planned to come home, nothing would stop her from flying here to be with you. In case you needed her."

When she was within reach, he peeled himself off his parents and pulled her into his arms, collapsing against her sturdiness. He broke the way his father had—minus the tears. Nuzzling into her neck, he murmured, "I'm sorry. You were right."

She ran a comforting hand down his hair and kissed his neck just beneath his earlobe. "Later," she crooned. "You and I will talk later. Right now, this is your parents' moment. Don't make it about us."

Right again. With a shuddering breath, he managed to pull himself together and stand apart from her. Thank God she was here! She was his rock, his anchor, his wings. She helped him soar above the petty and the miserable, then grounded him when he flew too high. She kept him balanced, focused him on the important things in life. In general, she made him happy. Taking both of his parents by the arms, he escorted them back to their table. Once they were seated again, he pressed one last kiss to his mum's cheek that drew an "Awww..." from the crowd, and he returned to where a smug Eliza stood with the microphone.

"Surprised?" she asked him in a low tone so the guests wouldn't hear.

"Congratulations. You pulled it off."

"Good. Because you owe me about eight hundred pounds for her travel expenses."

"Eight hundred...?"

"Listen, Romeo. Last minute lovers looking for forgiveness pay higher fees."

He took the offered mic and nodded. "I'll write you a check."

She stepped away, leaving him in the center of the room with everyone watching. He'd prepared a speech, all very neutral and unspecific, a speech he now realized was completely inappropriate. He needed something more, something personal and unique. He needed his muse. Lucky for him, she was here. Standing in her corner again, she must have sensed his turmoil because she nodded, and her encouragement surged through him.

He spoke into the mic. "For those of you who don't remember me, I'm Vanessa and Jack's only son and..." He dared a sharp glance at Sara. "...the oldest of the tribe. I...umm..." His thoughts scattered, and he rubbed his hand over his head. "I'm sorry. I had a speech fully prepared, but somehow, it...umm...doesn't seem to do this occasion true justice. So bear with me because I'm going to make this up as I go along." His brain fumbled for words, and panic set in when absolutely nothing came to mind.

Polina, sensing his need, mouthed three simple words, "Talk to me."

So, he did. "Growing up, whenever my sisters and I misbehaved or disappointed our parents in some way, the first thing that Mum would say was...?"

He scanned the crowd for his sisters, and they all chorused together, "'We love you, but...'"

He grinned and mimed applause. "That's right. 'We love you, but...' As in, 'We love you, but you shouldn't cut the hair off your sister's dolls. We love you, but you cannot keep a frog in your bed.'" Laughter rang out from the audience. "'We love you, but the damage to the car will come out of your allowance.' And yes, I was the guilty party in all those scenarios. But I'm not boasting. I mention these incidents because my sisters and I all knew that no matter what happened, our mum and dad would always love us. They witnessed our flaws, our mistakes, but loved us anyway. Unconditionally." He paused to draw a shaky breath. "A lot of people get married because they believe they've found their perfect *somebody*."

Polina must have caught the emphasis he placed on that last word, as he intended, and cocked her head in question. Unfortunately, she'd have to wait a little longer. Or catch on to what else he planned to say. If he could get the words out in some semblance of logic.

"Most times, these unions don't last. Because no one is perfect. Eventually, we all fail. We make mistakes. We say things we shouldn't, do things we know are wrong. My sisters and I...we were luckier than most kids. We learned firsthand that one of the most important aspects of love is the ability to forgive." He grimaced and tapped his temple. "Though, for one or two of us, the lesson took longer to sink in. I love you, Mum. Dad. I love you both. Thank you for being the example of true love every family deserves but few receive. Happy anniversary. Now, I know, the second I pass this mic to Sara, Mum will say to me, 'We love you, too, Rhys, but you should come home more often.'"

"That's exactly right," his mother shouted, drawing more laughter from the guests.

"I promise I will," he replied. "And for what it's worth..." His eyes locked on Polina's. "I'm sorry I made you wait so long for me to wake up and realize how extraordinarily lucky I am."

Applause erupted, and he passed the microphone to Sara. "Well, I can see a few things haven't changed," she quipped. "My brother's still a tough act to follow..."

The rest of her speech buzzed in the background while he strode toward Polina, but she shook her head and surreptitiously pointed at his parents. He cast a glance in their direction. His mother had melted into a puddle of joyful tears, and his father, a fragile shell of the man Rhys remembered, rubbed her shoulder with one hand while using a linen napkin to dab at his wet eyes with the other. Rhys nodded in their direction, but continued his path to Polina's side. The closer he got to her, the harder his heart hammered in his chest.

She met him halfway, a frown marring her features. "You should stay with your parents. They haven't seen you in so long."

"I don't want to steal the thunder away from my sister's speeches. They knocked themselves out putting this affair together. Getting them to work in harmony on any project is a Herculean labor. After all the arguing and planning they probably went through to bring this to fruition, they deserve my parents' full attention right now. Besides, I want to hear all about you. Where've you been? What have you been doing? How did you get here? Why didn't you answer my emails?"

She laughed at the barrage of questions he fired at her.

"Well, let's see. Where've I been? Massachusetts, for the most part. I've got a job at a brand new theme park, designing five big roller coasters for them, including my...ta-da!...Dragon's Tail."

"Wow. That's terrific. Congratulations."

"Thanks. And, get this. I found my father. Though,

that's not a hundred percent accurate. He's been with me the whole time. I just discovered his identity recently."

"Really? Who is he? Tell me."

♥

As they strolled the hallway outside the ballroom, Polina told him everything she'd experienced since leaving Poland. She told him about her arrival in Texas, her reunion with Uncle Leo and the carnival, Tiny's confession, the email from Riverside Entertainments, and their nighttime escape to Massachusetts. "And Rhys, I bought a house! A real house! With a yard and a porch and neighbors and everything. It needs work, a lot of work. But it's pretty and mine. All mine. No mortgage. No one can ever throw me out because it's mine."

"And Tiny? Is he still with the carnival?"

"Tiny—I mean my *father,* I still can't get used to calling him that—was a...what do you call him? A don, right? Tiny was a don for years before he joined the carnival. He lives with me now, and he's gone back to work at a local community college in the area. It's been a crazy ride the last few months."

He grinned. "I guess that explains why you didn't return any of my emails."

"I didn't think, after our last conversation, you'd care to hear from me." Not entirely true. She'd seen his emails, but hadn't opened any of them. She couldn't bear the hurt.

"I've been going out of my mind without you." He took her hand, kissed each of her knuckles in turn.

A tiny spark of hope flared inside her. "Really?"

"Ask Henryk. I've been nagging him and Bianka for weeks to tell me that you were all right. I was worried sick."

She glanced at the gold carpet beneath their feet. Maybe she'd been too harsh on him. Maybe he did care, after all. "I'm sorry."

"All my luck ran out when you got on that plane the day after New Year's. I haven't made a decent trade agreement since."

"Oh." The spark fizzled. She'd dared herself to believe

he actually missed her, that his pretty speech for his parents meant he understood the true meaning of love. And maybe, that he was including a secret message to her. Some kind of hint that he might be in love with her.

I am such a fool.

Uncle Leo's recriminations echoed in her head. *She's as dumb as her mother.*

No. Her mother wasn't dumb. Neither was she. Naïve, maybe. But learning. And unlike her mother, she wouldn't use her body or some kind of manipulation to get Rhys to admit something he didn't truly feel.

Slapping on a broad smile, she exclaimed, "The house takes up a lot of my time. Can you believe it, Rhys? I've got a *house*. A place where I can stay. And live forever. No more moving around from town to town. I'm going to get a pet— maybe a kitten. Or no, a puppy. Or both." Giggling, she wrapped her arms around herself and twisted back and forth. "I still can't believe it. It's like a dream. And if it is a dream, I don't want to wake up."

"It sounds like you've got everything you need. I'm thrilled for you."

"Oh, I'm a far distance from 'everything,' but I'm on my way." She lowered her arms to her sides. "It probably sounds crazy to you. I know how much you value your freedom and the ability to travel all over the world for your artifacts, but I've done enough traveling in my lifetime."

Did she sound condescending? God, she hoped not. She only wanted him to see her as she was beginning to see herself: confident, growing, becoming the woman she wanted to be. A woman worthy to give and receive love.

Another round of applause burst from the guests, and she realized she'd rambled while his sisters had all finished their speeches. "I'm glad you decided to attend your parents' party. You've made them very happy."

"I'm glad I came, too. But more importantly, I'm glad you came. I couldn't have managed to get through my speech without you."

A lukewarm feeling washed over her, but she knew all too well that the sensation wouldn't last long enough to become pleasant. She was still an object to him, a good luck token he could rub when he wanted to make magic. He still didn't see that love was the real magic. And that it took more than luck or a quick rub to nurture that power.

"Somehow," she said with a sigh, "I think you would've done just fine. All you had to do was speak through your heart." Removing her hand from his, she took a few strides ahead to put some distance between them. "Come on. The speeches are all done. Now you can really talk to your parents."

"Come with me. I'll introduce you."

They walked inside, headed to the small round table at the front of the room, and Vanessa Quinn rose from her seat, her arms flung open wide. "Darling Polina, thank you!"

She stiffened and backed up against Rhys's chest. "Thank me? For what?"

"For convincing my son to come home." After pulling her forward, Rhys's mother wrapped her in a hug filled with rose perfume and sleek fabric.

"Oh, no, honestly. I had nothing to do with his showing up here."

Aside from her brief time with Bianka, no woman had ever hugged her, and she found herself unwilling to let go. The warmth, the affection, the automatic *acceptance* from this woman soothed all her prickly edges. She only wished Rhys realized how lucky he'd been to grow up with this kind of luxury.

"Don't listen to her, Mother," Rhys cut in. "She had everything to do with it."

"Of course she did." Still holding onto Polina, she craned her neck to the table. "Jack, come meet Rhys's Polina."

"She's not *my* Polina. She's not a doll or a toy. She's Polina. Just Polina. Someone who means a great deal to me. But I don't own her."

Polina didn't know if she should be thrilled with his statement or upset by it. Had he really come to understand her in the few months they'd been apart? Or did he still think of her as just another possession—an artifact he'd found in the dirt, cleaned up, and now put on display for his parents?

"Oh," Vanessa waved a dismissive hand. "She knows what I mean."

Rhys's father approached, his open arms spread wide. "May I?"

May he what?

She looked to Rhys for a translation. "He wants to hug you, sweetheart."

"Oh. O...kay. Sure. I guess." While she found herself embraced by yet another stranger, Rhys stood back, grinning.

"Rhys!" a woman squealed. "Get over here and meet your niece. Bring your somebody so we can be properly introduced."

"Egad." He emitted a dramatic sigh. "I see Sara hasn't changed much. Still the bossy one."

His mother laughed. "What did you expect? She took over your mantle as eldest child when you took off after commencement. If you plan to seize that title again, you'd better make sure you visit a little more often than every fourteen years." She reached across her husband to pinch Polina's arm. "That goes for you too, Polina. We'll expect to see you often."

"You're seeing her now, Mother. Don't be greedy." He took her hand, drawing her away. "Come on, Polina. You've got a whole gaggle of women left to hug."

25

Another airport, another departure.

Polina had enjoyed her time with the Quinns, but every minute spent with Rhys pricked her heart. All too soon, each of those teeny holes would spurt blood, and she'd collapse, drained of life. She wanted him to love her, wanted to share a future with him, but saw too many obstacles in the way. Oh, she understood his need to travel to far-off places, to replace all the possessions he'd lost. She just didn't want to be one of his acquisitions.

At the entrance to the security checkpoint, the last few feet of space they could share together before her flight home would separate them by thousands of miles again, she took her backpack from him and prepared to leave.

"I'm glad you came," he said.

Keep it light, she warned herself. "I am, too. It was worth the jet lag I'm going to suffer for the next few days just to hear Eliza divulge all your childhood secrets."

He frowned. "I'm serious. You made a very difficult time easier for me. I don't know how to thank you."

"You don't have to thank me. That's what friends are for, right?"

"We're more than friends, Polina."

"We are?"

"Of course we are. You're my good luck charm."

She bit her tongue until she tasted blood. "I should go," she said at last. "It's been fun, but now I have to buckle down and concentrate on all my work at *home*." She placed heavy emphasis on the last word. "Lots of things to do with the house. Cleaning, painting, gardening." She swallowed hard. *Don't sound desperate. Don't let him see your vulnerability.* "Tiny and I want to plant lots of vegetables. When you've lived like we have, fresh vegetables are a luxury. What about you? What are your plans? Did you choose your next assignment yet?"

"I've narrowed it down. As a matter of fact, I'd appreciate your opinion on the matter."

Down, girl. Don't look eager. "Oh?"

"Yes. Rome or Mexico City?"

Her last hope snuffed out like a lit birthday candle in a blizzard. "What made you choose those two places?"

"The Rome office has a project they think I'd be perfect for, and if I time it right, I can be there in time for some new explorations planned around the Herculaneum. But my grandfather spent nearly a year in Mexico City. I could walk the same streets he did, and who knows what I'll find? What do you think?"

"They both sound great," she lied. "I'll...umm...I'll have to think about it and get back to you."

"Thanks. I know you'll help me make the right choice."

Disappointment churned in her stomach, and she glanced up at the clock overhead. "I should go. I don't want to miss my flight."

"Right." He dipped his head to kiss her, and her heart fluttered, sputtered, and cracked into pieces.

"Bye, Rhys," she managed. "Have a safe trip home."

"You, too." She turned to queue up with the other passengers, but he called her back. "Polina?"

"Hmm?"

"I love you."

"But...?"

"But what?"

"Your speech. You said your mother always said, 'We love you, but...' So, you love me, but...?"

"No but. I just wanted you to know how I feel before you got on the plane."

If he truly meant the words, she'd let the flight leave without her, but she knew better. He didn't really love her. He loved having her around, his good luck charm. He loved her the way a child loves a favorite toy—selfishly and without real regard.

"Well?"

She knew what he wanted from her. He wanted her to say the same thing to him. But she couldn't. Not because she didn't love him. She loved him the way a woman loves a man she wants to spend the rest of her life with, the way his mother loved his father—selflessly, wholly, flaws and all. Without that same love between them, they were doomed. So, she let him go.

"You have the world's worst timing," she said instead and dashed away to hide in the ladies room before he could see the tears filling her eyes.

♥

Rhys returned to Poland two days later, his head still buzzing with Polina's last words. *You have the world's worst timing.*

Not exactly the reply he expected.

The world's worst timing. Why? Had she fallen in love with someone else? Someone in Rhode Island? Someone from the carnival? What about that Tiny character she talked about? Was he really her father? Or had she said that to avoid hurting Rhys's feelings with the truth? Clearly, the man, whoever he was, had been a part of her life for a long time. And he wasn't going anywhere any time soon.

Tiny and I had to hide in the truck's cab under a tarp to escape before Uncle Leo found us.

Tiny was a don. He's living with me now.

Tiny and I want to plant lots of vegetables.

Tiny, Tiny, Tiny.

You have the world's worst timing. Since when? She hadn't exactly given him ample opportunity to pour out his heart to her. When should he have told her? At the anniversary party with dozens of strangers looking on? Afterwards, at his grandparents' house, while his parents hovered around them? Was he supposed to send her an email after they both left England for their respective homes?

Why exactly had she planned to return home immediately following the party? Leaving them little to no time together? In fact, she'd spent more time with his sister, Eliza, than she had with him on this trip. What was so important in Massachusetts that she had to return so quickly? Or was it a "who" that was so important all of a sudden? Had she shifted loyalties to someone else? Fallen in love with someone else?

The world's worst timing. Because, now, someone else had captured her heart?

Once in his Kraków flat, he checked his email. No message from her. Full radio silence.

Forget about her. Focus on other issues. God knew he had plenty of other things to think about.

Rome or Mexico City?

Although he wasn't due back at work until tomorrow, he decided to check his office email, get a jump on what might be waiting for him. His first attempt to connect went straight to a white screen with the message, "This account has been locked. Please contact administrator." His second and third attempts achieved the same results.

Strange. Had there been some kind of security breach while he was away?

Henryk would know. He dialed his friend's office number, but his call only reached voicemail. After the prompt, he left a message that he was back—nothing about Polina—and he couldn't access his work computer for some reason. He ended with, "Call me and let me know what's happening."

Now what? One more login attempt would lock him out and require dealing with the Help Desk to fix the damage. He hated the Help Desk. Every experience with the staff there began with the inane, "Have you tried turning your computer off and turning it back on again?" and ended hours later with Rhys fighting the urge to bang his head against a solid object to stem the frustration.

No, he'd pass on the Help Desk. That meant he'd have to pass on catching up with work, as well.

He paced the three small rooms of his flat, bored and agitated. What did other people do when they were alone and unable to work? Watch telly? Read a book? He was too keyed up to sit still for either.

His office building had a gymnasium for employee use, complete with free weights, machines, and a racquetball court. Maybe he could take out some of his frustrations by pounding the treadmill. First, he'd unpack his suitcase. Sort his laundry. Then, the treadmill.

He'd just stowed his luggage in the closet when someone knocked on his front door.

Henryk, probably. Good. He'd get some answers about whatever was going on with his off-site access, and maybe challenge the old goat to a racquetball game to get the endorphins up.

He opened the door to see a strange man in the hall. "Rhys Linsey?" the man asked in thickly accented English.

"Yes?"

"I'm Krzystof Bleich of the KNF. Would you come with me, please?"

The KNF was the Financial Supervision Authority, Poland's regulatory organization for banks and financial institutions. What did they want with him?

"Why?" Rhys asked. "What's going on?"

"You're under arrest, sir. For embezzlement and fraudulent investment practices."

♥

"Rhys was arrested last week for embezzling money from the firm."

Polina stared at the woman's image on her computer screen, forcing the words into her brain, past the wall of denials resounding in her skull. "I don't understand. What does this mean?"

"Stealing. They say he set up fake bank accounts to steal money meant to pay client transfer fees."

Stealing? Rhys? No way. A high-pitched buzz filled her ears. "He didn't do this," she insisted, shouting to be heard over the noise in her head. "He wouldn't."

Bianka nodded. "I no think so, either. But my Henryk says Rhys's name is on all the incriminating documents. Every account in question links back to him. The...how you say?...*indictment* was filed in criminal court. And the bank's investigators found out the truth about his father, so they think..." She didn't have to finish the sentence.

Polina knew. The prosecutors, upon hearing Rhys was the real-life son of the notorious Black Jack Quinn, automatically thought, like father like son. She knew that routine better than anyone. How often had her mother's black marks been used to stain her?

Poor Rhys. His worst nightmare was coming true. At least, he had his family now. Surely, they'd stand beside him at his lowest point. They were loyal, loving people. Then again, after what happened with Jack, would the Quinns be strong enough to withstand another storm?

"His mother," she said to Bianka. "Is she okay? His father's health seemed sketchy when I met them last week. How did he take the news?"

"They don't know. No one knows. Not yet. So far, the bank wants to keep this quiet. Bad for business, if people find out. After trial, if he's convicted, then they can publish in all the newspapers, make it into a big deal because they caught a big criminal."

Big criminal. No. Impossible. Rhys would never play fast and loose with money. Especially not after what his father did. She knew him too well, knew how he'd struggled to put his father's crimes behind him. He would never risk everything he'd worked so hard for to make a coupla bucks.

Rhys was *not* guilty. Regardless of what she knew about his father, she knew *him*. Rhys was honest, all the way down to his crystal clear heart. There had to be a way to prove it, to keep him from being convicted of a crime he didn't commit. "What happens now?"

"They will question all the people he works with. Investigate. His computer, his records, his past work history."

In other words, they'd rip open his life and study the contents. She shivered. He would hate that. "What happens to Rhys while all this is going on?"

"They will keep him in jail or let him go home and keep him under surveillance until he goes to court."

"And if he's found guilty?"

"He'll go to prison."

Prison?! Her heart lurched, and her shivers intensified. In her mind, she compared the photo of arrogant Jack Quinn from the online article Rhys had shown her to the frail man who'd asked permission to hug her at the anniversary party.

Working at the carnival, she'd seen her share of ex-cons. They either came out of prison big and mean, or broken like Mr. Quinn. What would happen to Rhys?

"For how long would he be sent away?"

"Don't know. If he's found guilty on the little charges, it

could be a few months. Big charges mean bigger sentence. Could be all the way up to eight years."

Eight years?

"They'll make him pay back the money, too," Bianka added. "Sell everything he owns or anything they think he might have bought with his illegal profits."

Another poison arrow to her chest. His artifacts. He'd lose his artifacts. Again.

"And they'll post his name and crimes in all the papers."

Making sure he never worked in the finance world again. Like his father. The entire cycle would repeat itself. Father to son. It all came back to his father. "This isn't a coincidence. Someone's framing him. Someone found out about his father and decided to use that information to their own advantage."

"Maybe." Bianka shrugged. "But he has no way to prove such a thing."

Not without help. And not if he was locked up in jail. "Someone has to help him. Who would be able to do that? A private investigator? Someone with experience at this sort of thing? Or someone in the finance world who could double-check the records and find the truth? Who can we hire to do that?"

"I don't know. Wait. I ask Henryk." She disappeared from the screen, leaving Polina alone to work things through in her mind.

She wept for Rhys, for what he must be going through. She couldn't imagine being alone in a foreign country and tossed in jail. She glanced up at the fireplace mantel where her Christmas gift from the Nowaks occupied a place of honor. Thank God he at least had them on his side. *You have to take care of him for me*, she told the smiling images of Bianka and Henryk. *Somehow, you have to help me help him.*

A flurry of activity on her tablet screen heralded Henryk's sudden appearance in front of the camera. "Bianka says it's best if I talk to you directly. You have a lot of questions, I'm sure."

"Yes, thanks. Rhys didn't do this, Henryk. You know he couldn't possibly have done this."

Henryk shook his head. "I agree. But the evidence must be pretty damning for the KNF to actually arrest him."

"Isn't there someone who can help him find the truth? A private investigator or an independent auditor?"

"He'll need a very good lawyer with a lot of experts in his arsenal. That kind of defense takes money, and right now, unfortunately, Rhys's funds are frozen, pending seizure after his conviction."

He couldn't access his money? How on earth was he supposed to mount a competent defense without the cash to hire a lawyer? "I'll contact his family. Maybe *they* can put some money together—"

"No! He doesn't want them to know. He didn't want you to know, either. He made me promise not to tell you."

"But Bianka told me anyway."

He gave Polina a mirthless smile. "Yes, well, my wife didn't promise."

Uh-huh. Well, if they could use that strategy, so could she. "I didn't promise, either. I'm going to get in touch with his sister. He should have his family with him right now."

"No. I agree with Rhys on that point. The KNF has already linked him to his father and those earlier crimes. His best defense now is making sure the prosecutors know he changed his name a long time ago and that he has no contact with them. Distance. He needs to show he keeps his distance from them."

"But, the anniversary party," Polina argued. "He was at their anniversary party a few weeks ago."

"I know. This fact will be difficult for him to overcome."

Cripes. Her fault. She'd convinced him to go. And now, he could wind up locked in jail for years because he'd been in the wrong place at the wrong time. He'd been right to stay away. She should have minded her own business, kept her nose out of it. But she didn't. And because of her, because she'd talked him into making peace with his father, Rhys was in jail.

She inhaled a shaky breath. O...kay. Only one thing to do. She'd broken this.

Now, she had to fix it.

"Henryk, can you gather the names and costs for the best defense lawyers available in Kraków?"

"Yes, of course, but who's going to pay for a lawyer? I told you, Rhys's accounts are frozen."

"I will."

Shaking his head, Henryk clucked his tongue. "A lawyer will be very expensive, Polina. Where will you get that kind of money?"

"I have...something...I can sell." The house. Her perfect dream. Like all dreams, she supposed, it was never meant to last. She'd scrimped and saved for a decade, lived on scraps, until she'd come to this small town in Massachusetts and found a job she loved and a house that she could make into a home. She'd bought it to ensure her future. Now, she'd sell her future to save Rhys's.

"Rhys won't let you do that."

She flashed him a wistful smile. "Rhys doesn't have to know. Promise me you won't tell him."

On a heavy sigh, he nodded. "Okay. I promise."

"I'm going to sign off now, Henryk. I have to talk to someone about getting the money together." Exiting the chat function, she called out, "Dad?"

Yes, she called him Dad now. She'd never liked calling him Tiny because she knew it was meant as an insult. He'd never pressured her to accept his presence in her life, but she'd welcomed the chance for them both to start again.

When he came into the living room, she gave him a brief rundown about Rhys's situation and concluded with the biggest part of the dilemma. "I could apply for a mortgage, but I have no credit rating at all. I think my best bet for quick cash is to sell it at a good price so someone will snatch it up fast."

"Below market value, you mean." Her father pointed a finger at her. "You're going to take a loss on this. You love him very much, don't you?"

She sat up straighter, looked him square in the face. "I do. I love him, but..."

"But, what? He doesn't love you?"

"Not the way I love him." She dropped her gaze to the black face of the tablet, tracing a finger over the empty screen as if, by magic, she could conjure up his image.

"Does it matter?"

She thought about that for a long time. Did it? Ever

since her mother died, she'd insisted she was done with halfway and temporary. After all these years, she wanted everything life had to offer. All the laughter, the joy, and the love she could possibly hold. Even if it meant she had to experience all the drama, the pain, and the sorrow that came as part of the package.

"Yes," she said at last. "It does."

"Yet, you're still willing to give up everything for him?"

She faced him again, her expression hard and determined. "He's innocent. I know it. And I couldn't live with myself if he was convicted and I hadn't done everything in my power to set him free."

"You know what?" He skimmed a hand down her cheek to cup her chin. "You're right. If he doesn't love you the same way you love him, it matters. You deserve someone who'll love you with that same passion. Do what you want with the house, Polina. It's yours. We'll figure out something for us. We've been in worse situations over the years. We'll make do. You and I are adaptable."

She put the house on the market the next day, had a buyer within a week, and used the deposit to retain Mr. Marcel Rudaski to represent Rhys.

26

Rhys sat at the steel table in the tiny brick consultation room, across from a smooth-looking stranger in a Savile Row suit. Quite a contrast to his bright orange prison uniform and matching steel leg cuffs, he thought bitterly.

"Mr. Linsey," the man said, "I'm Marcel Rudaski. I've been hired to handle your defense."

He quirked a brow. "By whom?"

"My retainer has requested to remain anonymous. However, I've been charged to do everything in my power to not only gain an acquittal for you, but to full-out prove your innocence to the charges. Clearly, you have a very staunch ally in your camp, Mr. Linsey."

Yes, he did. Henryk had certainly done his homework. Rudaski's reputation preceded him. If anyone could clear his name, it was this shark in lawyer's clothing. A flicker of hope woke up inside him. Maybe he hadn't destroyed his entire life. Yet. "How do you plan to do all that?"

"For starters, I need you to tell me everything," Rudaski replied. "Every detail, no matter how minor. I've already acquired the disclosure records of the prosecutor's case against you. You and I will be poring over those documents, looking for irregularities, errors, or inconsistencies." He opened a briefcase and removed a mini-tape recorder, a yellow legal pad and pen, along with several thick manila folders. After arranging the items on the table, he closed the briefcase with a snap and set it on the floor. "Let's start with your side of the story."

"I don't have a side. I'm not even sure why I'm here."

"The charges weren't explained to you when you were

arrested?"

"Yes, but they make no sense to me. I mean, all I was told was I was charged with falsifying documents and creating fictitious accounts to re-route client fees. I don't know what fees, where or how these accounts were set up, under what name..." He flipped his hands palm-up on the table. "I'm at a loss."

Rudaski picked up the first folder in the pile. "Then let's remedy that problem first. According to the charges, on or about January twenty-third of this year, a routine audit of your computer files showed several accounts opened with Interbank over the last ten months. Agents from Volker-Kellogg and their clients in Brazil, Ecuador, and Canada confirmed you had advised them of regulatory problems with their usual clearinghouse and that you had set up an interim account with Interbank to continue conducting business—"

"Adamiak!" The name erupted from his lips the second it came to his brain.

Rudaski looked up over the rim of his black-framed glasses. "I'm sorry?"

"I didn't set up those accounts. Jon Adamiak did."

"Jon Adamiak? The chief financial officer?"

"Yes." Rhys remembered the email back in December. How something about it nagged him at the time but, obsessed with finding Polina's perfect Christmas gift— which he'd botched, by the way—he'd ignored that tingle. He was an idiot.

"This is a very serious accusation. Do you have proof?"

"There was an email. From one of our clients that confirmed it." He read the defeat in Rudaski's eyes. "But I'm guessing it's no longer on my computer."

"Certainly nothing like that was found, to my knowledge."

Of course not. Because someone had scrubbed all the evidence before he even knew about the accusation. "I'm going down for this, aren't I?"

"Not if my retainer has anything to say about it." Rudaski removed his glasses and rubbed his eyes. "I won't lie to you, Mr. Linsey. The deck is seriously stacked against you. Jon Adamiak is a very powerful individual with a sterling reputation."

"So was my father, once upon a time," he replied dryly.

"And that's another strike against you, as I'm sure you realize. Mind you, we might be able to use your father's example to show no one is immune to corruption, but if we sling mud without some kind of shield, we're liable to get spattered ourselves. Can you remember who sent you the email? Perhaps, we'll get lucky on the other end."

Who sent the email? By God, his head had been so full of Polina at the time he barely remembered his own name. He struggled to recall the details of that day. If he could just figure out which country was involved, he'd know the name of the agent. "I think..." *Come on, baby. The information's there.* Right at the edge of his brain. He had to find a way to push it forward. "I want to say Brazil, which would mean Rochelle Chung, I think."

Nodding, Rudaski flipped through his paperwork. "Rochelle Chung." Looking up again, he frowned. "She was let go by Banco de Brasil at the end of last year."

His flicker of hope extinguished. "Great. I'm doomed."

"Not necessarily. This is a starting point. Don't get me wrong. We have a lot of work ahead of us. But we have a suspect and a contact to get the ball rolling." He picked up the briefcase and slapped it on the table again. "I'm leaving copies of these files with you. Study them. Find me more. Meanwhile, I'll have my staff begin looking into a connection to Adamiak and track down Ms. Chung. If there's anything there, we'll find it. Any questions in the meantime?"

"How much is all this going to cost?"

"Cost is not your concern right now."

That's what *he* thought. Rhys reached over and picked up the folders. "I'll find something."

Right now, Rhys wasn't footing the bill for the attorney fees, but he'd be damned if he let the one person who never gave up on him lose everything for him.

♥

Attn: Polina Kominski

Dear Ms. Kominski,

This letter is to inform you that Rhys Linsey has been cleared of all charges and all forfeited property has been returned to him. Jon Adamiak, former CFO of Volker-Kellogg Bank, was convicted on ten counts of embezzlement and securities fraud after pleading guilty in a plea-bargain agreement with authorities of the KNF early yesterday morning. In exchange, prosecutors dropped ten other counts against him. Adamiak will be sentenced next month. Effective on the date listed above, Rhys Linsey has been released from Meingo Prison.

Pursuant to our agreement, please find our bill for services rendered attached to this letter. Payment is due at the end of the month. Thank you for referring this case to our office...

Polina read the email at least a dozen times, each time expecting to see a different outcome. But, no. She didn't miss anything. Rhys had been cleared of all charges. As he'd promised when she'd discussed her requirements with him, the attorney she'd hired, Marcel Rudaski, had rooted out the true villain and managed to keep Rhys—and his family history—out of the public arena. Except for his attorney and several members of the KNF, Rhys's secret was still a secret.

She opened the attached bill and scanned to the bottom for the total figure.

Her stomach pitched.

"You okay, sunshine?" her father asked.

After two or three inhales, equilibrium returned, and she nodded. The attorney had been worth every penny.

"Rhys is free," she said flatly.

"Was there ever any doubt? You said the attorney had the Adamiak crook on the ropes with that Brazilian-Chinese lady's testimony, that she'd kept copies of all the incriminating files on a friend's computer."

"No. I mean it's official. He was released two weeks ago." She'd set him free. Now, it was time for her to do the same for herself.

Her father placed a hand on her shoulder and a kiss on top of her bent head. "Way to go. You did it."

"Yeah." She looked around at the kitchen she'd be packing up to leave for good at the end of the week. "Worth every penny."

Over the last few months, once she'd decided to put the house on the market, they'd scrambled like mad to come up with a new future. They'd been lucky their prospective buyer was willing to wait this long to go to closing.

"I gotta go to work," he announced. "You gonna be okay?"

"Don't be silly," she said aloud with a forced smile. "I'll be fine."

And they would be. One thing about carnies: they were always self-sufficient. They'd found a small two-bedroom apartment close to the theme park site.

After they settled in their new place, she'd email Rhys. Pretend she knew nothing about what he'd gone through since January. She'd apologize for falling out of touch and blame it on the demands of her job.

Getting in touch with him after all this time was a huge risk. He could turn around and tell her to go to blazes, considering she hadn't had any contact with him since he'd said he loved her and she blew him off with her remark about his poor timing. Not exactly a stellar place for them to pick up where they left off.

She re-read the email one last time and, satisfied that nothing had changed and ever would, she turned off the tablet.

"Okay, then." Her father headed out the front door, but seconds later, a knock sounded.

She rose from her chair in the kitchen, calling out, "What'd you forget?" When she yanked the door open, her father wasn't the man on the other side.

"Absolutely nothing. In fact, you're all I've thought about since the day I first met you."

The sun behind his head blinded her to his features. It didn't matter. Her other senses knew him well. He still wore that lime-sea breeze cologne, still had that same timbre to his voice. His height, his build, and the way he stood were all emblazoned on her heart's memory.

"Rhys." She scrambled to push open the screen door for him. The sun, not as bright from this angle, allowed her to drink him in for the first time in months. He was paler than she remembered, perhaps a bit thinner, too. And in his hands, he held an enormous bouquet of red roses draped with silver ribbons. For her? Why? "What are you doing here?"

He leaned forward and pressed his mouth to hers. All those familiar sensations rushed through her, whirling her insides, curling her toes, leaving her breathless. When he broke the kiss, she swayed on her feet. "Today's your birthday, sweetheart. Did you think I'd forget?"

Why not? She certainly hadn't remembered. "Oh. Right."

He laughed, another distinctive sound that had haunted her day and night. "You didn't remember, did you?"

Her cheeks flamed. "You know it's never been important to me."

"But it *is* important to me. Everything about you is important to me."

Liar. "You don't mean that."

"Yes, I do." He gestured to the roses. "Feel like bringing these inside, or were you headed somewhere more important just now?"

"No...umm...I mean, I thought you were my father. He just left."

"The man in the black and white checked shirt? I saw him. If I'd known who he was, I would've introduced myself. Taken the opportunity to thank him."

"Thank him? For what?"

He quirked a brow. "Are you going to interrogate me out here on the porch before you let me in?"

"No. Of course not. I don't mean to...Come inside." She reversed direction, leading him past the living room, into the kitchen.

When she reached the sink, she turned and leaned against the counter, suddenly shy. How did he get here? Why had he come? For her birthday? Had he really remembered her birthday when she hadn't? She'd have to believe him about that, she supposed. But, after all these months without her speaking to him, why would he show up now?

"Here." Once again, he offered the cut glass vase full of flowers and ribbons to her.

She took it, murmured a thank you, and placed it on the counter behind her.

Shifting his weight to one hip, he shot an index finger at her. "You're not comfortable receiving flowers, are you?"

"I don't know," she admitted. "No one's ever given me flowers before."

Silence permeated the room, broken only by the hammer of her heartbeat in her ears. Mouth dry, she licked her lips and dug up a small store of courage. "I'm sorry I've been out of touch. Things have been...crazy."

He smiled. "I know the feeling."

Yeah, she bet he did. She moved away from the sink, away from the flowers, away from his nearness. "Care to talk about it?"

"I don't think that's necessary."

Ouch. That stung. Then again, she reminded herself, she probably deserved his animosity. They hadn't exactly parted on the best of terms last time. "No, really. I want to know how you've been since we last talked."

"Mr. Rudaski didn't keep you informed?"

What? How did he know she was in touch with the attorney? She feigned confusion by furrowing her brow. "Who?"

He crept closer again, each stride a study of precise grace. "You don't have to lie, sweetheart. I know you hired Mr. Rudaski."

"You do? He told you?" Why on earth would he do such a thing?

"No. Bianka told me."

Her jaw dropped. "But, that's not fair. I made Henryk promise—" She stopped, recalled what Henryk had said about telling her the secret of Rhys's predicament. "Henryk promised. Bianka didn't."

He tapped a finger on his nose. "You got it one guess."

She burst out laughing. "Those two are unbelievable. No wonder they're so in love with each other. They're both sneaky and crazy..."

"And the best people I've ever met." One more step brought him to stand before her, and that familiar cologne wreaked havoc with her senses. He leaned forward, pinning her between his warm body and the wall. "Until you came into my life." She drew a shallow inhale, then another. Intensity blazed in his eyes. "Why, Polina? Why did you do it?"

"Because I knew you were innocent. Because it was my fault. Because you were about to lose everything that mattered to you. How could I not help you when you needed me?"

His head dipped closer, their lips a breath apart, his chest pressed to hers. "Any other reason?"

"Because..." Her heart pounded in perfect synchronicity with his in a rhythm older than time, deeper than the ocean, more powerful than the sun. "I love you."

"I love you, too."

Tears pricked her eyes. No. He really didn't. But she nodded rather than disagree.

He kissed her again, and this time, the world tilted. He didn't possess her. And she didn't possess him. They simply became one entity, united in love. By magic. By fate. When he pulled away this time, she wanted to weep. Love was so unfair. He was her world, her everything. But in his world, she was just a satellite—an artifact he'd picked up on the streets of Kraków, a good luck charm, his "Get out of jail free" card.

She forced herself to find her pride. Because she loved him, she'd given him his freedom. No matter how much pain it cost her, she would let him go. Let him find his happiness. She just wished his happiness had been her.

"I like your house," he said as he studied the freshly painted walls and the gleaming cabinets.

She'd spent the weeks after his arrest stripping off the old grime from the oak, then re-stained them and applied polyurethane. Her "keep-your-mind-off-Rhys" project. She loved the way they looked now, so warm and cozy and golden. Apparently, so had her buyer. Better this way, she supposed. Start fresh. No memories to haunt her.

"It suits you, you know."

The changes she'd made throughout the house suited her. But the house wasn't hers for much longer. Once again, she opted to lie—this time in case he developed an unnecessary sense of responsibility for her loss. "Actually, it's a little too big for me. Too much work. Dad and I decided to put it up for sale a couple of months ago and found a buyer right away. We're moving out at the end of the month."

Rhys gave her a speculative look. "And here I thought you were happy here. At least, that's what you told me the last time I saw you. How you were making plans for a garden and you might get both a kitten and a puppy..."

Right. No pets allowed in the new place, either. She attempted a shrug, but her shoulders felt too weighted down to cooperate. "It's no big deal. It's just a house. Dad and I found a great apartment closer to work for both of us. We'll be happier there."

"Are you sure? Because this place seems perfect for you. I can see you studying in the living room and spending afternoons on that pretty sun porch with a kitten in your lap. That big bay window in the living room is the ideal place for a Christmas tree..."

Why was he doing this to her? Every word, every description plunged a knife into her heart. Had he come here now to punish her? To remind her of everything she was giving up? Why?

She sniffed, fighting to keep her pitching emotions in check. When the tears threatened to overwhelm her, she turned away and fussed with the dishtowels hanging from the oven handle, aligning the design so it perfectly matched on both sides.

"You don't have to leave here if you don't want to." Rhys's voice was a warm, low hum in her ear.

She ducked her head, keeping her back to him. "Yes, I do," she confessed. "I sold the house to pay Mr. Rudaski's bill."

"I know," he replied. "I'm the one who bought it."

She whirled to face him. "You...what? How? That's impossible. You were in jail. Your money was frozen. Henryk told me."

He pulled her into his arms and held her close. Nothing

else would ever feel so welcoming, so soothing, so...devastating. She stifled a sob, and he tilted her chin up toward his face.

"Bianka told me you planned to sell 'something' to pay my legal fees. I knew it could only be the house, the house you told me all about at the anniversary party. The house you loved."

"You were innocent," she repeated. "They wouldn't let me call your family. Even Mr. Rudaski said any contact with them—especially for financial help—could jeopardize your case. Selling the house was my only option."

"Did you honestly think I'd be happy to know you were giving up your future, your security, for me?"

She gave him a disgruntled look. "You weren't supposed to find out."

"Well, I'm very glad I did. I couldn't let you do that. I had Henryk call my parents. They arranged to help me buy your house."

Wait. What? Anger rose within her. "You contacted your parents? You risked the prosecutors using that connection against you? For me?"

"You sold your house. For me."

"Yes, but that's not the same."

"You're right. Your sacrifice was greater."

She shook her head. "It's just a house. A thing. Things are easily replaced. People you love, not so much."

"I know. You taught me that. How could I not follow your example?"

"But that was so foolish! What if Mr. Rudaski's team hadn't been able to link Adamiak to the embezzlement? You could have gone to prison for eight years."

"And if I'd gone to prison for eight years, you would have lost your house for nothing."

"Not for nothing. I would've kept fighting for you."

He skimmed a hand down her cheek. "I believe you. Saint Polina would slay every dragon to rescue her errant prince."

With a frown, she pulled away. "Don't make fun. You shouldn't have bought my house, Rhys. Now, we're both in debt. Me, to Mr. Rudaski and you, to your parents."

"You're not in debt to anyone, *ukochana*. I already paid

back my parents. And I fully intend to pay Mr. Rudaski, as well."

"How?"

He didn't say a word. He didn't have to.

The answer hit her with the force of a lightning strike. "You sold your artifacts. Rhys, no! Why? Why would you do that?"

"Because I wasn't about to let you sell your future, not even for me. You were right, you know. The collection will never be the same as what I lost. It's more useful to sell it and use the money to gain my freedom *and* yours."

"I hope you got a lot of cash from the sale, then. You haven't seen Mr. Rudaski's bill. It's ginormous."

"Don't worry. I've got an excellent credit rating. Of course, it would be better if your name was on the paperwork, too."

He was teasing her now. He had to be. None of this made sense unless it was all a colossal joke.

"Yoo-hoooo!" her father called from the front door. "How's it going back there? Rhys, do you need reinforcements?"

He knew Rhys?

"Come on back, Morgan," Rhys replied. "I don't think our girl's fully aware of what's happening yet."

They knew each other? How? While Polina tried to iron out this new wrinkle, her father appeared in the kitchen, his face suffused with joyous expectation.

"What'd I miss so far?"

"How do you...?" She couldn't get the words out and tried a different tack. "Shouldn't you be at...?" No dice. She was stunned into stupidity.

Lucky for her, Rhys put her out of her misery. "I've been in touch with your father for weeks now. Unlike the Nowaks, *he* can keep a secret."

"But," she sputtered, glancing between the two men. "You should be at work."

"What, and miss your birthday surprise?" her dad replied. "Not a chance. I've waited twenty-nine years to celebrate a birthday with my baby girl. Not even this lug would keep me from missing another." His gaze traveled to the roses on the counter, and he turned to Rhys, shaking his head. "You should've checked with me, bucko. I would've warned you Polina's not a roses kind of girl."

"I know," Rhys replied with a grin. "That's why I saved one particular artifact from my collection." Reaching into his pocket, he pulled out a black velvet box, flipped the top, and displayed the golden dragon inside. "I'm an idiot, Polina. For years I've been searching for my happiness in a bunch of dusty old treasures. Until fate brought me you. I'm only sorry it took me so long to realize that you're my world. My everything. How could I ever be happy surrounded by cheap imitations when I could have the real treasure in you?"

"Smooth, Rhys. Very smooth," Dad said, arms folded over his chest, head bobbing with approval. "Keep going. I think you're finally getting through to her."

"You should know, sweetheart, I made a choice on my next job assignment. I left Volker-Kellogg. Took a position at a small American firm, about a half hour's drive from here. A permanent position. I know I said I'd wait while you pursued your goals and that I wouldn't pressure you. But I guess I'm more selfish than I realized. I don't want to wait to spend my life with you. And I have no right to make you change your dreams to fit my life when I could easily adapt my life to your dreams. What do you say, Polina? I'm ready to live up to the promise behind the ring. Are you?"

The aura of love encompassing the kitchen—*her* kitchen—expanded, surrounding the three of them in a circle of endless joy. They were, at last, a family.

She thrust out her left hand, ring finger extended to willingly accept her fate. "Let's do this."

ABOUT THE AUTHOR

Gina Ardito is the award-winning author of more than twenty romances in contemporary, historical, and paranormal sub-genres. In 2012, she launched her freelance editing business, Excellence in Editing. She's hosted workshops around the world for writing conferences, author organization meetings, and library events.

To her everlasting shame, despite all her accomplishments, she'll never be more famous than her dog, who starred in commercials for 2015's Puppy Bowl. For more information, to sign up for her newsletter, and to learn about all things Gina, visit her website at https://ginaardito.com.

OTHER BOOKS BY GINA ARDITO

THE MONEY SERIES
The Bonds of Matri-money
A Run for the Money
♦
That's Amore!
♦
THE NOBODY SERIES
Nobody's Darling
Nobody's Business
Nobody's Perfect
♦
Chasing Adonis
Duping Cupid
♦
THE AFTERLIFE SERIES
Eternally Yours
In Your Dreams
Waiting in the Wings
♦
THE CALENDAR GIRLS SERIES
Charming for Mother's Day
Duet in September
Reunion in October
Homecoming in November
Memories in December
♦
Even Now
A Love to Keep Me Warm
Kaleidoscope Hearts 2
Echoes of Love

www.ingramcontent.com/pod-product-compliance
Lightning Source LLC
Chambersburg PA
CBHW061607170626
46811CB00001B/348